The Good Children

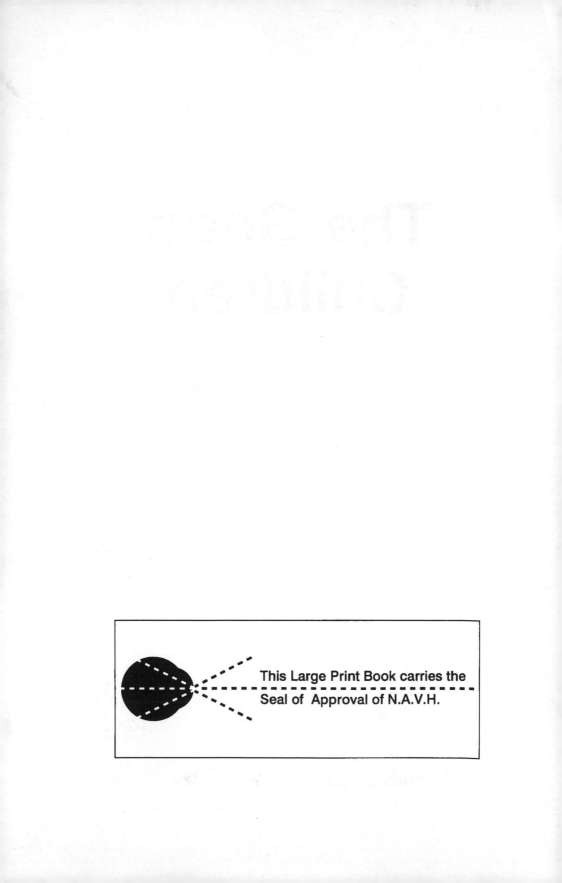

This Large Print Book carries the
Seal of Approval of N.A.V.H.

The Good Children

Kate Wilhelm

G.K. Hall & Co. • Thorndike, Maine

Published in 1998 by arrangement with St. Martin's Press, Inc.

G.K. Hall Large Print Core Series.

The text of this Large Print edition is unabridged.
Other aspects of the book may vary from the original edition.

Set in 16 pt. Plantin by Al Chase.

Printed in the United States on permanent paper.

Library of Congress Cataloging in Publication Data

Wilhelm, Kate.
   The good children / Kate Wilhelm.
    p. (large print) cm.
   ISBN 0-7838-0167-X (lg. print : hc : alk. paper)
   1. Large type books. I. Title.
  [PS3573.I434G6 1998b]
   813'.54—dc21   98-16351

For Gordon Van Gelder

1

Brian heard the van first and shrieked, "They're coming!" He was jumping up and down, no longer able to contain his excitement. I think he wet himself that afternoon, although he denied it and said the dampness was from spilled root beer. He had turned six a few weeks earlier, in May.

Kevin was sitting on the porch with both feet one step down, his arms resting on his knees, his chin on his arms, a very uncomfortable-looking position. He had not moved for a long time, praying maybe, or just willing things to work out, or planning his strategy if they didn't. Where Brian was open and transparent, Kevin had folded in on himself and become impenetrable. He stood up only when the van pulled into the driveway.

Amy had been perched on the porch railing, one foot on the floor, swinging the other one like a metronome. She stood up and moved closer to Kevin. They were like that, automatically drawing closer when there were problems, or in the face of strangers, or when there was simply a great change coming, as if they strengthened each other in a way I couldn't share.

Kevin was fifteen; Amy fourteen. I was eleven, an awkward in-between age, too young for their newly discovered secrets, their approaching adulthood, too old for Brian. I had been snooping all around the house, peering into windows, trying doors, tiptoeing to see inside the garage. I came to rest alone near the front door and watched our mother and father get out of the van and walk toward us, and I knew even before they said anything. I could tell by the way she was walking, her steps as light as a fairy dance on the wind; her eyes were sparkling, her cheeks flaming. I let out a long-held breath just as Dad yelled, "Let the wild rumpus begin!"

They had signed the papers and bought the house. It was ours, the first house that was really ours.

We all had noisemakers, pots and pans to bang on, horns to blow, a drum. . . . Mother led us in a wild dancing marching parade through the empty house, which echoed and magnified our exuberant racket. Into the living room, to the kitchen, up the back stairs, down the front, around and around, out to the porch, the covered walkway from the garage, the back patio . . . around and around and around, laughing, yelling, dancing.

Finally, exhausted, we collapsed in the backyard, where the grass was knee-high, and I lifted my face to let the breeze dry the sweat.

"Listen," Dad said.

"To what?" Amy asked after a second.

"Nothing! Not a goddamn thing!" He yelled and yelled again, a loud, exultant cowboy rodeo whoop.

Mother grabbed his shoulders and looked up

into his face. "You're acting like a child, Warden. Control yourself!" She was laughing. He swept her into his arms and danced her through the high grass, singing "Waltzing Matilda" at the top of his voice. He was wearing his dark gray suit, and she had on a blue dress with a swirly skirt and white sandals. They were beautiful, a king and his queen come home to our castle.

That was our first day in our new house. It was over a hundred years old, and Dad said it had started out quite small. He pointed out the two original rooms, seed rooms, he said, that had sprouted out in all directions. Narrow back stairs had gone up to a sleeping loft.

"Then they added the rest of the first floor and real bedrooms on the second floor, and probably discovered those narrow stairs just wouldn't do for a family with beds and bureaus, things that needed to go up. So they added the stairs in the front."

The master bedroom on the first floor and the finished attic on the third had been done at the same time, he said, pointing out the similarities in paneling and windows, things totally boring to me. I had my own room; that was interesting. And I could pick out the paint I wanted. Within reason, Mother had added warningly when they told us we could decorate our rooms ourselves. We all had individual rooms. Mine would be pale, cool green, with cream-colored woodwork and curtains. I had three windows; one overlooked the woods to the north, and two opened to the wooded hill out back. Brian's room was next to mine, and Amy's was across the hall, next to a mammoth bathroom, and the wide stairs to the living room, and the narrow ones up to the attic, which Kevin wanted. Dad said the partitions up there were temporary, easily removed, probably put in for servants back in the twenties. He knew about things like that. He was a structural steel-stress engineer.

Until we got beds and the movers brought the rest of our furniture, we slept in our sleeping bags on the floor, in our own rooms. The first night, I lay looking out an uncurtained window, listening to the sounds of the countryside, most of them unidentifiable — crickets and tree frogs, deer in the woods, raccoons. . . . I didn't know what all I was hearing; that night they were just noises. The sky was black, not the milky haze I had grown used to; the stars were sharper than I had known they could be, and the wind smelled so unfamiliar, it might have been a completely different combination of gases.

I was wide-awake, too excited to sleep, too aware of all the strangeness, too intent on listening for something that didn't happen — car noise, or a siren, or a plane overhead, doors slamming, people yelling . . . things I had grown used to hearing throughout the night.

It was June. For the rest of the summer, Mother had said, we would finish out the house, make curtains, buy furniture, paint, and we would all have to have bicycles, and register for school in the fall.

Another new school. I had gone to four differ-ent schools in four different states, and now number five. But this time I would stay, get to know other kids, make friends, go on to high school with kids I knew. . . .

I had left my door open a little; it came open more and Brian crept in. "Liz, can I sleep in here with you?" he whispered. He was dragging his sleeping bag.

"What's the matter?"

"Nothing. It's scary, isn't it?"

"No, it's great! You can stay in here, but you have to go to the bathroom first."

"It's scary," he said again, spreading out his sleeping bag as close to mine as he could. "It's haunted. I can hear footsteps."

"No you can't! Go on to the bathroom; the light's on."

In spite of himself, when he came back from the bathroom, he couldn't stay awake very long, but I couldn't go to sleep. I was too happy to sleep, overwhelmed by joy. I thought of how Mother had danced in the high grass, and I wanted to go out and dance like that under the stars.

Dad had told us houses got stiff and creaked and groaned before they settled down for the night. I listened to our house creak and groan, a board easing itself back into place, a stair step adjusting its position, a wall relaxing just a little, and I was filled with love for the old building.

Where Brian had heard ghostly footsteps, I heard our house grumbling to itself about us, the noisy new people.

Later I came to believe Brian had been more perceptive than I could ever admit to him.

2

Dad had the rest of June off before starting on his new job — a computer-chip plant near Portland. He worked for a big construction company that had sent him to Saudi Arabia, to Guantánamo, to Texas, Florida, California, Colorado. . . . This was to be his last job for them, a two- to three-year contract, and then he would supervise maintenance at the plant.

Was he sorry? He didn't act like it, but it was hard to tell. He always got excited before a new job, brought home books and magazines, travel folders, city maps, and treated each move like a great adventure. As far as I could tell, this one had been exactly like all the others.

Mother could have put a stop to our wanderings, but she didn't. Kevin did.

"I won't go!" he had yelled when Dad began to talk about the new project in Oregon. "I'll run away!"

Dad was a big man, over six feet tall and broad, with red cheeks and bright blue eyes. He laughed a lot, and cursed a lot; he sang and danced and played a guitar with enthusiastic abandon. He never had known his father. There had been a series of "uncles." One had broken his arm when he was nine, and for a short time afterward, he had been in a foster home. At seventeen, he had joined the army; his mother had signed without demur, and when he got out, home from Vietnam, she had moved. He never saw her again.

For the next five years he had put himself through school. He would never be poor again, never get drunk again, never do drugs again, never hit a woman or child. After finishing his education, he had started his travels with the construction company. He kept all the promises he had made to himself.

That night in Denver, he stared at his gangly son, and Mother screamed, "Hush your mouth! What are you talking about, running away!" She grabbed Kevin's arm and shook him. "You don't know what it's like out on the streets, boy! You think that's a picnic or something, scrounging for a bite to eat? You think that's the kind of life you want, when all you can think of is the ache in your belly? You've got food on the table, a bed to sleep in. We're a family!"

Dad could move faster than anyone. He got up from the kitchen table and put one arm around Mother, his other arm around Kevin's shoulders, separating them before she could lash out and slap Kevin. She looked as if she might, she was so angry.

"Hey," Dad said. "Hey, hey, hey! Let's talk." He looked at Amy and me, silent, staring, afraid to move. "Beat it, brats. Off to bed with you. Time for the big people to talk." He grinned and I knew it would be all right. He would make it all right.

But we didn't go to bed. Amy and I listened outside the door. It must have been a hundred degrees that night in our Denver apartment, but Amy and I huddled together, not moving, trying not to breathe, not to make a sound.

"What is it, Kevin?" Dad asked in his low quiet voice. He had many different voices; he could have been an actor. When he read to us, he did all the voices, even squeaky, tremulous women's voices, until we giggled so hard, he had to stop.

"It isn't fair," Kevin said. He didn't sound mad anymore, but maybe a little afraid, and he sounded younger than he usually did in those days. "Just when we start to know people, we have to move. I want to go to high school here, and then go to college. We keep moving all the time, until I'll never even finish high school." He stopped talking when his voice went high-pitched the way it did, embarrassing him every time.

"You think you can go to school, living out on the streets?" Mother cried. "You think that?"

"Now, Lee, let's hear him out," Dad said. "Make us some iced tea, why don't you. God, it's hot in here. What do you want to study, Kev? You got that far with your thinking yet?"

"I want to build things. Mr. Myerson looked at my drawings. He said I have talent, that I should study architecture. That's what I want to do."

"You want to show me your drawings?" Dad asked.

"You saw them already."

15

"The same ones your teacher saw? I don't think so."

Amy and I squeezed ourselves against the wall when Kevin came out of the kitchen to get his sketchbook. He scowled at us but didn't say anything, and when he went back to show Dad his drawings, he didn't give us away. We never gave one another away.

For a long time no one spoke in the kitchen. It was so quiet, we could hear the sound of papers being picked up and put down. Mother made tea; we heard her banging things about, then the refrigerator opening, water running on the ice tray. Finally, Dad said, "Listen, Kevin. I'll see to it that you get to start and finish high school in one place, just not here. *Sit down!* Have I ever broken my word to you? This job will be over in six or seven months. We'll all stay here and you'll finish out the year, and then we'll settle down. You hear me? After this year we'll settle down and stay put." His voice got even lower. "That's a promise, son. One more year." Then he said in a growly way, "Now beat it. Go to bed, and tell your nosy sisters to get their butts in bed before I warm them up good."

We kids shared a bedroom with two sets of bunk beds. Brian was asleep, but the three of us stayed up, whispering for a long time. Kevin didn't believe Dad could fix it so we would stay put, and Amy, as usual, believed whatever Kevin did. But I knew Dad would do it.

In April he came out to Oregon to look around.

Housing had always been a problem for us. There were few rentals that would admit a family with four children, and needing it for a limited time made it even harder. When he came to look, he said he would find a good place and buy it. In May Mother flew out to inspect the house. She stewed and fretted about leaving us overnight, but in the end she did, and we managed fine.

For years Dad had wanted us to stay in one place and let him go off to his various jobs, and Mother had said no. We were a family and we would stay together, no matter what. She was adamant about very few things; on this she would not budge. So we had moved from one state to another, then to another, and now we had our own house and planned never to move again.

During our first week Dad and Kevin tore down the temporary partitions in the attic, and Dad made him a built-in drawing table under a dormer window. We painted and bought furniture, and Mother said she would make curtains, then admitted that she didn't know a thing about sewing, and so we shopped for them, too.

After a few nights Brian was willing to sleep in his own room if he could have a night-light and the door stayed open, and after Dad explained again about the noises old houses made and sat with him to listen to and identify some of them.

We had picnics on the back patio, and explored our acreage — four acres, all of it rocky, hilly and wooded beyond a small, level backyard, and the level front. There were deer in the woods. This was a semirural area fifteen miles south of Portland. The nearest town, actually no more than a village, called South Hills, was three miles away, not an impossible walk, and a good bicycle ride. Our house was on a blacktop road that wound around the hills, and while there were neighbors, we met no one for more than two weeks. No other house was visible from ours; the road was hidden by fir trees and great rhododendrons and Oregon grapes. A massive tangle of blackberry brambles was one boundary, and an outcropping of rock was another. In the backyard, shading the patio, was a big, overgrown apple tree heavy with fruit. Dad said he'd bet that deer would come right in to eat the apples in the fall.

Dad started his new job, and we were still settling in when two neighbor women paid a call, Wanda Hennessy and Heather Larkins. Mrs. Larkins was beautiful, blond and thin, in tight jeans and an oversized sweatshirt. She had rings on every finger, and her nails were long and sharp and bright red. I decided I wanted to look like her when I grew up. Mrs. Hennessy, older, with gray hair, wore sweatpants and a sweatshirt. They had been taking their run, they said. Maybe when Mother was free, she would like to run with them; they did it three times a week.

"It's nice to get young people around here again," Mrs. Hennessy said. "My youngest is eighteen! Hard to believe how fast they grow up. But Margaret Larkins will be on the same school bus as your kids. She's how old now?"

"Sixteen," Mrs. Larkins said. "Do you have the school schedule yet, or the bus schedule?"

"I'll take care of all that next week. So much to do," Mother said. She waved her hand vaguely and Mrs. Larkins said of course, they understood. They didn't linger much longer.

Brian and I hurried out the back door and around the house to hide behind a bush and watch them leave. First they sort of jogged in place, talking, then they trotted out the driveway. It wasn't much of a run, I thought, watching until they were out of sight. I knew Mother would never go running with them.

When we went inside again, Mother was enraged. "Prying busybodies. She never did a lick of work in her life, from the looks of her. Those jeans get any tighter and they'll strangle her." She looked about the living room distractedly. We had started on the bedrooms and kitchen but had not done much downstairs. First things first, she had said. In the living room were unopened moving boxes, and the old furniture we had moved looked shabby and dirty, haphazardly arranged. "We'll get new furniture," Mother had said when the movers brought it in. So far we had bought a refrigerator and stove, a washer and dryer, a kitchen table and chairs, and five new beds. She had refused to bring the bunk beds, and she and Dad had a new king-sized bed now. Our dining room held boxes of good dishes and glasses, and the china cabinet. They had sold the rest of the dining room furniture before a move a few years earlier. The family room was still empty. "Three moves equal one good fire," she often said.

A few days after our two visitors had come, Mother hung drapes in the living room and dining room. To frustrate the snoops, she said, laughing. Dad began to teach Kevin how to drive and took him to get a beginner's permit. We located our schools and registered, and got the bus schedules. All three schools were in the same big complex, elementary, the middle school, and the high school, all separated by playing fields. We would be able to ride the same bus back and forth, and although Brian would get out earlier than the rest of us, they let the little kids play in the cafeteria at their school until it was time for the older kids to leave. It was an ideal school arrangement, the best we had ever had.

We didn't glimpse our neighbors again except in passing now and then. Dad and Mother bought a Toyota for her to use, and they spent days with insurance people and a lawyer, and laughed about that, too. As homeowners they had responsibilities, they said.

In September Mother took Brian to school on the first day, and if her usual pattern held, we all knew she would never go back. She was not a joiner, she said often. PTA, church groups, clubs, they were not for her. She had not set foot in any of my schools after the one time when she took me. From then on, Brian went out with us to the blacktop road and we all rode the same bus. We sat together, Amy with Kevin, I with Brian, and that was our usual pattern, too. Looking back, I can see that it was defensive — we felt alienated from the world of other children — but at the time, it just seemed the only way we were comfortable.

Two years earlier a counselor had told Amy that we were not unlike army children, who had to make friends quickly and adjust to new surroundings all the time. We knew the difference even then. Army brats were with other army brats. A best friend on Friday might be half a world away by Monday, but they might meet again later, and they were all in the same situation. We were always going into a community of children who had known one another for years, who had slumber parties, whose parents knew the other parents and shared car pools, were room mothers, went running together. If the schools we had come from had not yet touched on subjects, we were the new dummies. Amy and Kevin had taught me fractions. Dad had taught Amy how to diagram sentences. If our previous schools had been more advanced, we were stuck-up, snobs. We always knew more geography than anyone, often more than our teachers. We all learned not to volunteer answers. Our accents were always wrong — too southern, too northern, too midwestern. . . . We never knew the new recess rules, the pecking order. If we carried lunches in boxes, the other kids used brown paper bags. If we took drinks in thermoses, they bought milk at school. We were used to being out of step for weeks or even months.

Amy had cried when she left her elementary school in Dallas. None of us ever cried again about leaving. Neither did we make friends easily. We stuck to one another and told one another everything. We had little need for outside friends, and great need for the wariness that had become part of us.

The same counselor who advised Amy had lined up the three of us in her office one day and lectured: "If you move into a new neighborhood with a chip on your shoulder, you are just daring others to knock it off."

Two boys had jumped Kevin on the way home the day before, and Amy and I had joined the fight without hesitation. If anyone fought one of the McNair children, he had to fight them all. And we were good fighters.

I had been afraid of the counselor. She had tight gray skin with patches of white where the skin was stretched too tightly over bones. I thought she was dead and turning into a skeleton already. She sent a note home and said we all needed counseling. Dad went to talk to her. That night, we told him what had happened and he sang a song about the bone lady that made us all laugh. Mother went out and bought ice cream and root beer and we had a party.

"You children remember this," Mother said, spooning the ice cream. "Can't any power on earth touch a family that stays together and takes up for each other."

She'd never had any family until she met Dad and created one, and for her there was nothing else that had any importance.

"When you've got family, you've got the world's riches," she used to say, packing to move, or unpacking, trying to fit us all into a too-small apartment, or pretending she didn't notice the disrepair of a new rental house. "When you've got family, you don't need anything else."

3

The first official notice of Mother listed her as Baby Jane Doe. She had been discovered in a cardboard carton on a bench outside the bus station in Nashville. A healthy four-month-old female with light blue eyes, she should have been adoptable, but she had not been adopted. She was either cross-eyed or walleyed; she was always uncertain about which. Her earliest memory, she claimed, was waking up unable to move, unable to see, in a hell made up of screaming babies and children. They had operated on her eyes; she was four and a half years old, kept in restraints so she would not tear off the bandages on her eyes.

She had been weird-looking, she often said. Knobby and skinny, with big ears that stuck out like flaps, too big for ears, too small for wings, and glasses that never did fit right and usually had a broken temple, or were held on with a rubber band around her head, and were always dirty. She had been clumsy and awkward; without her glasses, she bumped into things and knocked over things, and with them she was a sight. Then she laughed.

Various foster parents had cut her hair in funny ways, most of the time keeping it short in a boy's haircut because it was so fine, it tangled too much to brush or comb, like baby hair, up to the time she was a teenager. It had darkened over the years to mud-colored, she declared. She probably lied about that. Her hair, as far back as I could remember, had been the color of wild honey, and it was thick and shiny, with enough curl that she never had to do anything with it.

"Oh, children, never, never, *never* let yourselves fall into the hands of officialdom. The things they do to children! Put them in homes they know perfectly well are unfit, and take them away from homes that are fine. I remember Mama Shelley, a big, fat, jolly woman who actually liked me. She used to make special treats for the two of us — gingerbread with raisins, and apple butter on top. She always said I needed fattening up. I can just taste it now. But they took me away. Said she drank. Maybe she did a little now and then, but she liked me."

She ran away when she was twelve. They found her and put her in a home for delinquent girls. "Delinquents!" she cried. "All I was doing was trying to protect myself!" She was in two more foster-care homes after that, and at fifteen she ran away again, but she was older and wiser, she said. She didn't get caught.

The first thing she did, she said, was make tracks out of Tennessee. She headed south, looking for warmth in the coming winter. The next two years were always left vague; she carhopped, waitressed, did this and that. She lost her glasses, or they were stolen, and she couldn't hold jobs after that. She was afraid of getting put back in the system if she asked for help, and she couldn't afford an eye examination and new glasses. Ten-cent store glasses were the best she could afford, and they simply made the world even fuzzier than it was without them.

She heard that anyone could get a job cleaning motel rooms in Miami, and she headed south again after spending a winter in Atlanta and nearly freezing. "Cold! You wouldn't believe how cold it can get in the nice sunny South!"

Another time she said, "I was scared the whole time I was in Atlanta. They didn't take kindly to vagrants or runaway girls. We all knew that the cops might pick you up, and . . . Never mind. I was scared and glad to put it behind me."

She found a job in Miami, but she couldn't find a room she could afford. "It wasn't bad at first. At night it was eighty degrees, better sleeping out than in, I'd say. But it rained a lot."

Every time she found a job, she used a fake Social Security number and a different name. No one ever checked, she said indignantly. In Miami she had become Leeanne Hobson.

"If you were real careful," she said, "you could spot people who got up and out at the crack of dawn, and you could slip inside a room and get a shower. Sometimes people even left food. Lots of times they never touched the towels or anything. Such pigs! You wouldn't believe what pigs can afford to take vacations, stay in motels. Pigs!"

When she got to the next part of her story, she always became dreamy-eyed. It was the part that we all loved the most.

"So I'd been half-asleep out under a bush near the pool, keeping an eye out for a departing guest, and darn if the rain didn't start. It didn't usually rain in the morning, just every afternoon, but there it was. You don't know what rain is unless you've been in the Deep South. Buckets and buckets of water dumped without letup. Like they were bailing out heaven. It just keeps coming like that, half an hour, an hour, and then the sun comes out and everything steams. I was soaked to the skin, I tell you. Soaked through and through. I ran to the motel and tried to take cover under a little tiny overhang, and this big blurry hulk opens a door and says, 'For God's sake, get inside here.' "

That was how Leeanne met Warden McNair.

" 'I'm on my way out to get something to eat,' he said. 'Go use the bathroom, dry yourself. Shirts in the drawer there. You can use one until your clothes dry out.' "

Very gravely, he would chime in here and say, "She looked like a drowned rat, and it happened I was in my drowned-rat-rescuing stage."

"He was just a big blur," Mother said, "but he sounded kind, and I was shaking with cold. I went in and used his shower and he brought back breakfast for two. When he came in carrying coffee and juice, sausage and toast and hard-boiled eggs, I snapped. Me, the tough kid on the block, out on my own for years, ready to take on the whole world if I had to, I snapped. I couldn't really see him, you understand, just a fuzzy outline of a big red-faced man. My knees got weak, and I felt like this was what I'd come to Miami for, that all my life I'd been heading for this blurry red man with his kind voice."

Warden McNair was exactly twice her age; he knew she was little more than a child, much too young for him. She needed a twenty-year-old, someone to grow up with, not a man approaching middle age. For a short time he treated her like a little sister. They talked over breakfast and kept talking through the morning. She was feisty and independent, street-smart and wise, and she made him laugh. When she told him he was the lonesomest man she'd ever met, he knew he needed her as much as she needed him. By late afternoon they were talking about their future.

He had gone to Miami to fool around for a week before heading out for Cuba, the job at Guantánamo. He had enough clout by then that he could take a wife with him, but an underage girl? Statutory rape, he said; the company would draw the line.

"We can lie about it," Leeanne said.

"No, by God! We won't start with a lie. Marry me, Leeanne. Will you?"

She would. She did. And she lied after all. She claimed she was eighteen. He took her to an ophthalmologist and she got contact lenses and saw him for the first time and fell in love for the second time. He bought her some clothes, and they bought a lot of books to take with them. They honeymooned for the next two years on the island of Cuba.

She wanted a big family, she told him, and he said so did he. "Will there be enough money so I won't have to go to work?" she asked cautiously.

"With a big family, I think you'll work," he said. "But no, you'll stay home and be the perfect mother of the perfect family, forever and ever."

He had been with the company for years by then, and his job paid very well, with hardship pay for working in strange places, generous relocation expenses paid, bonuses that were significant. He had lived frugally, never wanting much more than decent housing, good food, and a lot of books to read, and he had saved and invested his earnings over the years. Early on, he had wanted to buy a house and settle her and the children somewhere, but she had said no firmly and often. They were a family. They would stay together.

Mother never did become much of a reader. Bad vision in her early years, poorly fitted glasses, then for too long no glasses, and living in general chaos had not inclined her toward books. But Dad read everything. Every time we moved, one of the first things he did was locate a library and get a card, then take us kids there. And he read to us every night from the time we could hold up our heads. When we lived in smaller houses, I would often fall asleep listening to his voice rising and falling as he read to Mother in bed.

In Cuba, Mother had learned to prepare Cuban food and had bought cookbooks, and over the years she had become a real gourmet cook. Her collection of cookbooks numbered in the hundreds and she delighted in new ones, new food combinations, new dishes. No matter where we lived, she had always managed to find ways to make breads, pies, cakes, to fill our apartments or houses with food smells that made our mouths water at the door. She ranged from Indonesian to Indian, Spanish to French, Mexican. . . . There was nothing she would not try, and everything she tried was wonderful.

She would not join anything, would not participate in civic affairs, did not even vote; she made no friends and said she needed none. Sometimes she entertained Dad's friends, who were filled with admiration and probably envy at the quality of her food, and she would go to the company outings if Dad wanted her to. And that was more than enough social life, she would say. They rarely ate out; she criticized restaurant food mercilessly. For their nights out they went to movies and concerts. They both loved music, all kinds of music, but especially classical. And they talked. There was incessant conversation in our house; they talked about the books he read to her, about articles she read, about the music they had heard, about the house, about us, as if we were not even there sometimes. He talked about his work, about the car, now two cars, about the grass that seemed to need mowing constantly. And we talked about school, the bus ride, the other kids, the teachers. In our house, music was always playing and everyone talked all the time.

Over that first summer in Oregon, Kevin grew several inches; he never seemed to know where his feet were, and someone was stumbling over them all the time. His hair was darkening; probably it would be the same russet brown as Dad's hair, but his coloring was more like Mother's, with pale blue eyes and a creamy skin tone. And Amy was getting more like Mother. Her hair was the same honey color, with the same kind of curl, and she could wear some of Mother's clothes. Brian lost his baby look and turned into a little towheaded boy with red cheeks. I don't think I changed from an awkward eleven-year-old into anything else, and my hair was getting more mud-colored all the time. I was still all knobby knees and sharp elbows and just blah.

But Mother changed most of all. I thought it was magic how we were growing up and she was growing younger. She and Amy could have been sisters. She sang and danced through the days, and her temper, which could flare unexpectedly and be fierce when it did, hardly ever showed.

One day, just before school started, Dad caught up Mother in his arms and held her, and he said, "Oh, Lee, honey." That was all.

She laughed and said, "I have a right. The perfect family in the perfect house."

Later that night, lying in bed, I thought about that and realized that although she had not said so, what she had meant was that she had created all this — perfect family, perfect house, and herself, the perfect mother.

Then I thought she should not have said that, and I wished I had not heard it, had not brought it to mind again. I reached up and knocked on the headboard of my bed. I wished she had not said that.

4

We always referred to the second weekend in September as "that last weekend."

"Remember how Dad and I cut back the shrubs?"

There had been warnings about the dry conditions, possible fires. Kevin and Dad worked all weekend on pruning shrubs, cutting back bushes, watering everything, mowing the lawn and raking the grass into a big pile that Dad watered down. "Great compost for the garden next spring," he said. He had tilled up a little garden spot the week before. None of us knew a thing about gardening, but he said that, by God, if the information was in books, by spring we'd find out enough. He had started to accumulate garden books, and Mother got interested. She wanted to grow herbs. Overnight the grass pile got hot and steamed. Brian and I went out to feel it again and again, afraid it was catching on fire.

"Remember how Mother and I made pies and froze them for winter?"

Amy and I had picked blackberries for the final time; they were small and not very sweet by then. They knew it was time to hang it up, Dad said, the days were getting too short, not enough sun for them to make sugar now. But there were so many, too many to let go to waste, Mother said, and she set about to make half a dozen pies. She had made jam and jelly earlier and had frozen many bags of berries, and there were as many left on the brambles as we had already used. Amy fretted about the purple stains on her fingers. She soaked her hands in lemon juice and water; it irritated her skin and did not remove the stains. I liked my purple fingernails.

"Remember how Brian kept reading out loud until Kevin said he'd stuff a sock down his throat if he didn't stop?"

Brian had learned to read before he started school, but no one had thought to tell him that he was reading. He had come home from school after a day or two and announced that he had learned to read, and he wanted to demonstrate it. Dad took him to the library and let him pick out books all by himself, and he read them constantly to anyone within earshot.

"Remember how Kevin kept knocking over the garbage cans?"

Our driveway was a long, shallow curve, concrete from the road to the garage and the front of the house, then gravel back out to the road. Kevin was not allowed to drive on the road alone. He drove the length of the drive, made a laborious turn in the narrow space, drove back the other way to the road, and turned again. Over and over. Dad bought two plastic garbage cans and set them down and told Kevin he had to learn to park between then, with the wheels no more than eight inches from a rope he stretched out on the side of the driveway.

Kevin had wanted to learn to drive in the van, but Mother wouldn't let him. She said it was too big, which didn't make a bit of sense. He was at least six inches taller than she was by then, and she drove it.

Amy and I had sat on the front steps and watched him try to park until he got it right, then got it right again, and again. We cheered every time he did it right, and booed and groaned when he knocked over a can, or ran over the rope.

We talked about school with cautious optimism, already recognizing the difference it made, living in our own house instead of in the wrong kind of place in the wrong part of town.

"Remember how we talked about getting a cat and dog?"

At dinner Sunday night Kevin had asked if he could have a dog. He had always wanted a dog, he said, although this was the first time he had ever mentioned it. Neither Mother nor Dad had had pets, but she recalled a fat poodle in one of the homes she had been placed in. "Fat and stinking," she said. "I imagine its teeth were rotten. Mrs. Smollen used to buy special candy and feed it to the dog piece by piece and laugh because the little monster was so greedy. I stole a piece of its candy once and Mrs. Smollen beat me with a wooden spoon. She chased me all through the house, waving the spoon at me, and caught me in a tiny little hallway, and the little beast yapped and yapped while she beat me." She looked through us, the way she did sometimes when she was remembering. "Candy corn," she said. "It was candy corn. You know, those little orange-and-yellow candies you get at Halloween. I've hated them ever since."

No one spoke for a time. Then Dad said, "I think a dog would be a fine thing, out in the country like this. Not a yapper, though."

"A big dog," Kevin said. "A retriever, something like that."

Amy said she wanted a cat, and I said so did I, and Dad nodded. "I expect when the weather changes, mice plan to move right in with us," he said. When Brian said he wanted a horse, everyone laughed. "We'll talk about that later," Dad said. "I think this is getting out of hand."

We talked about that last weekend obsessively, endlessly, recalling every incident, every scrap of conversation, what we wore, what we ate, everything, as if we were compelled to commit it wholly to memory. And we never talked about the week that followed. I have so few memories of it, I might have gone through it in a stupor.

On Tuesday I was in history class when the principal, Mr. Karel, came to the room and spoke with the teacher, Mrs. Jesperson. They went out to the hall together, and when she returned, she came to my desk and said I should get my things and go with her. Her eyes were teary.

In the corridor, Mr. Karel put his arm around my shoulders and walked me to his office. Kevin and Amy were there, both of them as afraid as I was. I thought at first we all were in trouble again, but this was different. Mr. Karel said he would take us home. Someone had gone to get Brian and he would take us all home. There had been an accident at Dad's work.

We sat together in the backseat. Mr. Karel said Kevin could sit up front with him, but Kevin shook his head, and we sat together, Brian on Amy's lap. No one spoke on the drive home.

There were cars in our driveway, and strange men in the living room. Mother was sitting on the couch beside a strange woman. She had been sitting up so straight, staring, not crying or anything, but her face was as gray as the bone lady's face. She jumped up and ran to us when we entered, and she tried to hold us all, tried to get her arms around all of us at once, and she began to cry.

"They killed your father! My poor babies! They killed him! They killed him."

People came and left, strangers. Food appeared. The strange woman stayed overnight and slept on the couch. She was the wife of one of the company men, I learned later, but then she was just a strange woman on our couch. She saw to it that we had proper clothes for the funeral, and she managed the meals, but after the first night, she no longer slept in our living room. Mrs. Hennessy and Mrs. Larkins came and brought food, and they stayed in the kitchen, talking for a long time. Mother had been sitting with them silently, but suddenly she stood up and cried, "Why don't you leave me and my children alone with our grief? Do you want to see me break down, fall in a faint? What are you waiting for? Leave us alone!"

We fled up the back stairs, all the way up to Kevin's attic room, where we sat huddled together on the floor, not talking. After a few minutes, Mother came up and sat with us. No one talked; we just sat there until it grew dark.

No one prepares children for death and funerals. We didn't know what to do, what to say to the strangers who kept coming to our house. We wanted to be with one another and not have to talk. At the funeral, held in the funeral home, a preacher we never had seen before talked for a long time. Later I couldn't remember a thing he had said. Mrs. Larkins took me by the hand and said, "You have to tell your father good-bye. Be brave, Liz, for your mother's sake." I didn't know what she was saying, what it meant. She led me to the casket and I saw him, someone, and for a second I thought it was a mistake, all of it. A mistake. That was not Dad. I stared, not able to move, until Mrs. Larkins pulled me away. Other women were leading Amy and Kevin to say good-bye.

When someone tried to take Brian to the casket, he screamed, "No! That's not my daddy! No!"

Mother stood up and drew Brian to her and held him on her lap, and she stared straight ahead while he sobbed against her shoulder.

There was another short service at the cemetery, and then we went home. People were there, company men mostly, a few others. Mother walked past them all to her room, went inside, and closed the door. Again, we children didn't know what we were supposed to do. When someone on the patio laughed, Mother's door flew open and she ran out to stand, wild-eyed, with her chest heaving, in the kitchen doorway.

"Get out! All of you! Get out! You can't come here and laugh on his grave! Get out of here, all of you!"

A woman started to move toward her, with her hand outstretched, and Mother shrieked, "Don't touch me! Get out of my house and leave us alone!" She backed away from the woman, turned, and ran to her room and slammed the door.

The woman reached out toward Amy, who twisted away and fled up the back stairs. Kevin, Brian, and I followed. We went to Amy's room, where, clumped together at the window, we could see the driveway and the small groups of departing people, who met in twos and threes, then separated and got into the various cars. We didn't move until the last car was gone. Then we went down to Mother.

She came out to the kitchen and stood clutching a chair back, her face dead white, her eyes red and staring. "Children, promise you won't do that to me when I die! You won't let them paint me and put me in a box and let strangers come and stare at me." She started in a low harsh voice, but her voice rose until she was nearly screaming. "You won't let a preacher say lies about me. If there's a God, he doesn't need your father. He didn't greet him and embrace him. He took him away from us, and *we* need him. God doesn't need anyone. Promise me! Kevin, by the sacred memory of your father, promise me! Say it! Promise me!"

Huskily he said, "I promise."

She turned to Amy, who was sobbing. "I promise, Mother. I promise!"

I promised, and even Brian promised. Mother closed her eyes and drew in a long breath. Then she looked at the table spread with casseroles and a ham, other food.

"Girls, rake all that garbage out. We won't eat a bite of their food, the ghouls. After while I'll make us some dinner."

She put her arms around Amy, who couldn't stop sobbing. Stroking Amy's hair, Mother said, "We'll manage, children. We will. We're still a family. We'll manage."

I felt a surge of relief that she was taking charge, that she was able to take charge and be aware of us again. I hadn't realized until then how frightened I had been by her, her apparent disregard for all of us that week. We all knew how sometimes she had seemed to be looking through us, at something that wasn't there, at memories maybe. Those moments had always been brief, ended abruptly with a laugh, a joke, or a caustic comment. That week she had been like that most of the time.

The next day Mr. Martens, a lawyer, came to talk to Mother. She told Amy and me to take Brian out for a hike in the woods and said that, as the man of the family now, Kevin should stay for the discussion.

Afterward, he reported in full what had been said. Dad had taken care of us. There was mortgage insurance; the house would be paid for entirely, ours free and clear. There was a big insurance policy that would pay double for an accidental death. The company would settle for another large sum, to be determined by the legal department without a fight, since they would lose a court battle and have to pay even more and they knew that. Every month money would be transferred to Mother's bank account; she would not have to do a thing about that. The principal was to be managed by the lawyer's firm and was not to be touched except for emergencies. Money was in trust accounts for the education of all four children. Periodically they would review the family's financial position and make any necessary adjustments.

When Kevin was ready for college, he was to have the school send all the necessary papers to the lawyer, who would oversee the payment of tuition, housing, a monthly allowance, whatever else would be required. The same arrangements had been made for all of us.

Dad had thought of everything. He had known Mother was not to be trusted with large amounts of money and had seen to it that she would never have to worry about finances. She would never have to leave her family.

5

We went back to school the next week. Mrs. Jesperson put her arm around my shoulders and gave me a little squeeze and said she was so sorry. I ducked my head and didn't answer. I didn't know what to say. When I thought the other kids were whispering about me, about us, I stared out the window and pretended I was somewhere else, or I worked at my math or read my history, anything to keep myself far away from them. I didn't know how to cope with sympathy.

Mother couldn't cope with sympathy, either. She took Amy and me to the supermarket in the village where we usually shopped. When we were finished and had our basket at the checkout counter, the cashier told Mother how sorry she was and Mother walked out. Amy ran after her to get money to pay for the groceries and Mother sat in the car and waited for us. She never went back to that store, but drove several miles past it to a strip mall that had a Safeway where no one knew us. More and more often she sent us in with a list and she waited in the car.

She stopped going to the bank and used the ATM machine instead, or waited in the car for one of us to use it. We all had the PIN. She didn't open mail, and it piled up until one night Kevin and Amy started to go through it. Cards of condolence, bills, sales flyers . . .

"Mother," Kevin said, "you have to pay the electric bill. We owe for two months." When she looked at him with an absent expression, he said, "I can write the checks if you want, and you sign them."

Mother and Dad had paid bills together as long as I could remember. She would exclaim, "A hundred eighty dollars! For electricity! My God, turn off some lights." He would laugh and write the check, and she would open the next envelope.

"Mother, I need the checkbook," Kevin said anxiously, as if he was not certain she had heard him.

She went to her room, returned with the checkbook, and laid it on the table, then walked on past to the living room and turned on the television. Kevin and Amy went through all the bills. He wrote checks, she put stamps on envelopes. After three days, the checks still were not signed.

"You do it, honey," Mother said to Amy.

"I can't forge your name!"

"It isn't forgery if I give you permission." She wrote her name on a piece of notebook paper, then went to the living room to watch television. Every day, late into the night, she spent hours watching television, something she had never done before.

Amy and Kevin looked at each other, then at the scrawled name, and slowly Amy began to copy the signature. Mother's handwriting was as childish as Brian's. Amy filled a sheet of paper, another one, until she had a fair enough copy, and then she signed the checks. When we got our first report cards, Amy signed them, too. No one noticed or commented if they did notice.

Mother was a good housekeeper. It was all she had ever wanted to do, and she did it well. But our meals changed. No more gourmet dinners, no more exotic combinations of flavors, strange colors, and seasonings. Now it was fried chicken or hamburgers, mashed potatoes, baked apples, simple food. The other meals had been for Dad.

She never talked about him, and if one of us started to, she left the room. She talked very little and usually only about her early life before Miami. It was grim talk, full of warnings about "the system" and what it did to children. One evening at dusk Brian yelled that deer were eating apples off the tree. She nodded and said, "He knew they would." Then she left the room.

One day two men from Dad's company dropped in. "Just thought you might be needing some help," one of them said. "You know, firewood, something like that."

Mother stood in the middle of the living room; they were still by the foyer door, and she said, "Where were you when my husband needed help? We don't need anything." She turned and walked out.

A few weeks after the funeral Mrs. Hennessy came by. Brian went to the door when she rang. I was in the kitchen with Mother, peeling potatoes. When Brian told her who was there, she said in a loud, carrying voice, "Tell her I'm not home."

By November Mother's isolation was complete. She saw no one except her four children, and our isolation was nearly as complete. For reasons we could not understand, we became her accomplices in seeking seclusion. We participated in no extracurricular activities; none of us went home with other kids, or brought anyone home with us. When my teacher, Mrs. Jesperson, urged me to take a part in a play that would involve staying late for rehearsals, I said I couldn't because my mother was sick and needed me at home. Amy and Kevin used the same excuse. The three of us often sat in one of our rooms, talking late into the night while she sat in the living room before the television, sometimes with the sound off. We didn't include Brian in those late-night talk sessions; he was still too young.

Kevin was worried that Mother would not take him for his driving test in December, when he would be sixteen. He was desperate to start driving. He would take us to ball games, he said, and the movies now and then, things Mother always agreed to vaguely, things we never did. Amy was worried that maybe Mother really was sick, and we all knew she would never consent to going to a doctor.

Much of our talk started with the phrase "Remember when . . ." and we talked about Dad and life before, and that last weekend, things we couldn't talk about when Mother was around.

The fall had been very dry, although we had read enough about Oregon, and had heard enough by then, to know that winters were rainy. In November it started to rain on a Sunday and it rained every day for a week, never very hard, but without letup.

On Saturday Mother stood at the kitchen window, gazing out at the rain. There were still apples on the tree, high up, out of reach of the deer. "We should pick some more of them," she said absently. Then she said, "I've heard that it's so nice in Phoenix, warm and sunny most of the time. And it's a big city. There's always so much to do in a big city."

Kevin was at the table with Brian, drawing funny animals for Brian to color. Kevin looked sick at Mother's words. Silently he stood up and walked out of the kitchen, up the back stairs.

At dinner that night Mother said, "The best thing about a big city is that no one knows you. They don't pay any attention to you at all." She began to talk about Atlanta. "Most of the time, I felt like I was an invisible girl. Gliding in and out around people who never saw me. Isn't that strange, how they don't see you if they don't want to."

The rain stopped on Sunday. A few days later Brian had a cold and would have to stay home the rest of the week. Mother said that's what happened in such a cold, wet climate. On Friday,

Amy had to go to the library and I wanted to go with her; we would catch a regular city bus and be home a little late. Kevin said he would go straight home from school, and of course Brian would be with Mother. Usually we all got home a little after four. It started to rain again in the afternoon. None of us kids minded it at all; we had waterproof jackets and umbrellas and boots. Rain, no rain, it didn't matter. Mother would be upset, though, I thought gloomily. I hoped she wouldn't start about Phoenix again.

It was getting dark when we got home at about five. We walked around the house to the patio, where we always left our umbrellas to drip. The ladder was lying on the patio. Kevin met us at the door. His face was gray, even his lips were gray, and he was shaking hard.

"Mother," he whispered. "Mother." He began to cry.

6

Capricious memory, merciless or merciful, with no pattern. My memory of that evening has been merciful. I have snapshots, glimpses, no coherent sequence of unfolding events, and, strangely, no memory of what I felt, what I experienced.

Mother was in bed, with piles of blankets on her. Her hair was wet and muddy, her pillow was muddy.

Amy threw up, and they said I cleaned up the mess, but I don't remember. Kevin was shaking so hard, he couldn't hold a glass when he tried to get Amy a drink of water. I couldn't hold the phone when I tried to call 911.

"Remember our promise!" Kevin cried. His voice was so hoarse and broken, I couldn't understand what he was saying. "We promised!"

We stood around the phone, which was on the floor in the hall, until it began to make the noise it does when it's been disconnected too long; Amy stifled a scream at the sound. Kevin couldn't pick up the phone; he was shaking too hard from shock and from a physical chill. He was soaking wet. Amy picked it up and put it back in the cradle.

"You should get dry," she said in a faint voice, as if she was very far away.

He must have gone upstairs to take a hot shower and put on dry clothes, because the next snapshot is of the three of us sitting on the couch, holding hands, with Kevin in the middle, no longer wet and shaking uncontrollably. A tremor passed through him again and again as he told us about it.

He had come in through the back door, the way we always did, and had left his boots on the patio, then hung up his jacket to drip on a peg by the door. He went upstairs to put his backpack down and get on some dry shoes. Passing Brian's door, he saw that he was sleeping, and he assumed Mother was napping, too. Brian had been up with a cough several nights in a row and neither of them had slept much. He went down to the kitchen for something to eat and began to feel uneasy. Flour was out; a bowl of dough was on the counter, a rolling pin and a pie pan nearby.

He poured a glass of milk, put it down, and went to her door to listen. Sometimes she played music while she was resting. He didn't want to knock, in case she was asleep, but he opened the door a crack, enough to see that the room was empty. From the doorway he could see the open door to her bathroom, also empty. Maybe Brian had gotten worse and she had gone out for medicine or something, he thought then, and went to look at Brian, who was cool and sound asleep. Kevin went through the whole house room by room, out to the garage, where the car and the van were both parked, and by then he was desperately afraid. It was raining hard. She wouldn't be out in rain like that.

Returning from the garage, he saw the ladder again. He had seen it earlier without paying any attention to it. I had seen it and paid no attention. He found her not far from the patio, under the apple tree.

When he turned her over, her face was muddy; her mouth, nose, even her eyes were muddy.

All he could think of was to get her out of the rain, put her in bed and cover her up so she would get warm, and wash the mud off her face.

After he finished, the silence stretched on and on until Amy finally said, "We have to tell someone."

"We promised!" Kevin said. His voice cracked.

"It doesn't have to be that way," Amy whispered. "We'll tell them not to do that."

"They won't pay any attention to what we say."

"They'll put us in homes," I said, terrified. "No one will want four kids. They'll put us in a lot of different homes!" Kevin's hand crushed mine. It hurt, but I didn't want him to let go.

"We'll bury her ourselves," he said hoarsely. "We won't tell anyone."

We were crazy with shock, crazy to think we could do that, crazy to consider doing it. When Brian got up, we told him he must never tell anyone or they would take us all away and put us in homes, like the ones Mother used to talk about, where people would beat us with wooden spoons. We might never see one another again.

We all helped dig the grave. We moved the big pile of decomposed grass and dug it there. Amy and I washed Mother. We carried in pots of water and towels and cut her muddy, wet clothes off and washed her, even her hair. We dressed her in her white silk kimono that Dad had given her and that she seldom had worn because it was too nice for around the house.

We didn't know what to do about a coffin. There was nothing to make one with. Finally we put her in her sleeping bag and zipped it up all the way. Kevin took a door off the hinges and we carried her on it, and all four of us lowered her into the grave. Kevin read from the book Dad had been reading to her, *Madame Bovary*. It had been on the nightstand by his side of the bed. Everything of his was still where he had left it.

Reading, Kevin sounded exactly like Dad. I remembered listening to Dad's voice rising and falling, on the edge of audibility, when he used to read to Mother.

" 'Little by little these fears of Rodolphe's took possession of her. At first she had been intoxicated with love, had had no thought beyond. But now that it was indispensable to her, she dreaded losing anything of that love, dreaded the least difficulty that might befall it —' "

Abruptly, Kevin stopped; his voice failed after all, or his eyes did. He snapped the book shut and reached over to put it in the grave. Amy said brokenly, "Rest in peace, Mother. We love you."

When Kevin began to fill the grave, Brian screamed and ran blindly until I caught and held him as he kicked and screamed and fought to get loose. It was twilight; fog was drifting down through the trees, rising from the ground, merging — uneasy pale shadows like uninvited guests, shielding us from the world.

I half-carried, half-dragged Brian inside and held him while Kevin and Amy finished the burial. It was Saturday, twenty-four hours since Amy and I had come home from the library.

7

Few adults comprehend the depth of grief that children can suffer. Memories of their own grief-stricken days have been expunged or made tolerable by the passage of time. If confronted with a child's grief undeniably, they seem to consider a little pat or a friendly squeeze of a shoulder enough to assuage it, but if the confrontation is less than undeniable, they don't recognize the grief at all. It is as invisible as Mother was when she glided along the streets of Atlanta.

In school on Monday Mrs. Jesperson asked me if I was ill, and I said everyone in our family had a cold. There were a lot of absences that week; she let it go. Amy told her teacher she had cramps, and she was sent to the nurse's room to lie down for a while. Brian's red eyes and sniffles caused no comment; his teacher probably assumed his cold was still lingering.

We were afraid Brian would betray us. We told him to say Mother was fine if anyone asked, nothing more. That was the only foresight we were capable of until later that week, over the long Thanksgiving weekend.

Our newspapers nearly gave us away. On Friday after Thanksgiving the doorbell rang and Brian went to answer it. I was in the kitchen making myself a sandwich and I heard Mrs. Larkins's voice. "Is your mother home?"

I ran to the front door and pulled Brian back. "Your sandwich is ready," I said.

"Hello, Liz," Mrs. Larkins said cheerfully. "I just wondered if your mother is all right. I noticed the newspapers piling up in the box." She handed me several rolled-up newspapers. She was wearing a long fur-lined raincoat that came to the top of shiny pointed-toe boots. She pulled the hood of her coat down as if she expected me to open the door wider and let her in.

I had thought she was beautiful, but that day, I saw her as a prying, evil witch with bloody fingers.

"Mother's fine. She's taking a nap. She caught Brian's cold. He had to stay home all last week. Now she has it." I said this in a rush, hardly knowing what I was saying. I thought Mrs. Larkins was trying to look over my head, past the foyer and into the living room, and I pulled the door to close it. "We all have colds," I said desperately.

"Oh. Maybe your mother would like a little help until she's feeling better."

Then I heard Mother call out, "Tell whoever that is that we don't want whatever it is they're selling. And shut that door!"

I held the doorknob as hard as I could or I would have fallen, before I realized it had been Amy's voice. She had sounded exactly like Mother.

Mrs. Larkins's face changed and looked hard and tight. She turned to leave, then she paused and looked at me again. "Liz, if you kids need anything, I'd like to help. Remember that."

Nodding, I shut the door and locked it and then watched out the little window by the side until she pulled her car around the van carefully and drove out the driveway. Kevin had practiced driving the van all day Thursday and again that Friday. Mrs. Larkins might have thought Mother had been out shopping in it or something. I was still standing at the little window when Amy came to stand by me.

"She's gone," I said.

We turned toward the living room together, and I saw it for the first time in a week. Clothes were strewn about; books were on the floor, cups and glasses on end tables. Had Mrs. Larkins seen the living room? "She brought these," I said to Amy, holding up the newspapers. "There's probably mail in the box." Kevin had brought in the newspapers a few times, and the mail a time or two. Then none of us had thought of it again.

We went to the kitchen, where dirty dishes were on the table and counters, piled up in the sink. We had been living on sandwiches, canned soup, and cereal until the milk ran out a day, two days before; I didn't know when we finished the last of the milk. The soup was all gone, and there was one loaf of bread in the freezer, but I had scraped the peanut butter jar to make a sandwich. Brian was eating it. He was dirty, scruffy-looking. I doubted that he had had a bath all week, and his hair was stringy and matted. I felt guilty about him, and about myself. My hair was stringy, too, and I had had only the fast in-and-out showers they made us take in school after gym. The need to be squeaky-clean that had overtaken both Amy and Kevin had not yet touched me.

Kevin came in through the back door. He had ducked out of sight when he saw Mrs. Larkins. "What did she want?"

I showed him the newspapers. "She noticed them in the box. And probably she saw the living room."

"We have to clean up this place," Amy said. She sounded tired. We were all so tired most of the time.

"We have to buy some groceries," I said.

We thought about the four of us shopping, bringing bags of groceries home on the bus. Someone would wonder, we knew. Kevin said, "I can drive. We'll take the car."

Amy said no. The law was that he could drive only if a licensed adult was in the car with him. He had complained about that endlessly. "If you get stopped, and you might, they'd take away your permit, and they'd come here," Amy said in a low voice.

I thought of Mrs. Larkins in her long coat with her hood up. Mother had a long raincoat. It wasn't lined with fur, but it had a hood, and Amy had dressy boots. "You could pretend to be Mother," I said. "Everyone knows she let us do the shopping while she waited in the car."

Amy shook her head violently and jammed her hands against her ears. Kevin pulled one hand down and yelled, "You can do it! We'll all help."

We made Brian take a bath, and Kevin inspected him and washed his hair. I took a shower and washed my hair. We made a list of everything we could think of that Mother usually bought, and then added things, more milk, more cereal, more everything. We didn't want to have to do this again soon. "Real food," Amy said, writing. "We have to start eating real meals or someone will get sick."

We three older children could all cook. Mother had started teaching us as soon as were eight or nine. "You'd better know how to take care of yourself," she used to say, "because you'll have to sooner or later." We could cook and clean and do laundry, all the things we hadn't thought of that week.

When we were ready, we got into the Toyota because that was what Mother usually drove. Kevin clutched the steering wheel hard with both hands and was overcautious, taking no chances. He used the ATM machine in the front of the bank and Brian and I went next door to the supermarket. I started filling a cart; Brian pushed it, the way he usually did. When I looked out the window at the Toyota, it was scary; Amy was sitting exactly the way Mother used to do, her head bent over a magazine, the hood up over her hair. She had become our mother.

No one in Safeway paid any attention to us.

Scrubbed children are always reassuring to adults. The cashier at the checkout asked where my sister was and I said she had a cold. She said it was going around. Then we were done.

Going home, we passed Mrs. Larkins driving toward us. She waved and Amy turned her head away very quickly. Mrs. Larkins never came back to our house; she was polite when she saw any of us in the village, but she never asked about Mother. Her daughter, Margaret, never spoke to any of us again.

We cleaned the house and washed clothes and started cooking real meals, the way Mother had taught us, but we didn't cook onions. Mother always thought you had to put onions in nearly everything, but we didn't use them and we didn't miss them. We made rules about the chores, about baths, bedtime, homework, everything we could think of. Brian pouted at some of the rules and said, "You can't make me." And Kevin said darkly, "You want to go live with that lady and her fat dog, get beaten with a spoon?" Brian's chin quivered and he ducked his head. We used that threat anytime he seemed to be getting out of hand.

Off the kitchen was a family room that we never had used. Mother had meant to put our old stuff in there when we bought a new couch and chairs. The room was still unfurnished. Over the weekend, we moved the television in there, and one of the chairs from the living room. We would get pillows for the floor, we said, as soon as Kevin got his driver's license and we could go to Kmart or someplace. If anyone came by and happened to go into the living room, it would be clean because we would never use it. We kept the door to the living room closed after that, as well as the doors to the dining room and Mother and Dad's room.

The first and most important rule we made, and even wrote down, was never to draw attention to ourselves. Never cause anyone to question anything about us. Never get in trouble at school or anywhere else. Never give cause for a special parent-teacher conference. We knew the usual conferences could be avoided because Mother had avoided them for years. Don't get sick, no doctors. Brush your teeth, no dentists. Brian was never to open the front door again to anyone, and never to answer the telephone.

During our rule-making session, I told Brian he had to go back to sleeping in his own bed in his own room. After Dad died, for weeks Brian had crept downstairs night after night and slipped into bed with Mother. After we buried her, he had come to my bed every night. Twice I had gone down to sleep on the couch because he was a restless sleeper.

"You can go around the house with me and watch me check all the doors and windows to make sure they're locked," Kevin told him. "No one's going to get in here."

"They're already in," Brian said.

Getting Kevin's license raised a hurdle we thought impassable. He had to have a regular driver's license. It was too risky having Amy pretend to be Mother. If she kept it up, sooner or later someone would see her and know, or someone would go up to the car window to speak to her, or the police would stop Kevin just to check his permit. We consumed enormous amounts of food and we couldn't carry it home on the bus. I thought of carrying the big packages of toilet paper on the bus. We couldn't do it. We had to use the car. But Kevin had to be accompanied by a licensed driver to the DMV office for his test; that was the law. One of the boys at school told him they would ask who had brought him. They always checked. He didn't have a best friend to ask, much less the older brother or parent of a best friend.

We solved the problem by having Amy pose as Mother for one more time, we hoped the last time. The day after Kevin turned sixteen, Amy put on her high-heeled boots and Mother's raincoat, and we all went to the DMV office. Kevin left the three of us by the car and went inside to ask a clerk how long he would be; he said his mother wanted to know if she had time to take the kids shopping. The clerk glanced out the window at us, Amy with her back to him, Brian and me facing his way. The clerk told Kevin he'd be done by five, and Kevin came out and told us to move it. We walked away, I on one side of

Amy, Brian on the other.

After the tests, Kevin drove us home legally and we had cake and ice cream, his birthday party.

During the period between Thanksgiving and Kevin's sixteenth birthday two weeks later, it seemed that we were all adjusting. Our grief was there, and it came out unexpectedly sometimes. More than once Brian yelled at Kevin, "Mother said I could!" and burst into tears. Now and then he yelled and cried over being told trivial things — to scrape his plate, or turn the television off, or to go to bed — or over nothing. Amy would start to cry without warning, or I would. But we were keeping ourselves clean and part of the house presentable; we were eating real food most of the time; we were going to bed at a reasonable hour. For a while, no one had wanted to go to bed before midnight or even later.

Fear was the authority that held us in check; its power was awesome.

During those weeks, several times Brian came to my room in the middle of the night and tried to crawl into bed with me.

"I can hear people walking," he said. "They're in my room, watching me."

"There isn't anyone here and you know it. Come on, I'll go back to your room with you."

"Listen," he said.

I heard the house noises, and I was sleepy and cross. "You little creep. That's just the house settling. Come on."

He started to cry, but I took him back and sat on the side of his bed for a while and said things like "That's the wind blowing the fir trees," or "That's what the stairs do at night. They creak." Those were the things Dad had told him. He cried himself to sleep, with the cover pulled up over his head.

I couldn't go back to sleep for a long time. The house noise sounded different. It sounded like people walking around.

As Christmas got closer, we debated putting up a tree. Only Brian wanted to. He asked if Santa was going to come, or if he was mad at us the way God was. Amy said, very gently for her, "Honey, no one's mad at us. Sure, Santa will come. Have you decided what you want?"

Brian still half-believed in Santa Claus. I remembered the year I decided it was a myth, my dismay and indignation when I confronted Mother and Dad. "You lied to us." Mother said, "Hush, Liz. We never said there was. Maybe the world lied to you. It does that, you might as well learn now." None of us would tell Brian; he would learn how the world lied soon enough.

On the next Saturday we went up into the woods behind the house to find a little fir tree. I loved the woods, so drippy and cool and calm, with mosses everywhere. With the coming of the fall rains, the moss had turned from dull gray to emerald green, sparkling on tree limbs, on fallen trees, rocks. Deer had made crazy, meandering trails through the woods and we had enlarged the trails, made them our trails. The woods went up a little hill, down the other side to a distant road; our property ended at the top of the hill. I liked to pretend it was all ours, as far as I could see, and it might as well have been; we never saw anyone else up there.

That day Amy led us to an area with a lot of seedling fir trees. She had spent more time in the woods than any of us. Very early she had discovered slugs, and she was fascinated by them, especially the long banana slugs, yellow-and-buff-colored, with dark spots, up to eight inches long, trailing their silvery slime wherever they went. Sometimes she tracked one of the trails until she claimed to find the slug's nest. She had decided to become a naturalist, then a biologist, and finally said she would be a zoologist one day. "A slugologist," Kevin had said in disgust. "The word is malacologist," Amy said scathingly.

We cut a little tree, carried it home, and decorated it, and we opened the drapes enough so it could be seen from outside. Afterward we went back to the kitchen and closed the living room door.

That night, after Brian was in bed, we sat at the kitchen table and talked about the check.

The first week of December a letter had come from Mr. Martens, the lawyer who was the keeper of our money. There was a check for a thousand dollars enclosed. We had gaped at it in awe. The letter was dry and brief. "Following your late husband's instructions, we are forwarding a check for one thousand dollars to defray some of your additional holiday expenses. If you have any questions . . ."

We were not rich, but neither had there been a real pinch. Dad had known how much was needed to run our household and had covered it. Mother had not been a good money manager, and we were worse, but even so, sometimes at the end of the month a little money was left over, and it had grown to nearly a hundred dollars. But a thousand dollars was beyond our comprehension at first. And it was a check, not a transfer to the bank account. Amy was afraid to sign it, although no one had ever questioned her signature on the monthly checks to pay bills.

"Dad wanted us to have it," Kevin said. "Mother would have spent it on us."

In the end we deposited the check. Every day for a week, until it was all withdrawn again, one of us used the ATM machine and took out two hundred dollars, the limit for one day. And we spent it all. Brian got a bicycle, Kevin a television for his room, Amy got clothes and a CD player, and I got a violin.

I had been taking music for more than a year by then, a year in Colorado, and the first half of this school year. Dad had promised that if I stuck with it and proved I really was going to keep it up, they would get me my own violin. I had been using one furnished by the school, but to have my own violin at home was my dream.

We bought the little things that Mother and Dad used to stuff in our stockings — cheap watches, calculators, puzzles, games, crayons and paints for Brian, earrings. . . . We had not wanted to hang stockings, but we did after all, and surprised one another with our gifts, bought and wrapped secretly.

That Christmas was a turning point. Grief and terror had penalized us harshly. Amy had lost weight and liked being thin. She often had trouble sleeping. I was thinner than ever and hated it, all elbows and knees and bone, but I was growing taller at last. Sometimes I had nightmares that made me sit up in bed, shivering until daylight. Kevin had turned moody and often was surly and mean, especially with Brian. And Brian had become afraid of him, afraid of noises, afraid of everything.

After I began practicing at home at night, Kevin sometimes yelled at me to take that thing someplace where he couldn't hear it. One night he yelled down the stairs, "Shut your damn door!" And I yelled back, "Shut your own damn door!" Both doors slammed simultaneously.

But whatever annoyances and arguments arose, no matter how bitter, we were all united in our deception, and in our grief and terror. We were fearful of "the system," of "officialdom," of Mrs. Smollen and her wooden spoon.

We should have done something about Brian.

We all sensed that, but we didn't know what he needed, what to do for him. Sometimes I heard him crying and went to sit by him and read until he fell asleep again. When the three of us talked about him, Amy said despairingly, "He'll just have to get over it. Give him time, he'll get over it." Kevin scowled and didn't say anything. I felt inadequate, and resentful that they, the older ones, seemed to relegate the care of Brian to me. Just as Amy had always turned to Kevin, now Brian always turned first to me, and I knew I was useless to him.

Then, a night or two before the long Christmas holiday ended, after practicing, I opened my door and saw that Brian's door was closed. My first thought was that I had been keeping him awake, that he disliked my practicing as much as Kevin did, although he said he liked to hear me. He always slept with his door open, and I left mine open, and we kept lights on in the upstairs hall, in the bathroom, the kitchen. Our house was never dark. Now that I was done practicing, I took the few steps down the hall to open his door, in case he came awake and got frightened later, and I heard him laughing.

I opened the door and saw him kneeling on a chair, looking out the window. He turned to look at me with a smile. "She's dancing," he whispered.

I ran to the window. It was not very dark that night. Thin clouds reflected moonlight, making the backyard almost visible. Of course it was empty. "You must have seen the deer," I said. "Get back in bed before you get chilled."

He peered out the window for a moment, then left the chair and climbed into bed. Light from the hall fell across his bed the way he liked it. I wanted to tell him again that he had seen the deer in the backyard, but I didn't want to make a real issue of it, maybe have him start crying. "I'm sorry if I kept you awake," I said, tucking in his cover. "I'll practice down in the living room from now on."

"No, we like it," he said, and yawned. Then he pulled himself up on one elbow and caught my arm. Light from the hall now fell across his face. He looked serious and intent. "Don't tell Kevin. Okay? Please."

"Tell him what?"

"Nothing," he said, and lay back down. "Just don't tell him."

"I won't tell him," I said. "Go to sleep."

I left his door open, and a little bit later when I looked in, he was sound asleep.

He had been an open, cheerful, biddable child until that fall, when he started throwing temper tantrums occasionally, and showed fear of the dark, and cried a lot. After that night, he sometimes closed his door when he went to bed; he didn't come to my room during the night, didn't mention the noises he heard, and rarely cried. If his door was closed, I never opened it again.

I didn't tell Amy and Kevin anything, and I convinced myself that Brian, too, had had a turning point, that his fear and terror had subsided, his grief was ebbing. He was getting over it, exactly as Amy had said he would.

The holidays ended and we returned to school filled with confidence for the first time that it was going to work. There had been crises that we had managed to get through; there might be more, but we would manage them when they came.

We never thought of what we were doing as evil or wicked. We knew lying was bad, but sometimes you have to lie. We were protecting ourselves as best we could. We knew how all this had started, how it was continuing; none of us had given utterance to a thought as to how it would end. That came later.

8

That year, after an indeterminate period of immobility, of terror, Kevin had started to hang out with boys who had been in trouble in the past and seemed to be headed for more trouble. They accepted Kevin as one of them, as if they recognized there was something pent up within him, something wild and reckless, with a savage need for release. They recognized it because they shared it.

With mobility, freedom, access to whatever money was in the bank account and few scruples about using it, and no one to check his behavior, he spun out of control. When he was home those days, rarely, he was bad-tempered and mean. While I didn't share Brian's fear of him, neither did I like him any longer. Brian and I kept out of his way.

One day the counselor at school called Kevin into his office for a long talk. He got through when he said, "I understand your mother is not well. Can you imagine what it would do to her if she had to go to juvenile court with you and be lectured about your choice of friends? If she was forced to oversee a curfew for you? Or promise to keep the car keys if your license is suspended?"

Later Kevin figured out that the PE teacher and the counselor had been in collusion that day.

It didn't occur to him at the time, and when it did, he had already threaded his way through the minefield of unlicensed adolescent freedom. They suggested he try out for football — he was big enough — or basketball — he was fast on his feet. He hated all contact sports, and said no, but he agreed to try out for the swim team and was accepted almost before he got wet.

He had given up all thoughts about architecture and never went near his drawing table after Dad died. Then he took a computer class and became a nerd/hacker convert.

He felt about a computer the way I had felt about my violin; he had to have one at home.

He called the lawyer. We all stood around him one day and listened.

"Mr. Martens," he said, "I have to ask you something. I've changed my major to computer science, and I need my own computer at home. I haven't mentioned this yet to Mother because I don't want to worry her if we can't afford it." He sounded very mature, understanding, and concerned. His eyes were closed and he was gripping the phone hard. No one else made a sound as he talked about getting a summer job and helping pay for it, or using part of the money set aside for his education. He answered questions politely, listened a long time, and finally hung up. Then he whooped exactly the way Dad used to do.

He bought the computer and set up the system in the dining room on a desk he bought at Goodwill. Afterward, we all used it with the under-standing that it really was his. He joined a computer club at school, and between that and the swim practice and meets, he kept out of trouble.

Another crisis that year arose when Amy and Kevin became panic-stricken when they realized someone had to file income tax returns. Our crime, if we had committed a crime, suddenly could become a federal offense. Finally Kevin called Mr. Martens and we all listened to him lie about Mother. She was ill; she couldn't locate any records; she had no idea about money, taxes, any of that. He went on at length, until Mr. Martens said irritably that his office would fill out the forms, since he did have all the records. If he had been the old family retainer, friends with Dad and Mother for years and years, it never would have worked, but we were simply a piece of ongoing business for him. He did the paper-work and sent it to us for Mother to sign and it was done, a federal offense as soon as Amy signed everything.

Kevin and Amy had gotten into a power strug-gle that first spring. Neither really wanted the responsibility of being head of our household, but neither was willing to concede authority to the other. They had started yelling at each other a lot. At first I was secretly glad they were fight-ing; now Amy would turn to me instead of him. But when I took her side, she yelled at me to butt out and mind my own business.

Things eased between them as summer drew

near, either because of a secret treaty or simple weariness of the bickering. We reverted to committee decisions most of the time. We were a committee of three, automatically barring Brian from major decisions.

It was not only his age that made us leave him out. He was spooky. Kevin said it first, and neither Amy nor I had denied it. Brian was spooky. The first summer we were alone, we told him we'd start taking him to day camp, since he was bored at home all summer; he said he would have to ask Mother if that was okay. He went out to the grave and sat down cross-legged on the ground and stayed a long time. When he came back in, he said it was a good idea.

We had planted flowers on her grave; the deer ate them. He demanded to be taken back to the nursery and asked the nurseryman what plants deer would leave alone; then he told Amy to buy azaleas and rhododendrons. He tended the grave, kept it weeded, watered the plants, and spent a lot of time out by it.

Whenever any of our decisions involved him directly, he claimed he talked it over first with Mother. Sometimes she told him it was okay, sometimes she said no. If she said no, we couldn't sway him. He was spooky.

Once Dad said, *"Tempus fugit,"* and Mother said severely, "Don't use that kind of language in front of the children." But it really does. Not in a reasonable way, though. The minutes, hours, days can be interminable, and a week is gone, a month, even years. Agonizingly slow in its passage, magically swift in retrospect.

It was time to consider how to handle Kevin's graduation from high school.

"It's not a big deal," Kevin said. "I just won't go. I'll go to the parties and the prom, but the graduation itself is dumb. Who needs it?" There were going to be a lot of parties, and he had a date with Carol Kaminsky for the prom.

Once I asked Amy if Kevin and Carol did it. She told me to mind my own business in such a sharp voice that I suspected that she and her boyfriend, Max, probably were doing it, too, even if I couldn't imagine Amy doing anything with Max, who had the personality and brain of a used charcoal briquette. I never mentioned it again, but I watched for signs. Since I didn't know what to look for, I never found evidence; I guessed they were doing it somewhere in private where no one would know.

"You could say Mother intended to go but took a bad turn that afternoon," Amy said doubtfully at the kitchen table that night.

We considered it. But if she was too sick to see her oldest son graduate, was she too sick to take care of the younger kids? Would anyone raise the question? Mother had been dead for two and a half years; we could talk about her like that by then.

We had managed to keep people out of the house for the most part, and when someone did have to come in, a repairman, someone like that, even a classmate, we always said she was taking a nap and to please be quiet. But we never knew when her nervous condition would bring someone to investigate, someone we wouldn't be able to deceive.

I said, "Maybe we could say she had to go to California to see her sister, who's in the hospital."

"Why didn't her sister come to Dad's funeral? Or afterward?" Amy said. "Maybe a more distant relative, someone like a cousin. Someone who just recently got in touch."

We invented Mother's cousin Harriet Downs, who lived in Riverside, California. She was forty-seven, never married, had had polio as a child and couldn't walk, and sometimes needed someone to stay with her for a few weeks. Now that Kevin was eighteen, Amy seventeen, and I was fourteen, Mother felt we were responsible enough to take care of Brian for a week or so.

We were vastly relieved. We had a place to send Mother from time to time. We could have friends come over, even spend the night, no questions asked. Amy and Kevin began to plan a party.

Kevin would take Mother to the airport in Portland and would pick her up in three weeks. After she returned, we would all go camping at the coast. A whole month of not worrying.

The next day Amy told Brian the plan after we got home from school. Kevin wasn't there.

"No," Brian said. "She won't go away."

Amy looked exasperated. "No one's going any-where. That's just our story to tell people why she can't go to the graduation."

He shook his head. "She won't go."

"You little dope! It's a story, a made-up story. Look, you can have a party with your friends here. We'll get cake and ice cream and every-thing. You can invite anyone you want."

He went into the family room and turned on the television. Amy was red-faced and looked murderous. "You go talk to the little shithead. Maybe he'll listen to you."

He did listen to me sometimes. The last time Kevin had threatened him with Mrs. Smollen and her wooden spoon, Brian had looked blank for a second; then he said, "Mother won't let anyone hit me." We had no other threats with any power. Apparently, he had forgotten the ter-rifying stories Mother used to tell. Now and then, however, if I reasoned with him, told him exactly why we were doing this and not that, he listened.

I didn't go to the family room right away. I was reluctant, because the last time I had ex-plained how children weren't allowed to live alone without an adult, he had said, "But we have Mother."

It was my day to cook dinner and I was teach-ing Brian to cook by then. He hadn't been in-terested in learning until I said, "Mother always told us we'll have to take care of ourselves one day, and cooking is part of taking care of your-self."

76

I fooled around in the kitchen, trying to remember how Dad had talked about ghosts once or twice. When I thought I had enough of it in my head, I called Brian to come help with dinner. He liked to make meatballs and spaghetti; he liked to squish the meat between his fingers before he formed odd little shapes. I waited until we had reached that point; he was happily squishing the hamburger mixture, and I said, "You know why so many people believe in ghosts?"

His hands stopped moving for a moment, then he squeezed the hamburger again and watched it ooze between his fingers. "Why?"

"It's what Dad told us," I said. I had to cite authority; he might argue with me, but he never refuted a word passed on by Dad or Mother. "You have to imagine you live in a cave — you know, it's caveman times. And the guy down a cave or two, Bignose, got killed and eaten by a saber-tooth tiger. Okay? Got that?" He grinned and nodded. Sometimes when he grinned like that, for a moment I glimpsed how Dad must have looked as a boy. Brian had the same high coloring, the red cheeks and bright blue eyes; his hair was getting coarser and darker much sooner than mine had changed from baby-fine, nearly white hair. He was as knobby and bony as I had ever been.

I put a finished meat ball on a plate and took another lump of hamburger and began to shape it. He was still just playing. "So there you are in your nice snug cave, wrapped in your bearskin cover, sound asleep. And you dream that you and Bignose are out hunting. He's there with you, big nose and all, swinging his club just like you're swinging your club, and you can see him big as life. In those days people didn't have many words yet. They didn't know what dreaming is. What they saw in their sleep, dreaming, was as real to them as what they saw when they were wide-awake. So naturally, when you dream of Bignose, you think you really see him, not eaten up at all."

Brian had stopped moving, but I kept on making meatballs and telling the story Dad had told us at a campfire in another lifetime. "The problem is that even though the tiger ate him, you and your pals saw it happen, and you went after that tiger and killed it later, sometimes you see a shadow or something that reminds you of Bignose, and you see him again, almost like you were dreaming with your eyes open. You can't talk about it to anyone because you don't know a word for what you saw. So you have to invent a word and you come up with the word *ghost*. Now you can talk about it, and the other guys say, 'Yeah, me, too, I saw Baldy's ghost once,' or 'I used to see Snaggletooth's ghost all the time after he fell over the cliff.' Things like that. They still don't know about dreaming; they just know what they saw. If they saw it with their eyes open or shut was all the same to them. They believed that people they knew had died were still walking around now and then, doing things, and they called them ghosts. Those cavemen told their kids about it, and they told their kids and so on."

Brian made a meatball and poked his finger through the middle of it to make a doughnut shape. Sometimes he made them like sausages, or neat little cubes.

He glanced toward the door, as if to make certain no one else was listening, then he whispered, "I see Mother all the time."

"Like the caveman saw Bignose," I said. My voice was shaky. I knew that, I thought, yet when he said it, I felt like I did the time I picked up a radio that had a bad wire and the electric shock made my heart race and made goose bumps crawl up and down my back, my arms and legs. "It isn't real unless someone else sees it, too," I said almost desperately. "No one else can see Mother."

Matter-of-factly he said, "You don't want to see her." He was making another hamburger doughnut.

"Brian, if anyone comes to the house and wants to see Mother, we'll be in real trouble, because no one can see her. No one. You dream about her, and see her in your mind, but that's all. We all miss her and dream about her, but no one can ever really see her. Can't you get that through your head? How many times do we have to tell you?" I was getting angrier and angrier as the words came out. I couldn't help it. "We have to say she's going on a trip so no one will come and ask about her. That's all we're doing. If anyone asks, you have to say it, too. She's going on a trip and will come home in a couple of weeks. That's all you have to say."

He began to scrape the gloppy meat off his fingers. "I can say it, but she won't go away."

That night I realized we had to put a stop to this. It had to end somehow. I was afraid Brian was crazy, not just creepy or spooky, but crazy.

There wasn't a time in the next weeks for the committee of three to get together and discuss anything. There were the school parties, two proms, junior and senior, and Kevin had a last swim meet. He worked at a part-time job at Safeway. He graduated. We had our party. It was out of control from the start, with beer and booze and pot. I fell in love with Johnny Waterson when he danced with me; he was seventeen, an older man. I fell out of love with him when I saw him kissing Sue Rothman. I had determined to watch Amy and Max; instead, I drank beer and got sick and went to bed early. I thought Max stayed the night, but he was gone in the morning, and I couldn't be sure. Then we cleaned up the house and packed up for our camping trip to the coast.

During those weeks I had been trying to think of a way to put an end to our deception. We would find a way when we had time to talk it over, really explore every possible way out, I told myself. But I was despairing. I had not been able to see how we would extricate ourselves.

9

We had always camped, for as far back as I could remember. In the Rockies, in Big Bend National Park in Texas, Kings Canyon in California . . . Wherever we lived, we found the best camping places and headed out. For a long time the whole family had shared one big tent, then Dad and Mother bought a second one for them to use, and the kids stayed in the big tent. If it rained too hard, we played Monopoly or cards. On pleasant nights, we sat around a campfire and told stories. Everyone had to tell a story.

The first summer we were alone, one day Kevin had exploded at Amy, then at Brian and me, and Amy had said, "Why don't you shut your fat mouth. We need a change. Let's go camping at the coast."

We had been afraid it would be a disaster, but we went. We did need a change, and camping was just right. We struggled with the tent and the camp stove. Our fire wouldn't burn; the wood at the coast was too wet; we ran out of food, and we hadn't brought clothes to change into when we got soaked. But strangely we had found peace for a time. We went again a few weeks later and took firewood with us, and it was better. Since then we had gone camping every month or so, summer and winter. Kevin decided the big tent was too crowded for all of us, and he bought himself a small tent, one he could set up in a minute. No one yelled or got mad. Kevin and Amy were patient with Brian. We even sat around the fire and told stories and jokes. We laughed.

During our camping trips, after the long day in the open, after Brian went to sleep, we three older kids sat around the fire and talked quietly, usually about before. It became the only time we talked without plotting and scheming.

This time, we arrived at our campsite in the afternoon on Monday, two days after the wild party. We set up camp and ran around on the beach for a while, then went back and roasted hot dogs and potatoes and heated some soup. Kevin had a beer. Amy, Brian, and I had hot cocoa. We were subdued, ashamed of ourselves, and not at all talkative. The night was cold; the fire felt good. Brian went to bed as soon as he finished his cocoa, happy with Amy's promise that the next day he could go with her to investigate tide pools. She had changed her major, no longer interested in being a slugologist. She would be a marine biologist, and she was already keeping a meticulous record of all the animal life she found at the beach in the tidal zone.

Although others were in the campground, it wasn't filled the way it was every weekend. We could hear a radio, and a guitar, voices, nothing close enough or loud enough to intrude. Trees were dense all around us; it was easy to ignore the other human noises and listen to the trees rustling in the wind and the low rumble of the surf half a mile away.

It wasn't a good night to bring up problems; we were too tired, but I had to. I felt as if I had been carrying this worry alone for a long time. If they couldn't come up with a solution, at least they could share my worry.

"How are we going to get out of all this?" I asked in a low voice.

Kevin poked the fire with a long stick; sparks flew up, settled again. "Jesus," he muttered. "Not now."

"Then when?" Amy said in her sharp voice. She huddled down lower, closer to the fire. It lighted her hair and made it glow like gold. "It's time we talked about it," she said.

I realized that they had shared my worry after all, they had talked about this without me. I felt resentment and relief all mixed together.

"We don't know," Amy said. "We used to talk about Kevin applying for guardianship when he got eighteen, but we can't do that. Mother would have to be legally dead."

"I have to go to the john," Kevin said. He snatched up the flashlight and stomped away in the darkness, keeping the beam of light low on the trail ahead of him, careful not to shine it into any of the other camps. Amy and I watched until he rounded a curve and trees and darkness swallowed the light.

"I'm freezing," Amy said. "I'll get our ponchos."

She went into the tent, returned, and tossed

mine to me. I shrugged into it. We both held them open in the front to let heat from the fire get inside, warm our backs, the way Dad had shown us. We had bought them in a little town across the border from El Paso. Then, mine had dragged the ground; now it was just right, knee-length, very warm. I remembered how Mother and Dad had laughed when they read the labels: MADE IN TAIWAN. I hadn't known why that was funny.

"We can't produce her body," Amy said in a very low voice. "We can't say she died over two years ago and we've been lying about her ever since. They'd lock up all of us. Maybe even accuse us of killing her."

I hadn't thought of that. I edged closer to the fire, shivering.

"We did such an awful thing," Amy said, almost too low for me to hear. "It was so dumb. Dumb and crazy. She probably had a lot of insurance, just like Dad. Mr. Martens probably would have hired someone to come to the house and look after us, since there was enough money to pay for it. We doubt that we ever were in danger of being placed in foster homes. But we didn't know that then, we didn't think of it."

I hadn't thought about what we might have done, what we should have done, only about what we could do now. I had thought about confessing, explaining everything, encountering sympathy and understanding; now I thought of the accusations that would certainly follow any

84

confession, the suspicions that would haunt us forever. The way the other kids would treat us, the way their parents would treat us, even if we didn't get locked up. But now I really believed we would be arrested; we would be put in prison. Kevin would be raped and tortured, beaten; Amy and I would be raped and beaten by tough women who had nothing to lose. Brian would be put in a hospital with crazy people, crazy children, drugged, maybe given a lobotomy or shock treatment. Irrationally, I began to think it was all Mother's fault; she had done this to us.

"We have to think of a way to make her disappear," Amy said, still in such a low voice, it was a strain to hear.

Kevin came back, got his poncho, and sat by the fire with us. Amy put the pot of water back on the rocks by the fire to make more hot cocoa.

"We thought of burning down the house," Kevin said that night. "But they would expect to find her body. Then we thought that maybe we could find a place where I could run the car off a cliff into the ocean and claim that she was in it, that she must have fallen asleep or something, lost control."

"It would have to be at night," I said. "Too many people are around every day. They would have helicopters and the Coast Guard out there in no time, divers. You'd have to walk back here, and we'd all have to act shocked or something." I knew we couldn't pull it off. We couldn't fake the kind of shock that had made us crazy. "Besides," I said, "they almost always find the body in the ocean. You read about it all the time."

"See," Amy said in a way that made me know they had talked about doing this and she had vetoed the idea. "No death, just a disappearance. We can handle that. We couldn't take a death." She poured water into the cups, stirred the cocoa mix in them, and handed one to me.

"Okay," Kevin said in a mean voice. "But we have to do something soon, this year."

I understood his urgency. He had decided to go to Portland State College, an easy drive to downtown Portland. But he didn't want to stay there more than a year. He wanted to go to Stanford, or Caltech, or even MIT, someplace with a good computer science department. And Amy would graduate in one year and be ready for college. She wanted to go to UCLA to study marine biology. With great reluctance she had agreed that she would go to Portland State for a year, until I was sixteen and could drive. We hadn't really talked much about their plans, partly because I was disbelieving that they would both go away and leave me with Brian when I would be only sixteen and he would be eleven.

"If we report her missing," Amy said after a lengthy silence, "then Liz, Brian, and I can move down to California and you can go anyplace you want. You can be a guardian now, and after I'm eighteen, I can apply for guardianship."

"They won't let you be our guardians," I said. "You don't know that will happen. What if it doesn't? You and Kevin will go away and Brian and I will be in foster homes." I felt tears hot in my eyes and ducked my head. "Besides, we couldn't afford another house, rent and all."

"We'll sell the house here," Kevin said flatly.

"We can't! We don't even own it."

"We can't, but after a few years, Mr. Martens probably could," Amy said.

I shook my head. "No way. We can't ever sell it. What if the new owners decided to dig up the backyard and put in a garden, or plant trees or something?"

Kevin said, "Fuck!" He stood up abruptly. "I'm going to bed." He left us and crawled into his little tent and pulled the flap shut.

I felt a bitter satisfaction that I had thought of something they apparently had not considered. "Amy, wait a minute," I said when she stood up. "Promise me something."

"What?" she said warily. She started to rake the fire apart.

I picked up the shovel and began to put dirt on the glowing wood. "Promise you'll find out first if you or Kevin can be our guardian. Before we do anything else, find out."

She hesitated a long time, and we worked at extinguishing the fire in silence. Finally Amy said, "Okay. I don't know how, but I'll find out. Satisfied?"

I should have been satisfied. Dad had taught us never to make a promise we couldn't keep, and never to break a promise we made. I never did, and I didn't believe Amy did either, but she had not said she promised. I lied and said sure.

It was a long time before I could go to sleep. I could hear the surf like a soft whisper rising and falling, and the wind gossiping with the trees, and Brian's breathing. I thought Amy was awake a long time, too; she was as unnaturally still as I was.

I realized that night that I was afraid of my brother and sister. Kevin was free; in another year Amy would be eighteen and free. I had just turned fourteen, and Brian was only nine, and the two of us had become a burden to Amy and Kevin.

I had meant to talk about Brian, how he was haunted by Mother's ghost. I was afraid to, afraid of what they would do.

10

The next day we climbed cliffs and slid on sand dunes, and when the tide went out, we hiked down a steep cliff to a newly exposed cove where Amy started her investigation of the tide pools. This was her favorite spot. When the tide was in, the water beat against the cliffs many feet higher than our heads, but at low tide, the little crescent beach was sheltered on three sides, and stacks appeared out in the water, where there had been only disturbances of waves earlier. It was as if the stacks and columns had waited for a chance to raise themselves and have a look around. This stretch of coast was basalt; the beach was mostly tide pools, with small patches of sand between them. The shallow pools warmed under the sun; we waded in them with the crabs and fish and starfish all around.

Kevin liked to swim in the cove, but none of the rest of us would swim in the ocean; it was too cold, and it was dangerous with riptides, erratic waves, hidden rocks. We stayed with the little tide pools while he swam.

I tagged along with Amy and Brian for a while, then sat with my back against a warm rock and watched Kevin swimming, and I daydreamed. I did a lot of daydreaming; everyone complained about it. I was sliding by in school, with decent grades, nothing spectacular, nothing to be proud of. The music teacher, Mr. Montoya, had talked to me more than once about my playing. I had talent, he said, I just wasn't applying myself. He wanted to talk to my mother about arranging some private lessons, about a recital or two — to get me over my stage fright, he said. I played much better at practice, and even better at home alone, than I did with the school orchestra when there was an audience. "Music is to be shared," he would say solemnly. "It isn't a private endeavor." For me it was. I had to be in the orchestra at school, or I wouldn't have been allowed to continue with music; I hated it. Being on stage with people looking at me made my hands tighten, my stomach hurt.

"Mother said I could decide about lessons," I told him.

In my English composition class I hated to write the essays that were assigned. Reading them aloud, as required, was torture.

The teacher, Mrs. Corman, made us keep a journal. At first, when she gave us the assignment, I wanted to drop the class; then she said no one would ever read what we wrote, unless we wanted to share it. She would check, just to make sure the pages were being written in, but the content was personal; we could write whatever we wanted to, as long as we did it every day. I censored myself severely. Everything I wrote in the journal had to pass the test: What if someone reads this? I made sure that neither I nor any of my family appeared in the pages.

Instead, I wrote weather reports, book reports, silly things like filling a page without using the letter *e*. As a diary it was hopeless; there was no diarist.

Mrs. Corman assigned a story to be written over a weekend, fiction this time. She taught us how to outline a story, beginning, middle, end, how to plot it, problem and solution, how to do the whole thing. And I froze. On Monday when the stories were turned in, there were only a few of us who weren't prepared. Mrs. Corman said, "Liz, I'm very disappointed in you." I felt that every eye in the class had turned to focus on me; I could feel the heat in my face, feel myself shrinking, and in that moment of shame, I suddenly had a story in my head, all of a piece, complete. "I'm working on it," I said. "I'll have it done tomorrow."

I wrote it that night. It was about a girl who lived in a world where everything was made of glass — the houses, the big buildings, everything. No one paid any attention to anyone else, as if they were all blind and couldn't see into every room, watch every movement. The girl found that if she crushed a white rock into a powder and mixed it with water, it made a white paint. She painted her walls. When she went inside her white room and closed her door, she was happy.

It wasn't much of a story, but when I finished, I felt exhilarated, too wound up to sleep, and I didn't know why. I didn't care that Mrs. Corman praised the story, or that the other kids were pitiless in their criticism. My story, like my violin, was for me, not for them, not for anyone else, just for me.

When I sat daydreaming, I was telling myself bits and pieces of stories, fantasies, wish-fulfillment stories, adventure stories in which I was the hero. Early on I wrote some of the fragments in the journal, then stopped when I realized how personal they were.

Kevin came out of the water, spread a towel, and stretched out in the sun down the beach from me. Amy and Brian were nearly at the far end, squatting over a tide pool, and I knew she was pointing out everything in the pool to Brian, who was entranced.

It was peaceful, easy to imagine that back at camp our parents were getting things ready for dinner, knowing we would be ravenous. I was playing the happy little reunion scene in my head when Kevin stood up. Silhouetted against the bright sky, he was very handsome, tall and muscular. I realized how seldom I saw him, or Amy or Brian, for that matter, and I wondered if Kevin really saw me, saw any of us. Kevin yelled, "Hey, Amy, let's go."

She waved and called back, "You go on. We'll be done in a little while."

Kevin picked up his towel and walked past me without a glance and started to climb back up the cliff trail. I felt as invisible as Mother had said she felt in Atlanta, and then I thought it was true that we all saw what we needed to see, things important to us, and the rest was a blur of shadows without substance. Then I heard myself mouth the words: "We probably will never do this again, not the four of us like this."

This part of our lives was coming to an end — "phase two," I called it — and we were rushing into phase three, wherever it might take us.

We didn't talk that night, and the next night a light rain began to blow in on a cold wind; we played hearts in the big tent. Kevin and Amy were both bored. As soon as Brian crawled into his sleeping bag, we switched to penny poker, which held Kevin's interest, since he always won. I ended up owing him four dollars and fifty-two cents. He said the grand total I now owed him was $350. It might have been.

On Thursday night Kevin said, "I have an idea." Amy got up to make sure Brian was sleeping, and when she came back, we drew a little closer together.

"Okay," Kevin said in a low voice. "In a few weeks Mother goes back to visit her cousin Harriet. I drive her to the airport, like before. We say she'll be back in one week, then when she doesn't come back, we say she called and said it would be another week or so. At the right time I go pick her up, just like we did before."

"You just want another party," I muttered.

"Shut up and listen! Then we say she's back home again. Okay? But in August she takes off again. I drive the Toyota to the airport and put it in long-term parking and Amy picks me up and we drive home. We tell people she drove herself this time. We take it for granted that Cousin Harriet called her and she had to leave without telling anyone, that she'll call us and let us know what's happening. After a few days we get worried because she hasn't called. I try the number she gave us for Cousin Harriet, but there's no one there by that name."

Neither Amy nor I was moving. It was clear that he had thought this through, and that there was more to come.

"So I mention it to some of the guys, and someone's bound to say I should go talk to the sheriff. If no one does, I'll bring it up myself. Or I could call Mr. Martens and tell him about it. However it goes, I end up telling the sheriff that we haven't heard from her, and Cousin Harriet's number is the wrong number. That's all. We're just a little worried."

That was the general idea. Amy and I began to question the details. Had we ever met Cousin Harriet?

"Never," Kevin said. "Mother spoke of her now and then, and said Harriet got in touch with her back in the spring."

"Didn't we ever call Mother when she was gone before?"

"No. She always called us when she said Harriet was sleeping. We weren't to call there. We might wake up Harriet, and she was pretty sick."

"They'll check the airlines and find out she

never took a plane anywhere," I said.

He had thought of that. "Both times I took her she got out at the departing passenger entrance and I didn't go in with her. She said I wouldn't be able to get through security and there wasn't any point in parking and hanging out with her for a few minutes."

They would find the car at the airport, he said, and no trace of Mother. They would discover there was no Harriet Downs in Riverside, California, and they would assume Mother had lied to us about it. She would disappear and never show up again.

"I don't want to drive the van," Amy said in a faint voice.

"It doesn't matter who drives what," Kevin said savagely. "Drive the fucking Toyota to the airport; I'll follow in the van."

I knew Amy's protest had not been about driving, it had been about this conversation, what we were planning, ghouls sitting around a campfire plotting to get rid of their mother, who had become a problem.

We talked about it a long time, adding details, firming up our stories. We would have to say what she might have been wearing, what clothes were missing. We had to pack an overnight bag and get rid of it somehow. Everything in her room was as she had left it; Dad's things were as he had left them. But that fitted. She had never stopped mourning, never gotten rid of anything of his.

We would have to vacuum and dust her room, put fresh sheets on the bed, just as if she had been living there all this time. Amy said she would buy a few magazines Mother used to read, and leave them around, maybe clip out a recipe or something. We had to search her room, make sure there wasn't an out-of-date calendar or TV schedule. It would be a little thing like that that might betray us. We watched *Columbo*; we knew a sharp-eyed detective would spot a small anomaly and confront us with arrest warrants. We would not leave anything for him to spot.

I asked why Mother had to go away and come back again. Why didn't we just have her disappear next week?

"Ground work," Kevin said. "Make it look like maybe she was thinking about not coming back this time."

So Mother went down to Riverside again in July and stretched out a one-week trip to nearly two weeks.

Amy and Kevin had reassured me about foster homes. No one would consider such a thing, not if Mother might walk back in any day. Mr. Martens might want to hire a housekeeper temporarily, and that was okay, as long as she didn't stay overnight. At our ages, we would say, we didn't need anyone around the clock and it would be a terrible expense. I thought that would be the most persuasive argument we could bring up, the expense.

It would be my duty to inform Brian. I was the only one he would listen to. Kevin hardly ever talked to him, and he never asked him to do anything, or suggested that he might do anything; he ordered him brusquely, as if expecting instant obedience, and became angry when Brian was recalcitrant. More and more often, Brian had become absent-looking when Kevin gave him an order. He seldom argued, or refused outright, he simply withdrew, as if he had become deaf. It infuriated Kevin. Amy was friendlier, and even kind to Brian most of the time, but although she included him as a passive audience when she talked about school, her friends, or her adventures driving, she never really talked with him except at the coast, where I suspected she didn't talk with him as much as lecture about the creatures they found in the tide pools.

The day before the event I would tell him what we were planning. I dreaded it.

Meanwhile, Amy and I cleaned Mother's bedroom and packed an overnight bag. We would say we didn't know what she was wearing, but we would know what was missing. We put her purse in. I remembered to put in her toothbrush and hairbrush from the bathroom. None of us ever used her bathroom, although it was downstairs, and we had to go upstairs to the other one. There were spiderwebs and dust in the sink and the bathtub, and a crusted mineral deposit at the water level in the toilet. Her special castile soap had turned gray and opaque, with a deep crack in it. We cleaned the bathroom, threw away the old soap, and got out a new bar. It looked too new, unused.

"We should soak it," Amy said faintly. She put it in the sink with hot water. We both stood staring at it until she took my arm and said, "Come on. We've done enough for now."

I went back later and found the soap soft and eroded in a sink of cold milky-looking water. I put the soap in the dish, cleaned the sink with Mother's washcloth, and dried my hands on her towel. The bathroom looked used.

That final week before the event, Kevin put rocks in the suitcase, and one night he drove into Portland, parked, and walked across Steel Bridge carrying the overnight bag. When no car was in sight, he let the bag fall over the side into the Willamette River. We withdrew six hundred dollars from the checking account, two hundred dollars at a time. We would keep two hundred and put the rest in a safe place to be used later a little at a time. We would say Mother had told us to get the cash, that she wanted us to take Brian shopping the end-of-season sales, it was time to start getting all of us ready for school. We would say she had kept the rest of the money, four hundred dollars.

Then, Sunday afternoon, it was time to tell Brian. I waited until Amy started to cook dinner. Kevin was working at Safeway until seven; he worked three days a week and every other Sunday. We had chosen Monday to carry out our plan because it was one of his days off. I walked out the back door, crossed the patio, and strolled to Mother's garden. That's what we all called it. Brian had enlarged the garden until it was nearly as big as the space Dad had tilled up.

There were rhododendrons, azaleas, some dwarf mahonia bushes, a spreading dwarf golden yew, shrubs with tough leaves that the deer didn't like. Sometimes, at the supermarket, Brian would put a potted plant in the basket. The first time he did that, Amy had glared at him and started to say something, but he had regarded her silently, and she had not said a word. It bothered him that everything bloomed in the spring, and now in August there were no flowers. He had started to read the garden books, looking for late-blooming, deer-resistant plants. He had placed rocks here and there in a way that suggested a master pattern in his head, one that I couldn't see. At a garage sale a year earlier he had spotted a redwood bench and talked Amy into buying it for Mother's garden. A path of pale gray beach stones, all smooth and rounded, each one carefully fitted into its own little hollow, led to the bench. In the rain the wet stones looked like a stream flowing through the garden.

I walked to the bench and sat down. I knew he would join me. He seemed afraid that someone would move something, alter something.

I had to wait only a minute or two before he showed up. I patted the bench and he slouched down next to me. "It's going on three years now since Mother died," I said, then I paused, hoping he would speak, but he didn't. "It's been hard lying all the time," I said. "It's been hard on all of us and we can't keep it up."

"You're going to send her away again, aren't you?" he said.

"We don't send her away. She's dead, Brian. We can't send her away. We just tell people that. We have one more lie to tell, and that will be all. We'll tell everyone she went down to California again, but this time she won't come back. We'll tell people she didn't come back and we don't know where she is. That's the last lie we'll have to tell anyone. We don't know where she is." I glanced at him; he was distant and unmoving. "Nothing else will change," I said. "We'll be just like we are now, but we'll say we don't know where she is this time."

He tensed, as if gathering himself together, getting ready to stand up, leave without another word, the way he often did.

"Brian, people will ask you questions. They'll ask if she told you where she was going, or when she'd come back. You have to say no. She didn't tell you anything. Will you do that?"

He stood up, then gave me a sidelong look. "Yeah. She didn't say she was going anywhere, because she isn't. She's going to stay here forever. She promised me." He walked away.

I watched him and I thought it was no wonder he was crazy. We talked about Mother among ourselves and to everyone else as if she were with us all the time. We had given her a presence in the house, referred to her constantly as if she were alive. No wonder he was confused.

It was a hot day, but I was chilled suddenly and felt I shouldn't be sitting in Mother's garden. I got up and hurried indoors.

"He went upstairs," Amy said, peeling potatoes at the sink. "Did you tell him? What did he say?"

"What can he say? He'll go along with it. He'll be okay. He says Mother told him she'll never leave here. She promised." Despairingly, I added, "Amy, he's sick. He needs help."

She glared at me. "Don't you think I know that? What can we do about it? If you think of anything, let me know. You want to turn him over to a counselor who will get him to confess all? Purge his conscience. Wash away his guilt. Shit! When you think of something, clue me in." She went back to peeling potatoes furiously.

Staring helplessly at her, I realized she knew, maybe had known as long as I had. She must have talked it over with Kevin, too. All three of us knew, and none of us did a thing for him.

11

On Monday we left the house at ten in the morning, Amy in the Toyota, Brian and I in the van with Kevin. Our story would be that Kevin had driven us in to shop and we had left Mother home alone. Amy had refused to drive the interstate and go directly to the airport, and after yelling a lot, Kevin had given in. She would follow us, and after he dropped us at the Pioneer Square Mall, she would follow him through city streets to a strip mall near the airport. Because he didn't trust her to park the Toyota and find her way back to the van, they would swap cars and he would take the Toyota to the parking lot himself while she waited for him to walk back. They would return to the mall and join Brian and me.

"Just keep the van in sight," Kevin snapped before we all left home. "You don't have to tailgate me, just keep me in sight."

"I know!" she screamed. "Leave me alone!"

Of all of us, only Brian appeared unaffected by what we were doing. I was as jittery as Kevin and Amy, and they both looked and acted as if they wanted to strangle each other. I thought she was too nervous to drive alone, and then I thought, *Well, tough! Just do it!*

It was nearly ten-thirty when Kevin dropped us off. At twelve-thirty we were to go to the food court and get something to eat and wait for them.

We would all fool around at the mall for another couple hours and drive home in the van. Everyone should buy something, socks, shoes for Brian and me, a sweater or jeans for Amy. . . . We should have something to show for the hours we would spend at the mall.

Kevin had cursed Amy for being too chicken to drive the interstate, and I silently echoed him. Wimp. I couldn't wait until I could drive, and I planned to cover the country. Every summer take off for a new place, Arizona, Michigan, New England. . . . I told Brian he could go with me if he wanted to, that we'd start with Yellowstone Park. The next day, he had said sure, he wanted to go, too. I supposed he had talked it over with Mother first.

I learned about the trip to the airport in bits and pieces later. Kevin led the two-car parade. It was slow driving through the city, with many stoplights and heavy traffic. It was nearly an hour before they reached the strip mall where they could change places. From there it was half a mile to the parking lot by the circuitous auto route, less than half that far on foot. Amy sat in the van and waited for him to walk back. She had a book, but she was too nervous to read; she held it open, kept her head lowered, and counted the minutes.

Kevin drove straight to the parking lot, stopped for the machine to spit out a ticket, then began weaving up and down rows of cars searching for an empty spot. He found one and parked, and he was walking toward the pedestrian exit when he heard a horn and someone called, "Hey, Kevin!"

He spun around and saw Travis and Mark Jacoby in a car being driven by their mother, who was searching for a parking place. Travis was a couple years younger than Kevin, a member of the swim team. "We're off to stay with our dad in New Orleans for a month," Travis called, twisting to get his head out the window as their car rolled past Kevin in slow motion. "Where you heading?" The car jerked forward and he laughed and said, "Whoops!" and pulled his head back in.

Amy said Kevin was too furious to tell her what had happened when he drove back to the van. All he said was, "Go on home. I'll pick up the kids." She drove the Toyota home and didn't find out until later why he had aborted the plan.

Brian and I had bought shoes and socks. We had spent an hour in the toy store. We had had chili dogs and Cokes in the food court, dawdling as much as we could. When I spotted Kevin stomping toward us, I knew something had gone wrong.

"Come on, let's beat it," he said roughly.

"Where's Amy?"

"Home. Come on!"

In the van he said, "Travis Jacoby saw me, and maybe saw the Toyota." No one spoke again as he sped home, where he stopped long enough for us to get out, and then took off with a squeal of tires.

Although he didn't come back until after midnight, Amy and I were up waiting for him. "Tomorrow," he said brusquely. "We'll do it tomorrow."

Amy shook her head. "I can't drive out there again. Not yet." She had gotten lost in Portland that afternoon.

"Shut up and listen to me. While Brian is in day camp, you two will go to Portland. The story is that Mother knew you couldn't try on clothes with a little brother tagging along. You'll say she drove you in and let you out downtown and said she'd be back at three. She had a few errands of her own to take care of. You drive straight to the train station; there's a parking lot there. A machine will give you the parking ticket and you park and walk downtown. It isn't far. Then at five minutes to four you call me at work and say Mother hasn't shown up and someone has to pick up Brian at four." He drew in a breath and continued. "I'll tell Mike there's an emergency at home and I have to leave, that I have to get Brian and then pick up you two."

He had it all figured out. He had spent the afternoon driving around Portland and had the street directions laid out for Amy and the name of the coffee shop where we should call him from and then wait until he came. He told her exactly how to get to the train station, where to park.

"Why downtown?" I asked. "We never go downtown to shop."

"Because you can walk there from the train

station," he said curtly. "You'd never make it to the mall, you'd get lost or something." He cast a mean look at Amy.

We went over it all again, then he said, "Get there by twelve-thirty. Two Amtrak trains will be pulling in about then and a lot of people will be around. No one will pay any attention to you."

Amy said she didn't want to drive to town on I-5, and he said, almost gently, "It's a snap, Amy. Just take your time. If people want to pass you, let them. Once you leave the interstate, it's only a few blocks to the station. A snap. The long roundabout way would have you in Portland traffic for more than an hour, and you'd probably get lost again."

It was hard to tell which was more frightening to her, getting lost in Portland or driving the interstate. Reluctantly, she opted for the interstate.

The next morning Kevin took Brian to day camp and came back home. We took another hundred dollars from our cache. Kevin had to be at work at twelve and we all left at about the same time, Kevin in the van, Amy and I in the Toyota. She was a nervous driver, and with her at the wheel, I was a nervous passenger. It would be my job to watch for our exit and then to watch for the streets we needed to take in Portland. I had written them down: "Exit on Front Street, left on Columbia, right on Sixth . . ."

It was simple, and would have been even simpler if Amy hadn't been so nervous. We pulled into the train station parking lot at 12:25. There were many cars coming and going, and taxis were lined up at the front of the station, edging forward one by one. No one paid any attention to us and we didn't see anyone we knew.

After we left the car, we walked across the street and passed the Greyhound bus station. My steps faltered. As an infant, Mother had appeared outside a bus station, and now she would disappear outside another one. Amy pulled on my arm and we walked silently to the downtown commercial section.

There were big expensive stores downtown: Frederick Nelson, Neiman Marcus, Nordstrom's. . . . I had never been shopping in any of them. We went from one store to another and tried on clothes, and finally we both bought jeans and a sweatshirt, because we had to have something to show for our shopping trip. Then it was time to go to the coffee shop and call Kevin.

Forty-five minutes later he drove up to the coffee shop, where we were waiting out front, and we all went home.

We had arranged for our dead mother to vanish.

12

On Wednesday we hung around the house after Kevin took Brian to day camp. Kevin looked up the Riverside telephone exchange and made up a number to go with it, and Amy, in Mother's childish scrawl, wrote Harriet's name and fake number in the address book.

On Thursday morning at eleven Kevin called the number. We stood at his elbow and listened. "Hello," he said. "Who did you say this is? . . . Oh, sorry. I must have the wrong number." He hung up. "A dry cleaner," he said. There was a line of sweat beads on his upper lip. He waited a few seconds and redialed. "Sorry to bother you again," he said. "I'm trying to find a Harriet Downs. Is she at this number?" He put the phone back. "He hung up on me." He called information and failed to get a number for Harriet Downs, then he placed a call to Mr. Martens, the lawyer.

He sounded very nervous when he said, "Mr. Martens, it's Kevin McNair. I didn't know who else to call. Mother's gone somewhere and we don't know where she is. I'm supposed to go to work pretty soon, but we're all pretty worried, and they won't have a car here if I take the van to work. I don't know what to do. Should I call the police?" He held the phone away from his ear so Amy and I could hear.

"Kevin, I don't know what you're talking about. What do you mean she's gone somewhere?"

"She took the girls shopping and was supposed to pick them up, but she didn't, and she hasn't come back since."

"Since when?" Mr. Martens sounded exasperated. "Calm down, Kevin. When did she leave?"

"Tuesday. We thought she'd call like she did before when she had to leave, but she didn't."

"For God's sake! Tuesday? Why didn't you call? Never mind. Don't go to work, just sit tight. Don't call anyone else yet. I'm coming out there. Be half an hour or so. Just sit tight and wait for me."

When Kevin hung up, we stood motionless around the telephone, until Amy moved closer to Kevin and touched his arm. "It'll be all right," she said. "It'll be all right." She was so pale, she looked as if she might faint.

Mr. Martens came. He asked us questions, then stalked around the house angrily, his mouth a tight lipless line when he went into Mother's room and saw all of Dad's things about, his hairbrush, his slippers, his toothbrush and shaving things in the bathroom. Clearly he was very disapproving of anyone who carried grief to extremes.

Kevin always called him "the Suit," but I thought of him as one of the Gray Men. His hair was gray and combed straight back, his suit was gray; he was over fifty, and looked ancient, with a deeply lined face, a furrowed forehead. I thought his expression was gray, as if he never smiled, never found anything to smile or laugh about. He didn't even try to disguise his displeasure with us, with Mother, with the situation. He was a corporate lawyer who dealt in trusts and securities, wills, partnerships and corporations; this was beyond his scope.

He tried the number in the address book and hung up without speaking. He tried information, then hung up again. Finally he called the sheriff's office. He said they'd send a deputy.

While we waited he asked Amy to find a picture of Mother. She looked at me in fear. We hadn't thought of that. "We haven't taken any in the last few years," she said almost inaudibly.

"Whatever you have. They'll want a picture. A snapshot will do."

Amy left to find a snapshot, and Mr. Martens asked Kevin for the make and model of the car, the license plate number, and he wanted to know the exact dates Mother had been gone before. I sat on the couch and listened to Kevin answer questions. He didn't remember the dates, he said, but we had marked them on the calendar. When he went to the kitchen to get it, I heard water running. His mouth must have been as dry as mine was.

When the deputy arrived, he and Mr. Martens talked on the porch for several minutes before they came into the house. The deputy was fat, sunburned, had white hair and a friendly smile. He seated himself comfortably, pulled a notebook out of his pocket, and asked us the same questions Mr. Martens had asked. When Amy mentioned Brian, he looked up. "Who's Brian?"

"Our little brother. He's in day camp now. He's only nine."

"I see," he said. I thought he looked sad.

He asked more questions that we already had answered for Mr. Martens; then he asked what Mother had been wearing.

Amy looked frozen. We hadn't discussed that. The original plan had been that we didn't know what she had put on. The deputy looked at me.

Almost desperately I said, "I think her blue pants, and a white top." We had put them in her overnight bag.

"Shoes?" he asked.

"I don't remember." I wasn't even sure we had packed shoes.

"Well, no reason you should have paid attention," he said kindly. He asked a few more questions, then stood up. He regarded us for a moment, sitting together on the couch, and he said, "Try to relax, kids. People do this kind of thing now and then. People need a break. They mean to call, but time slips away. You kids going to be all right out here?"

Mr. Martens hadn't asked anything like that. I doubted he had thought of it. I nodded silently. Amy said, "We've been alone before. It's okay."

Kevin got up then and asked, "Is there anything I should do?"

The deputy shook his head. "We'll handle it." He gave Kevin a card. "When she gets in touch, give us a call. If we find out anything, we'll let you know. Try not to worry. Just take it easy, okay?"

Mr. Martens walked out with him and they talked again on the porch. When Mr. Martens returned, he said, "I think for now it's best not to say anything about this. As you say, you've been left alone before, and Kevin is going on nineteen, a responsible adult. Now, we have to discuss a practical matter. Is there any money left in her account?"

"I don't know," Kevin said.

"Yes. Well, what I think would be a wise course is for us to go to the bank and find out, and establish you in a joint account with your mother. If the account is low, we'll transfer funds to tide you over until this is straightened out. Shall we go?" He looked very unhappy, as if the thought of dipping into the principal of our trust account was paining him.

"I'd better drive the van," Kevin said. "It's nearly time to get Brian."

Mr. Martens seemed relieved that he wouldn't have to come back to the house. He cautioned us again not to talk about this. "You don't want malicious gossip to circulate," he said, "and perhaps have reporters turning up."

As soon as they left, Amy burst into tears without warning. And I did, too. Release from

112

nervous tension. We held each other and cried. They found the Toyota that night, and the next day the deputy drove it back; a detective came in a separate car. Mr. Martens was right behind them. The deputy sheriff was concerned for us; Amy and I were both haggard-looking by then, and Kevin was so nervous, he twitched now and again. Mr. Martens was impatient; the detective, Walter Levinson, was grim-faced and thorough. I was afraid of him and half-believed he could tell by watching us that we were all lying. He asked a question, then snapped his mouth shut and leaned forward, staring intently as if dissecting the answer. He asked questions neither of the other two had brought up. He wanted to know why we had waited two days to report her missing. All we could say was that we had thought she would call. He seemed to think that was a lame reason. He wanted to know what was missing, if she had packed a suitcase. He had Amy look over her clothes and tell him what was gone. Hadn't we seen her put a suitcase in the car? In the trunk? When did she tell us she would take us shopping? Had she planned it ahead of time? Why was she driving with an out-of-state license that had expired? I hadn't given a thought to her driver's license, and I had no idea how they had found out anything about it. He wanted a list of her friends and was openly disbelieving when we said she had no friends. On and on.

Once or twice, Mr. Martens interrupted ineffectually. Then he said angrily, "For God's sake, can't you see these kids have told you all they know?"

The detective ignored him, but he finished soon after that, then prowled around the house, outside to the garage, and all around the grounds.

The deputy patted Amy's arm. "Don't take it personally. That's just his style. Doesn't mean anything by it. Why don't we go out and get a drink of water?"

We went to the kitchen, and he poured a glass of water and handed it to Amy, then gazed out at the backyard. "That's pretty," he said. "Your mother do all that?"

"It's Mother's garden," I whispered.

He nodded. Very soon after that everyone left. "You kids try to rest," the deputy said at the door. "You look pretty worn down."

Mr. Martens said he would keep in touch.

"Can't wait to get back to his wills," Kevin said when the cars pulled out of the driveway.

"I'm glad he came," I said.

"He had to. He's our lawyer," Kevin said derisively. "Besides, it all goes on the bill, every second of travel time, every second with us, all on his bill, two, three hundred bucks an hour. Out of our money."

The detective came back a few times; once he called first to find out when Brian would be home. He wanted to ask him a few things, he said. Kevin called Mr. Martens, who turned up and told the detective he couldn't question a child who was only nine years old. "I just wanted to ask him if his mother told him where she was going," the detective snapped.

From the doorway Brian said, "She didn't say anything like that."

After that we were left in peace. Word had gone around the village that our mother had abandoned us, and there was a lot of sympathy for a short time. Then it was forgotten. The deputy dropped in occasionally, not to ask questions, but to see how we were doing. He told us a woman had reported seeing our mother racing toward Portland several times while we were in school last winter and spring.

A few days before school started, Mr. Martens came back again, and he brought another "Suit" with him. "This is our associate, William Radix. He'll be handling your affairs from now on." He was getting rid of us and our problems.

William Radix was too young to be a real lawyer — that was my first impression. He was slender, and shorter than Kevin. His eyes were such a dark blue, they looked black at first; his hair was dark, not black, but close, and cut neatly. And he was dressed in a dark gray suit and a maroon tie. A Suit. But not yet a Gray Man. He was twenty-five, we learned later.

We sat in the living room, where I listened to Amy and Kevin and the two lawyers discuss what was to be done about us. It took them a very long time to come to the decision the committee of three had already made. We would need a part-time housekeeper, someone on school days from about one or two in the afternoon until five or so, or until one of the bigger kids got home from school. Brian wouldn't be left home alone. She would have to be available in case of illness, Mr. Martens said. She would tidy up and prepare our dinner, and see that the property didn't fall into disrepair, he added. He already had a woman in mind, Elinor Inglewood, a widow who needed to supplement her pension.

"This is quite temporary," he said. "Yes, temporary. Until your mother returns. Since Mr. Radix lives over in Lake Oswego, it will be convenient for him to drop in now and then to make certain everything is all right."

Not just a Suit, I thought in disgust. A rich Suit. Lake Oswego was where rich people lived; it was only a few miles away, on the east side of the interstate. We were on the west side.

I tuned them all out as the discussion droned on. I wondered if this was a billable hour or three, if William Radix's visits would come out of our money. Probably, I thought glumly. But maybe he wouldn't charge as much, since he was so young, and obviously new at lawyering. I glanced at him and my disgust deepened. He was gazing at Amy in a way that made me wonder how he would look at her if he knew that she and stupid Max did it every chance they got.

I imagined a scenario in which Amy and Max had made themselves a little bower up in the woods and were doing it. Radix came climbing up the hill from the other side, holding a stopwatch, timing every minute so he could bill us. He came over the top of the hill and stumbled on them, and they all three began to roll down our side in a confusion of arms and legs. I ducked my head and couldn't look up again until I heard Mr. Martens say, "Well, I think we have concluded our business."

We all stood up. Phase two of our lives had come to an end. Phase three was starting, bringing with it two new people into our sphere, Elinor Inglewood and William Radix. I heard myself silently mimicking Mr. Martens: "This is quite temporary. Yes, temporary. Until your mother returns." Right, I thought.

13

Mrs. Inglewood arrived on a Monday, Labor Day, to get acquainted, she said. She was a tall, strong woman with short gray hair as straight and crisp as wire; she was very tanned and wrinkled, and she was dressed in faded, soft jeans, a man's plaid shirt, and slip-on canvas shoes. I never saw her in any other kind of clothes, although I supposed she must dress differently when she went to church. She told us first thing that she didn't work on the Sabbath, the Lord's day, then grinned at us and said we shouldn't hold it against her. She and her husband used to have a ranch out in the Blue Mountain area, she said, until he got sick, and they moved near Portland for the hospitals and doctors. Now she had only two horses. She smiled at Brian. "One day maybe you'd like to come out and see the horses, take a ride?"

He nodded.

"Every morning I get up real early," she said, "and tend to my babies. I call them that, but they're getting on. Betsy's eighteen, and Billy's nineteen. I helped deliver them both. They want some coddling now, but they've earned it. I ride one of them every morning, rain or shine, take turns, you know. Don't want one to get jealous or anything. Then they need grooming. But by noon I'm done. So this will be good for me, too.

Something to do with the afternoons."

Amy and I showed her around the house, with Brian tagging along, evidently fascinated by her, or maybe by the idea of the horses. He watched her the way he might watch an alien. And so did I. She was the strongest-looking woman I had ever seen, yet her voice was gentle, and her eyes were a warm chocolate-brown color. She looked as if she could handle a wild horse, a tractor, a shotgun, or a kitten with equal ease, as if nothing would surprise her. Her eyebrows were like thick, straight woolly-bear caterpillars that nearly met. Perhaps we had been expecting a Mary Poppins or a bustling little woman in a house-dress and apron; we were not expecting a sixty-year-old cowgirl.

When she looked at the shelves filled with cookbooks, she shook her head. "I don't do much fancy cooking. Afraid my suppers might not be what you're used to."

"No one's really used them since our father died," Amy said quickly.

"Well. We'll see how you take to my food." She was examining other titles, but she didn't comment again.

Two walls in the living room were covered by floor-to-ceiling bookshelves, all crammed full, with books on top of books, and a stack of books on a table. There was a row of books on religion: Buddhism, Hinduism, Islam, a Catholic Bible, the Koran, a Torah, a King James Bible as well as a modern-language Bible. . . . Dad always said everyone should have a religious education and learn something about every religion. I was afraid Mrs. Inglewood might take offense and walk out.

When we finished our tour, she asked a few practical questions: When was garbage pickup? What kind of furnace did we have? The names of our doctor and dentist. When I said we didn't have either, she looked shocked and stern.

"You haven't had a dental checkup in the last couple of years? Well, we'll make some appointments and take care of that."

She asked what foods we absolutely did not like, and Brian said, "Sauerkraut and coleslaw."

She threw her head back and laughed, such a loud, raucous sound, we were all startled. No one had laughed in our house like that since Dad died.

"Forget kraut," she said. "I don't like it, either. What else?"

There were many things we never made because we didn't like them, but I couldn't think of a single one. Tentatively Amy said, "Beets, and canned spinach."

Mrs. Inglewood nodded. "Well, we'll see how it goes. I'll get here between one and two and stay until five or six and I'll make your supper for you to eat when you're ready for it. I know how different the schedules can be with kids in school and all."

She gave us her telephone number and address and said she would be there the next day, then she left, driving away in an old pickup truck with rust on the sides. I wondered if it had a gun rack.

Our patterns changed. Kevin found Portland State much more demanding than he had anticipated. He had complained about a wasted year, but on the first day he came home loaded with homework, a dazed look in his eyes. Amy was taking advanced classes that would earn college credits, and she had a lot of homework. She had gotten straight *A*'s all through school, and even with her extra load, she still did. And I drifted along. I had signed up for a fiction-writing class with Mrs. Corman, who required a story a week from us. I spent more time on my one story every week than with all my other homework combined.

Having Mrs. Inglewood gave us all freedom we hadn't had in years. I could stay after school for orchestra practice or go to the library after school. It was all right; Mrs. Inglewood was with Brian.

After she had been with us for only a week, I went to bed one night and found clean sheets. Luxury, I thought. I sometimes had let changing sheets go for weeks, even months at a time. And her meals were good: pot roast with potatoes and carrots and onions, chicken and dumplings, a baked ham, lasagna with fresh pasta. . . . We ate everything she prepared, even the onions.

In the middle of September on a Saturday afternoon, I was in the kitchen looking over the food that Mrs. Inglewood had left to tide us over until Monday. She seemed to think we might starve if she didn't prepare our weekend meals ahead of time. The doorbell rang and I went to see who it was and found William Radix.

I gaped. He was wearing shorts and a tank top and high-top sneakers. He had on wraparound sunglasses, which he removed when I opened the door. A bicycle was leaning against the porch, a helmet dangling by a strap from the handlebar.

"Hi," he said. "Anybody home?"

"Amy's upstairs," I said. "I'll call her." I opened the door wider for him to come in, then I started up the stairs. We were using the front stairs most of the time, now that we didn't have to keep the living room clean.

"Don't bother her if she's busy," he said. "I just dropped by to see how you guys are doing."

On his bike? I turned and looked at him suspiciously. "Is this going to be billed to us?"

He laughed and shook his head. Amy appeared at the top of the stairs; she probably thought I was talking to Max. It never sank in with her that I didn't talk to Max. I sometimes thought I might grunt at him, but I didn't. He would grunt back, and then what would I say? Kevin came from the hall to the dining room, where he had been working at the computer.

I shrugged. "As you can see, we're here. We're doing okay."

He was gazing past me, up the stairs at Amy, who was continuing down slowly. "I was exploring the hills on my bike and decided to come by.

I'm supposed to check in with you guys now and then. Part of my job description."

I scowled at him. He was laughing at us, a kid checking up on other kids. He didn't look a day older than Kevin.

"We're all fine, Mr. Radix," Amy said.

He held up his hands. "Please. If you call me Mr., then I have to call you Ms. McNair, and your sister Ms. McNair, and your brother Mr. McNair. I guess the twerp would be Master McNair."

"Excuse me," I said as coldly as I could. "I'm making dinner." I went down the few steps I had gone up and swung around to go back to the kitchen.

"Why don't you call me Bill," he went on, as if I hadn't spoken. "Make it easier all around." Then he said in a very serious voice, "I really wanted to tell you they still don't have a lead concerning your mother. I checked with the sheriff's office yesterday."

I felt every organ inside me try to curl up. He must have thought we were all monsters; no one had even asked about her.

Belatedly Kevin said, "I've called them a lot. They said they'd let us know if anything turned up." I doubted that he had called even once.

I went to the kitchen and stood gazing at two casseroles without seeing either one. We should have asked about Mother. We still might give it all away. I wondered if Mrs. Inglewood thought we were too carefree to be abandoned children.

I felt as if the entire burden that had eased off my shoulders had come crashing down on me again.

Kevin and William Radix came to the kitchen for a beer. I shoved one of the casseroles back into the refrigerator and made my eyes focus on the instructions Mrs. Inglewood had taped to the other one: "Bake at 325 for an hour and a half. Just needs salad and bread."

I put it in the oven and started to make the salad while Kevin and William Radix sat at the kitchen table and talked about bicycles and riding trails. Kevin said he had found a place on the Internet that listed trails in every state, and they wandered in to have a look, closing the door behind them. After a few minutes, I heard them laughing. There was something about men's laughter that infuriated me. It was a low and dirty sound, I thought, a dirty secret shared, a dirty joke. Maybe they were looking at something sexy. Mocking women.

From then on, Kevin, Amy, and Brian all called him Bill. I didn't call him anything to his face, but I thought of him as Radix. Just Radix.

A few weeks later he came back, again on a Saturday. It was raining. Brian let him in and yelled up the stairs to Kevin. I went to see what was going on, and Radix grinned at me.

"Just happened to be pedaling by?" I asked.

"Nope. Kevin wanted to talk to me, so here I am."

Business, I thought morosely. He would bill us this time for sure. Kevin came down the stairs and said hi; then he said, "Amy's out in the kitchen, her turn to cook. Let's go out there and talk."

Amy's cooking consisted of heating up whatever Mrs. Inglewood had prepared, but she made a show of looking domestic at the sink and counter.

Kevin brought out two beers, and he and Radix sat down. Brian went back to the family room and television. I remained at the kitchen door to listen.

"First thing," Radix said, before Kevin could start, "let's agree on tactics. See, if you call me at the office, that call is on record, and it goes on your bill, however long we talk. If I call you from the office, same thing. If I call you from home, or any phone except at the office, that's personal. Any paperwork I do is recorded. First I review whatever has come up, then I write a letter or something, then a stenographer has to retype the letter, and one of the senior attorneys has to review everything and okay it. All on record. All billable."

It turned out that Kevin had called him at the office to ask for some advice. Radix had said he couldn't talk then, that he would call back. He called that same night and suggested this Saturday meeting. He said he had the figures Kevin had asked for. This was the first I had heard of any of it.

Amy wiped her hands and joined them at the table.

"Okay," Radix said, "your father was thorough and he covered nearly everything. But he couldn't anticipate the inflationary rise in school costs. That's maybe the one area he misjudged. The trust is bringing in nine and a half percent, very respectable, but college inflation is running close to thirty percent."

He talked about yield and total return, about diminishing principal. . . . After a minute or two I started to leave. He was looking at me.

"Boring?"

"Terminally."

"Your time will come," he said, "but for now it's not your concern."

Condescending bastard, I thought back at him, and left. I went upstairs and did some homework while they talked. When Amy called me to dinner, there was a place set for Radix. "Why am I not surprised?" I muttered under my breath.

They talked about college and expenses throughout most of the dinner. "You take as many as you can of the mandatory undergraduate courses that don't interest you much, at the lowest-possible cost," he said. "Like the way Amy's earning college credit now, for free. Take only things that are transferable, though. That way, when you go to the school that has the best teachers for your field, you'll have to pay top dollar, but it will be for those things you really want."

Amy asked where he had gone, and he said Andover and Yale.

Then he said with a perfectly straight face, "But you have to understand that my old man's rich as Croesus. And as bossy as Jehovah. I went where he sent me. You guys are laying out your own future."

"Or someone is laying it out for us," I said under my breath, and I caught a glance from him that seemed amused. Maliciously I said, "Since you've got a date tonight, Amy, I'll do the kitchen for you." I pretended not to be watching for a reaction on Radix's face. His grin broadened. Hypocrite, I thought.

Radix came once or twice a month after that, always on a Saturday or a Sunday. He played chess with Kevin, then asked me to play one night. He beat me, but he had to work for his win. Now and then he played hearts or crazy eights with Brian and me or he asked me to play chess again. During the Thanksgiving holiday he played penny poker with us; afterward Kevin said I now owed him five hundred dollars. Radix owed him a dollar and twelve cents and paid up.

Amy said he was lonesome; his family lived back east in Philadelphia. He had moved to Oregon the previous winter, and very likely, she said, the law firm hadn't left him with much time to make many friends yet. I thought she was a real dope. One smile and he was hers, but she kept fooling around with Max, although they were fighting a lot these days.

Radix had moved in on us, I thought one night when he was there talking to Kevin in the dining room, playing around with the computer. Kevin had decided to take his advice and attend Portland State for two years. Amy hadn't decided yet, but it appeared that she would do the same thing. For the first time we all worried about money. There wasn't as much in the education trusts as we had assumed, and good schools cost a bundle, then graduate school, at least for Amy and Kevin.

That night Amy and Max went to Portland to see a movie; I watched a dumb monster movie with Brian for a while, then wandered upstairs to my room and closed the door. The school orchestra was in rehearsal for the Christmas program, and I had messed up twice that week. Mr. Montoya had told me sternly that I'd better spend a little time practicing over the weekend. He seemed to think I never touched the violin at home. I started.

In a little while the door opened silently and Brian crept in with a book. He often sat in my room while I practiced. He colored or read, or just sat with his eyes closed, a dreamy expression on his face. He never made a sound and I could ignore him.

We were going to play a medley of familiar Christmas music, seamlessly moving from one piece to another, Mr. Montoya had said almost mournfully, as if he suspected that when we played the songs, no one would recognize any of them. Also, we would not be allowed to play anything that smacked of religion; we were too enlightened to force religion on nonbelievers.

So we played "Rudolph," and "White Christmas," and "Frosty the Snowman," and in the middle of things, we moved from "Silver Bells" into a bit lifted from the overture to *Der Rosenkavalier*, and from that to the waltz in the ball scene. It was a tricky transition. I started with "Silver Bells" and stumbled the way I had done at rehearsal. I started over, then again, and again, until all at once it seemed that the notes changed even as I played them. I stopped and started over, hearing it now, how it should be, why it had been wrong before. Same notes, same transition, but suddenly I understood it. I played through the waltz and into "O Tannenbaum," the final piece.

I did the whole thing again, from "Silver Bells" on to the end, then I put the violin down. "There," I said.

As silently as he had come in, Brian left.

I went out to the hall and started down the front stairs, then stopped when I saw Radix rising from a lower step. He stood up and looked at me. "I didn't know you were a musician," he said.

I felt my cheeks burn as I realized he had been sitting down there listening. He moved aside, and I went down and around him to go to the kitchen.

"Are you taking lessons?" he asked, coming after me.

"In school," I muttered.

"No private lessons? Why not?"

"It's none of your business." I yanked the refrigerator open and got out milk.

"Sorry to inform you," he said, "but I'm sort of a temporary pseudoguardian for you kids. Mr. Martens made it my business."

"Well then, try this. I don't want lessons." I pulled a glass from the cabinet.

"Stop acting like a baby," he said angrily. "Look at me. When the music your hands make sounds like the music in your head, you won't need lessons anymore. Now you do."

I looked at him. "You listen to me, *Mr.* Radix. I'm not a performer. I don't ever want to be a performer. What I do with music is none of your business."

Kevin walked into the kitchen, looking mad. "What's going on?"

"Nothing," I snapped. "Just butt out."

Radix said, "I'm leaving. I'll ask around about teachers, and we can talk about it again later."

"I can't afford private lessons," I said furiously. "Why don't you listen!"

"It will come out of your education trust," he said. "This is as much a part of your education as the computer was for Kevin's."

He left and I cursed him. Kevin stood listening with a thoughtful expression for a while; then he interrupted. "I didn't know you knew such words," he said. "I wonder if you know what they mean." He grinned and went into the dining

130

room and shut the door.

All that night I thought savage thoughts about Radix, how smug he was, a rich Suit, filthy-rich parents, prep school, Yale, know-it-all smart-ass. . . . Trying to make himself indispensable, using me to get to Amy. . . . If he only knew how little we needed him, I thought, and I wished I could tell him, rub it in. He was just a pampered rich kid; we were self-sufficient in a way he never would be. Pretending he knew what was in my head. If he knew what was in my head, he'd tuck in his tail and start running, and keep running.

I was determined not to let him boss me around, tell me what I needed, but when he came back with the name of a recommended teacher, he said, "If you never perform before an audience, it doesn't matter a damn. You are your audience, and the music you play has to satisfy you, and only you. Will you give him a try?"

A week later Amy drove me to Portland and I met Mr. Kimmelman, a gnome of a man, hardly taller than I was, with a shiny bald head. He told Amy to wait in an anteroom, took me to his studio, and asked me to play for him. He sat in a chair facing away from me and listened, and afterward he said, "All right."

The world opened a new door to me that day. I entered a new space that was bigger than I had dreamed, more beautiful than I had imagined, and much more difficult than I had dreaded.

Shortly before Christmas Radix came by with a family present, a care package, he said. He had to go back to Philadelphia for the holidays; he wanted to give us his number, just in case we needed anything.

He didn't stay long, but at the door, almost as if he had forgotten until the last minute, he said to Amy, "I was able to get three tickets for a concert in January. Would you and Liz like to go?"

"Who's playing?"

He reeled off some names that none of us knew. "I'm afraid it's a string quartet, chamber music," he said.

"I guess not," Amy said. "But thanks. Liz might like it, though."

He turned to me. My heart was thumping. To hear a string quartet in a hall! I would have gone with anyone, even Max, to hear it. I nodded.

"Want to round up a friend, help me use all three tickets?"

I didn't know a single person I wanted to be with me to hear chamber music. I said, "Maybe Brian? He'd like it."

He looked surprised, then asked Brian, "Do you want to go?"

Like me, Brian could only nod.

"Good, the three of us. I've got to beat it. Merry Christmas!"

When he was gone, Amy turned to me in disbelief. "Brian? For heaven's sake! Brian? You'll make Bill feel like Big Daddy, shepherding kids to a concert."

"You're an idiot," I said. "He asked you. Anyone who would stick with stupid Max when someone like Radix is available is really dumb."

"Don't be a dope," she said. "He's engaged. That's why he has to go home for the holidays. She's probably a true blue blood with a couple million bucks, an old Philadelphia family, the works." She was eyeing the care package. "Let's not wait for Christmas."

Brian was lifting the package, trying to guess what was in it, sniffing at it. "Let's open it as soon as Kevin gets home," he said. We agreed.

I thought about Radix. Pseudoguardian or not, he didn't have to hang around us the way he did. He didn't have to bring us a present, offer to take Amy and me to a concert. We had something he wanted that he wasn't going to find back in Philadelphia. "He might be engaged, but he won't marry her, whoever she is," I said. "And if he does, it won't take."

Amy gave me a scornful what-do-you-know look.

The care package contained pâté de foie gras, truffles, imported cheeses, dried wild mushrooms, Godiva chocolates. . . . As we stood examining item after item, exclaiming how much it must have cost, that he must have picked out everything himself — what do you do with truffles? — I realized what it was we had that the rich kid lacked. We were a family. We were still united, still moved in unison, still ready to do battle for one another. In spite of everything, we were a family, just as Mother had always said.

In spite of everything.

I should have felt a premonitory chill then, something to make me knock wood, but I didn't. I was too happy.

14

It was the first string quartet I ever heard live. The difference between this and a recording was the difference between the sun and a sunlamp, between an original painting and a picture in a book. Samuel Barber's Adagio for Strings brought tears to my eyes. I turned away from Radix so he didn't see. It might have been the only time I moved. Brian sat transfixed. When Radix took us home, he said we were the best concert companions he'd ever had and that we would do it again. He went to the door with us but didn't come in.

I didn't know what to say, how to thank him. When I did, it sounded phony. "Thank you. It was a lovely evening." Right out of a paperback romance novel.

He must have read the same novel; just as formally, he said, "It was my pleasure. Good night."

A few weeks later, one night when he was there playing cards with us, Brian asked shyly if we could afford music lessons for him. Amy and Kevin were both doing homework; just the three of us were at the table. Radix put his cards down. "What do you want to play?"

"The violin, like Liz."

He nodded. "Kimmelman says Liz needs a new violin. I guess we can arrange it. You could start with hers."

Kimmelman probably hoped a new violin would inspire me to play better, I thought morosely. Then I was angry that Radix was checking up on me, but I guessed he had to, part of the job description.

Brian began taking lessons from a woman in the village, and after a year he began going to Kimmelman with me. And every month or so, Radix took us to a concert.

Brian seldom mentioned Mother anymore, but it came up unexpectedly one day when Mrs. Inglewood asked him if he'd like for her to pick him up on Saturday and go ride the horses, and spend the night. She would bring him back on Sunday. His eyes lighted up in excitement; he thought she had forgotten. But later he told her, "No thanks." She seemed disappointed.

After she left, I quizzed him. Had she ever done or said anything out of line? Didn't he like her? What was wrong with her? Didn't he want to ride after all? If Radix and Mr. Martens had both checked her out, she must be okay.

He said Mother told him he shouldn't go.

To my surprise, a few weeks later Brian asked Mrs. Inglewood if it would be all right if Amy or Kevin drove him to her house to see the horses on a Saturday afternoon for a little while.

"Well, sure," she said. "You just let me know ahead of time which day you're coming."

As it turned out, neither Kevin nor Amy got around to taking him week after week, and one Saturday afternoon, Mrs. Inglewood turned up in her truck to collect him. It was clear that she had become very fond of him and felt sorry for him. I overheard her mention him to Radix once and call him "the poor little motherless feller."

She picked him up again a few weeks later on a Saturday, and after that he spent two or three hours every other weekend with her and her horses. He learned to ride, and to groom them, and he helped her clean out their stalls.

I hoped that she would fill an empty spot in his life, even as I understood that she could never replace Mother, or be a real mother to him. Then I thought, But Mother had not permitted him to go overnight, not if it meant he would go to church with Mrs. Inglewood on Sunday. I denied the thought, but it had formed exactly that way. Mother had not permitted him to go. . . .

Amy graduated with honors and won a scholarship to Portland State. She gloated; she would be able to save her education money for UCLA later, and she could afford to apply the next year for a place in a marine biology summer workshop.

As soon as she graduated, she ditched Max. I wondered if he had been her security blanket, her reliable date for movies and the prom. She said he was too possessive; he wanted her to move in with him. I suspected that now she would notice Radix, but she said she was through with men. She didn't have time to fool around.

"I'm going to save myself for later, for the right man," she said.

"Better late than never," I muttered. She invited me to leave her room.

Brian caught up and surpassed me in music. Sometimes we played duets. Once, wandering by his door, I saw him sitting at the window playing, and I knew he was playing for Mother.

I turned seventeen. Kevin had transferred to Stanford, and Amy would go down to UCLA in the fall. She tried to talk Brian and me into going with her, and Brian said no almost reflexively. When she turned to me, I shook my head.

"I have to go," Amy said. "Please, I can't leave you both here alone."

"We're not alone," Brian said.

"You can't make that decision," she said. "What if Mrs. Inglewood quits, what then? I'll ask Bill. He'll back me up."

"I'll run away if you make me go," Brian said. "And if you catch me and take me back, I'll run away again." He wasn't yelling or getting excited, just stating a fact.

I had a flash of memory, of the night Kevin had cried that he would run away. Amy looked so much like Mother, the same wild honey-colored hair, the same stance, and now the same anger firing her cheeks. "Amy, forget it," I said. "We're not going. That's final." I wondered if she had deliberately misinterpreted what Brian had said, what he meant. I wondered if she thought he was a normal kid, if she knew he was still haunted, if she had managed to put it out of mind, and if so, how.

But most of the time Brian was a perfectly normal boy, if a lot quieter than most. He was a precocious reader, and he already was reading things in the house I hadn't gotten to until I was thirteen or so. He was reading all the books on religion, and the Bibles. He talked with Mrs. Inglewood about religion; he talked with Radix and me about philosophy and psychology in such a way that the difference in our ages simply was not applicable. He had expanded Mother's garden, and apparently he intended to keep expanding it to the edge of the woods. And he had become friends with the nurseryman, Mr. Wilcox, and no longer bought supermarket plants, but consulted with Mr. Wilcox and took his advice.

He had turned down the idea of day camps that summer, saying he had too much to do. And he kept himself busy most of the time: he practiced on the violin, read a lot, rode his bike to the library frequently, or to the swimming pool in the village, tended the garden, rode and helped tend the horses. . . . He kept busy, but he was a solitary boy. No wonder Mrs. Inglewood called him "the poor little feller." She thought he was staying close to home, waiting for Mother's return.

Amy had gone to the coast on study trips several times, but we hadn't been camping for over two years, and we wanted to go again. She wanted to photograph tide-pool life, and Brian and I simply wanted to go camping. Kevin had been with us briefly that summer, then had gone back to Stanford. He and a friend were writing a computer program that had him enormously excited, and we were reluctant to go camping without him. Two girls and a twelve-year-old boy — it didn't seem like a good idea, but we talked ourselves into it. My biggest worry was a flat tire. I was a better driver than Amy, and I didn't object to driving the van; we could manage the tent and everything, but neither of us wanted to have to change a flat tire. We studied the tires and finally decided they were okay, and Brian said that if we got a flat, he would change it.

Amy mentioned it to Radix, warning him that we would be gone from Wednesday until Sunday. He invited himself along.

"Do you know the first thing about camping?" she asked.

"Nope. But I'm a quick read. And you guys can't go alone. What time Wednesday?"

"Don't you have to work or something?" I asked crossly. A green camper would be a pain in the neck, I thought. We would end up waiting on him, and our campfire talks would have to be guarded.

"I'll play hooky," he said, ignoring the tone of my voice, the way he so often did. "Tell me what to bring."

15

We arrived at our camp by ten, and Radix wasn't as helpless as I had feared, although he had to be told just about everything. He said he had been to the coast a couple of times, and it turned out he had gone to the touristy places that we shunned. We intended to show him a different coast, trails in the forest, dunes, tiny unused beaches; our first stop was Amy's cove.

We stood shivering on the cliff, watching the tide go out. Amy wanted to go down as soon as there was enough room to stand.

Mist and fog drifted at treetop level; the water directly below us turned from dark green and frothy white to black as the basalt basins were uncovered; farther out, sea and sky were gray, without a horizon. On top of the cliff, a cold wind was blowing, but we knew that in the cove there would be no wind.

We were burdened with a tripod, reflectors, cameras; Amy and I had backpacks. A net was sticking up from Amy's pack.

As soon as a walkable stretch of beach was exposed, we hiked down. At the bottom, Amy and Brian assembled her gear; then she began to pick out the first pools she would investigate. The tide was running out fast; the entire beach would be uncovered very soon; more and more tide pools appeared. Radix followed Amy, watching in fascination for a time, then came to sit by me on a rock. Soon there would be enough dry sand to shift to something more comfortable, but not yet. Amy had located a tiny basin and set up some of her gear, had begun taking pictures. Brian was her obedient servant, steadying the tripod, shifting reflectors, doing whatever she told him.

"She's really dedicated, isn't she?" Radix said when he joined me.

"Fanatic," I said.

He shook his head. "A fanatic is someone who's dedicated and won't stop talking about whatever it is."

I shrugged. "See that stack, the one that looks hunched over? That's Papa Bear." It had just emerged from the receding water. Waves sent spray high over it; water streamed down its flanks. "Next there'll be Mama Bear, and then Baby Bear." We watched as a shorter basalt stack rose from the water; the pair looked poised, as if considering whether they wanted to come ashore. "When Baby Bear goes back under, it's time for Amy to start getting her stuff together. When Mama Bear goes, it's time for her to high-tail it back this way. And if we're still down here when Papa Bear takes a dive, we'll probably get wet. The tide seems to come back in faster than it goes out." Without changing my tone at all, I asked, "Are you still engaged?"

He was surprised and took his time answering. "No. Haven't been for over a year. She broke it off. Why do you ask?"

"Just wondered. Is Karen Walsh your girlfriend now?"

"She's a friend," he said coolly. "Is Boyd Symington your boyfriend?"

"He's a friend." I was brooding about Karen Walsh. She had been at the Mozart Players concert he had taken Brian and me to for my birthday in May. She had come up to speak to him during intermission, a tall, obviously rich, very elegant young woman wearing an ankle-length ecru-colored silk dress cut low in the front and with long sleeves. Her high-heeled pumps had matched it exactly. Everything about her had been perfect, from her smooth platinum hair cut short and straight to the diamonds in her watchband. . . .

Poor Amy, I thought, as elegant as a crabber. She was squatting over a tide pool, focusing her camera. Her hair was pulled back in a bandana; she was wearing scrungy cutoff jeans and a gray sweatshirt so frayed at the wrists that she used rubber bands to keep her sleeves up out of the water.

"I'm surprised you even remember Karen's name," Radix said, "the way you went tearing off when she showed up."

I gave him a mean look. I had stayed long enough to be introduced. "Oh, William," I said, mimicking her exactly. We could all do voices, a legacy from our father. "These must be the charming children you've taken under your wing."

He laughed, and kept laughing a long time. Ignoring him, I moved to some dryish sand, and when he was over his laughing fit, he did, too. "Baby Bear?" he asked, pointing.

I said no, not yet. It would be closer to Mama Bear. Lazily, he asked, "What are you going to be when you grow up, Liz?"

I groaned. God, I hated that question. I was getting it from Amy, from Kevin, from teachers. "A generalist," I had snapped at Kevin the last time he asked. "I want to know a little bit about everything, and if and when I ever find something interesting enough to become fanatical about, I'll tell you." Brian had said, straight-faced, he thought we already had enough generals.

To Radix I said sourly, "I'm stuck with being me. What are you going to be when you grow up?"

He didn't laugh. When I glanced at him, he was gazing out at the water. "My great-grand-father got caught up in one of the political disputes in Poland, and had to run for his life, taking what he and his wife could carry — precious little, as it turned out. He had been a professor, well known, respected, and he ended up a butcher in Philadelphia, a mean and bitter man, from all accounts. They changed his name from something unpronounceable to Radix when he entered the United States, and as a constant reminder of his humiliation, he kept the new name. His son, my grandfather, was named William, and was prodded to become respectable, at the very least.

He became a lawyer and started a law firm, and fathered three daughters, whom he despised, before he finally got a male heir, my father, who was William Radix, Jr. My father was fifty-two when I was born," he said after a brief pause, "and my mother was forty-one. They had given up hope of ever having a child by then. My father built up the law firm, made it important, significant, powerful. From the day I was born, William Radix the Third, I've known what I was supposed to do. I was some kind of prodigy, I guess, ready for college at sixteen. But I'd never been camping."

He stopped, longer this time, then continued in a monotone. "My mother was afraid to let me go to college at that age, afraid I would be seduced by a bar girl, take up dope, take up drink, learn swear words. . . . She took me to Europe for a year instead."

I was afraid to look at him, afraid he would stop and not start again. He never had talked about himself in anything but a self-mocking, derogatory way. His voice was lower, almost dreamy when he went on.

"We saw art. I wanted to cry when I saw *David*, the original in those days. It's a reproduction now. *The Pietà* . . . We saw the Duomo in Milan, like a wedding-cake decoration, all white lace filigree done in stone. I'd always hated Rembrandt, you know, muddy, murky colors on a muddy, murky background, but then we saw *The Night Watch*, and the hordes of people came alive on the canvas; they glowed with life. You feel like if you touched them, they'd squirm away. Van Gogh, the passion and madness of van Gogh. I couldn't breathe in his presence. On to Gainsborough, such cool precision, such control, so British. Castles and mansions, cathedrals, châteaus, monasteries with tiny dark prison cells and stone beds. I could imagine the countless monks who suffered there for the glory of God. Outside Aix-en-Provence, we were passing yet another castle, and I said I had to use the rest room. My mother didn't like the castles, too much walking, too many stone stairs, too gray and gloomy.

"I went in alone and she waited in the car with the driver. It was near closing time. A tour group passed me going the other way; the guide was speaking in Japanese. Then I was alone. Alone in the castle," he said.

He had been digging up sand, sifting it through his fingers; now he began to gesture. "You see the pictures, the Hollywood productions, and you think you know what the castles are like, but you really don't. The chambers and halls are so vast, the ceilings so high, as if they had been built for giants. You go into a room as big as a basketball court, with one door at the far end and narrow, high windows. The wind sighs and moans passing through. It's all gray, gray stone floors, so polished in places, they're treacherous underfoot, gray stone ceilings. I populated the halls with knights and princesses, hung tapestries on the walls, carpeted the stone floors with Persian rugs. . . ."

He laughed. "I was having an adventure, alone in the castle, wandering from hall to hall, down long corridors that led to rooms I hadn't seen before, or took me back to ones that I had been in, or ended at narrow stairs that led up or down into darkness. I was lost. And I got scared. I kept hearing other steps, and the wind began to sound like voices whispering, crying. I was afraid my mother would send the driver in for me, and I didn't want anyone calling my name, drawing attention to me. Finally I stumbled into a courtyard that I would have sworn hadn't been there before. On the opposite side there was an arrow pointing to an exit sign. I was saved."

I let out my breath when he stopped talking. I had seen it all as he described it, the gray corridors lost in shadows, the massive stones, the empty halls. I had heard the whispers and moans.

After a moment, he said, "When the rosemary blooms, the hills turn powdery blue, like seeing the sky upside down. The bees get drunk with nectar; they stagger and fall off the blossoms. Rosemary honey is the best in the world." He was gazing off at the sea again. "Is that Baby Bear?"

I said yes and glanced down the beach. Amy was carrying something in her net to the small basin where she could photograph it. I was supposed to keep an eye out for the tide change, but I had been lost in a castle. I had no idea how long Baby Bear had been out of the water. "What else did you see?"

"On to Spain," he said. "The Prado, *Guernica*, a lot of Picassos. Bosch. My mother didn't like them. She thinks art should be about things that are pretty, or at least human. She said no one should paint ugliness, like pictures of war and suffering. Or things that looked crazy."

He shrugged. "Then Granada and the Alhambra. After all the massive castles, the marble palaces, the mountainous cathedrals, stuff that's like bread pudding, meant to stay put, heavy forever, the Alhambra is like a soufflé, light and airy." He was gesturing again, making sweeping curves in the air. "Arches everywhere as far as you can see, like a forest of pale winter trees touching the tips of their branches together. They decorated the walls with carvings, geometrical patterns, swirls more and more intricate the closer you get, and with script, beautiful flowing Arabic script. You pass through one garden after another, masses of flowers humming with bees, and bird-song all around. It smells good. On both sides are ruins, and you wonder what marvels have been lost, what mysterious rooms and passages are gone now. And everywhere you can hear water running, or splashing from fountains, trickling over stones, miniature waterfalls tumbling down channels at the side of stairs, like soft music."

He became silent and we listened to the constant, ever-changing sound of the surf crashing against stacks and cliffs, and closer, wavelets hissing around stones. "Then what?" I asked finally.

"We came home and I went to school," he said flatly.

I realized then that he didn't want to be a lawyer, but I didn't dare question him; that was too personal.

"Waves are breaking over the top of Baby Bear," he said after a moment.

We stood up, and I began to get dry sweatpants and sneakers from my backpack for Brian. Radix watched. I had one more question. I didn't look at him when I asked it. "Do your parents call you William?"

He laughed, but it was not a happy sound. "You better believe." Then he yelled at Amy to start back. "I'll go help with their gear," he said.

I watched him trot off down the beach, and I thought with satisfaction that although Karen Walsh was the most elegant woman I had ever seen, she meant nothing to him. She called him William, too. And he hadn't answered my question of what he wanted to be when he grew up, only what he didn't want to be.

It rained a little the next day, not enough to keep us from hiking but too much for Amy to take her cameras out. We led Radix up a mountain to an abandoned railway bed, then followed it to a wooden trestle that spanned a narrow gorge with a waterfall. Trees were so dense, not enough light could penetrate to make shadows, and it was so still that the raindrops could be heard, their energy spent on the passage through fir trees until the drops were like tiny sighs as they fell and landed. Rocks, boulders, downed trees, logs, everything was covered with emerald mosses, dripping diamonds. That night we played Scrabble in the tent while the rain fell.

The next day the sun was out again; a bunch of Cub Scouts had gathered on the cliff above Amy's cove to wait for low tide. Without comment, we went somewhere else. We looked for gold in a stream and found agates that we didn't keep. We had boxes of agates at home. Brian found a nice piece of picture jasper and a perfect rock for Mother's garden, and Radix found a chunk of petrified wood. They kept those. We built a fire on the beach and roasted hot dogs. We built sand castles and played Frisbee, and drove down to Newport to have lunch in a seafood restaurant on Newport Bay, where we watched fishing boats returning and harbor seals at play. Radix bought us all kites and we flew them on a wide sandy beach. He, Brian, and I had a kite war and tore up all three kites.

Then, Saturday night, we sat around the fire, our last night at the coast. Amy and I had our ponchos on, Brian wore Kevin's, Radix wrapped himself in a blanket, and we stayed close to the fire.

Brian asked Radix, "Do you believe in God?"

Radix took his time. He always talked to Brian as if he were grown-up, answered his questions in a direct way, without a trace of condescension. He thought about this before he replied. "I used to just accept that there is a God. You know, it was a given. Then I stopped believing altogether. God became a myth to keep the peons quiet, no more than that. But now I'm not certain. Sometimes it seems there must be, then it seems not only impossible but also unnecessary. So I guess I come down in the agnostic court." Then he said in a lower voice, "I think there's something in us that makes us desperate to believe there's more than a brief fling at life, followed by nothingness. We've reached a level of consciousness that forces us to contemplate God, that makes us yearn to discover what might have come before a physical body, what might come after its dissolution. It apparently is universal, perhaps a universal archetype that is part of our psyche, but can archetypes get implanted without a basis in reality? That's where I usually swing toward belief. Then I think, But that's assuming that we've evolved all we're going to, and I don't believe that. Maybe when humans are finished, if a finite state is possible, maybe they'll recognize the archetype as something other than God. Maybe it's no more than a yearning not to be alone in our skulls. A yearning for meaning."

Brian had listened with attention. He nodded, as if satisfied. "Mrs. Inglewood believes in hellfire and damnation and heaven. I don't try to talk her out of it, but I don't believe it. I think back in the old days, when people tried to think of the worst thing they could do to each other, they thought of fire, burning, and they used it as a threat to keep people in line." He was watching Radix's fire-lighted face closely, as if trying to gauge his reaction to heresy. Radix was listening to him as attentively as Brian had listened. He went on. "And the heaven she believes in is dumb. I think a God who says worship me day and night is pretty lame. Why does he need that? If there's a God, he should have enough self-confidence not to need to be told all the time how great he is. I think it's really the priests and preachers who keep saying we have to sing praises day and night because they know no one can do that, and they'll be afraid enough to think they need the priests to intercede for them."

I wanted to applaud. Radix looked at me. My turn.

I dodged. "Kevin says that when they build a big-enough computer, with enough memory, enough speed, God will be born. We'll all be bytes in the God computer."

"Kevin's full of it," Amy said disdainfully. "Modern medicine took God out of illness. Spells, curses, God's wrath, gone. Replaced by microbes, viruses, genetics. Meteorology took God out of storms and floods, earthquakes and tsunamis. Astronomy took heaven out of the skies. Geology took hell away from underfoot. Understanding how synapses fire undermines visions and prophecies, even dreams. Science keeps pushing God out farther and farther, and one day he'll be so far out, we'll close the door, and conversations like this won't happen ever again." She stood up. "I'm going to bed."

Radix looked at me, smiling slightly. "You still avoiding the issue?"

Amy paused at the tent flap as I said, "God is an idea people had a long time ago. No one knows when. 'In the beginning was the Word, and the Word was with God, and the Word was God.' A word, a symbol, an idea. African natives created gods, South American Indians created different ones, Asians yet different ones, and so on. They created the gods they needed, gods who accounted for the mysteries of the universe, of being. It's backward to say God created Adam in his image. Adam created the God he needed, in his image, a God like him, who would give him dominion over the woman, over the whole world. And God kept growing and changing because people kept adding to the idea, until a priesthood stepped in and codified the God idea and said this is the true God. They said it in Egypt, in Africa and South America, in Japan and China. Everywhere. They said it in Israel and Rome. They say it now in the neighborhood church, but ideas don't stop because people tell them to. So God is evolving with us, changing with us, growing." I glanced at Amy, who was still standing at the tent flap. "You can chase the idea out the front door, but it will come whistling back through a window. Ideas are stronger than your science. The God idea will live as long as people think and feel afraid and alone."

Suddenly I felt embarrassed and self-conscious. Radix and Brian were watching me intently, and Amy had become motionless. I picked up a stick and poked the fire and made it spark up, then added the stick. The moment ended.

Brian looked at Radix and asked, "Do you believe in ghosts?"

Amy went inside the tent and closed the flap.

"Not your standard horror-story ghosts," Radix said. He gazed at the renewed fire and said, "We had a friend, my father's friend actually, a retired appellate judge, who claimed that a little girl about eight or nine years old hovered around him most of the time. He would look up from his desk and catch a glimpse of her, or he would turn on a light in a dark room and see her for a second or two. He said he didn't know her, had never known anyone like her; she never spoke to him, or touched him, or did anything except be there. No one else ever saw her, which was frustrating, because no one believed him. He had told a few people, not many. He died without ever discovering more than that. A little girl lived in his house with him for sixty or seventy years."

Radix leaned forward with his arms on his knees, his face closer to the fire. He looked very serious. "This man told us the story at dinner one night; he was old then, and angry because he had come to suspect he would die without a solution to his mystery. I was thirteen or fourteen. I've thought about it a lot since then, read

154

the various theories — projection, hallucination, a visual impairment, fabrication — but none of them seemed to answer the question, Why a little girl for such a long time? I finally decided I couldn't solve the puzzle any more than he had." Then very softly he added, "I wish to hell I could."

I stood up with a jerk. "That's the perfect ending for the day, a ghost story told around a campfire. I'm going to bed." If he had asked me if I believed in ghosts, I would have said no. But what would Brian say? I didn't want him to talk about ghosts with Radix.

I started to rake the fire apart and Radix said quietly, "Leave it. I'll see to it in a little while."

I looked at Brian, who was sitting straight up, gazing fixedly at the fire. After a moment he raised his face toward me. His eyes gleamed in the firelight. "You'd better come, too," I said. "Or you'll walk all over us later when you go to bed." We were sleeping in the big tent; Radix had Kevin's tent.

Brian's face was expressionless, as if he had fallen asleep with his eyes open. I realized he was deciding, and whatever he decided, there wasn't a thing I could do about it. Finally, he nodded and pulled in his legs to stand up. He had decided: Not now. I knew his decision had not been about going to bed, and I was afraid because it was so obvious that it had been his decision, not something he felt he had to do because I told him to. He had crossed an invisible barrier, and on the other side he had become a person who made his own decisions.

We broke camp before noon the next day, but we stayed at the coast, and Radix bought us all dinner, then he drove the van home. After we unloaded our gear and Radix put his stuff away in his car, he came to the door with us. He held Amy's shoulders and kissed her cheek. He gave Brian a bear hug, hesitated at me, and then turned toward his car.

"That was the best weekend of my life," he said. "Thanks." I walked out with him when he left; I still had to put the van in the garage. At his car door he hesitated. "Thanks, Liz, for letting me talk. I didn't know I wanted to talk about that stuff. I never did before."

I didn't know if he meant talking about God or talking about his travels. I nodded. Then, inanely, I said, "It was a great weekend. I'm really glad you came."

"Me too." He started to get in the car, then stopped again. "I wish you could trust me, Liz. I wish to hell you could trust me. See you," he said, and got in the car and left.

16

Radix had assumed that Boyd Symington was my boyfriend, just as everyone else assumed it. Actually, during the past year, Boyd had changed from a casual acquaintance, another student at Mr. Kimmelman's school, to a friend, and then suddenly to best friend. In preparing us for a recital, in addition to the solos we would have to perform, Mr. Kimmelman had teamed four of his sixteen-year-olds in a string quartet. Boyd played the cello and was an exceptional musician, gifted the way Brian was. I was embarrassed to have to play with him. The other two students were also fine. Our quartet was working well enough until we had a rehearsal before an audience of the other students, and I froze.

"See!" I cried. "I told you I can't do it!"

Mr. Kimmelman frowned at me; his bald head seemed to catch fire, it was so red. "You will learn to play with an audience," he said. "You will."

"I won't!" I said, and walked from the rehearsal room to go to the bathroom. I washed my face, which was nearly as flushed as Mr. Kimmelman's head; then, looking at myself in the mirror, I whispered, "I can't."

When I went back into the hallway, Boyd was lounging against the wall. He was a tall, thin boy, six months older than I was, with curly black hair and brown eyes that always looked enormous and a bit surprised behind his thick glasses. I never had paid much attention to him; he was just another student. He was drinking a Coke from a can. Wordlessly, he handed it to me and I took a long swallow.

"You're really good at practice," he said.

"I'm not afraid of you and Angela and Peter," I muttered. "You don't watch me."

"We're too busy trying not to screw up," he said. He grinned and I grinned with him. Imagining any of them screwing up was impossible. "Can you pretend the audience away?" he asked. "That's what I do."

I shook my head. "I tried, but they're there all right."

"I'm supposed to drag you back," he said, "and you're supposed to kick and scream." He gave me the Coke again.

We shared the Coke, then he tossed the can into the recycle bin. "Will you try something else?" he asked. "Let's rearrange the chairs so when you look up, you'll just see me. Will you try it?"

Without explanation we moved the chairs in the studio, and when I looked up, it was at him. His jaw was tight and his forehead furrowed slightly; I realized how focused he was, how hard he was concentrating, and, strangely, knowing he was working so hard helped me. The rehearsal was okay, an ordeal but okay. The night of the recital, I stared at the music or at him, and I got through that, too. After the recital he introduced me to his parents, who were so happy to meet me that I became suspicious. Amy and Radix took Brian home and I went out to dinner with Boyd; he would drive me home later, he told Amy, as if asking her permission, which was annoying, but I was too hungry to care much. I hadn't been able even to think about eating all that day.

At dinner he asked me very tentatively if I had a boyfriend. I didn't. When I went out with other kids from my classes, it was always in a group; I'd had a couple of real dates, but somehow it never seemed to work out. Then, shyly, he said, "Mom and Dad keep trying to get me to go out with this girl, the daughter of a businessman Dad knows. I don't even like her. I sort of told them I knew this really neat girl. . . ." Then he said in a rush, "They think you're my girlfriend. Is that okay?"

We both thought that was funny, and I realized that I could say he was my boyfriend. He lived in Portland and went to school there; I lived out past South Hills. We could have a long-distance pseudoromance. He would be my security blanket. We became friends that night.

We went to the movies once in a while, or out for hamburgers or tacos after our music lessons. And he came to the house sometimes to play with Brian and me. We set up chairs in the living room, a chamber group of three, two violins and a cello. Even though I was outclassed, we all enjoyed it.

We would both graduate the following year, and he planned to go down to the San Francisco Conservatory of Music afterward; he could hardly wait. He told me about his family, his grandparents in Monterey. We talked about school and the dumb classes we had to take, how he hated math and would flunk right out if his parents didn't have him tutored. And I talked about my family, about the good times we had had long ago, the many different places I had lived. I let him read my stories and we talked about them. But we both had secrets. I sensed it, and I thought he probably did, too.

For my birthday he brought two packages, one he had chosen, a CD of Isaac Stern, and one he said his mother had bought and insisted he give me. It was a bracelet, not fabulously expensive, but a costly gold band.

"She said it would look so pretty on your wrist when you play," he said miserably. We both knew I would never wear it when I played.

"Want to take a ride?" he asked then.

Brian rolled his eyes in an appropriate little-brother way, and I said, "Sure."

After driving aimlessly for nearly an hour, he parked somewhere near the Willamette River in Portland; the city lights were more beautiful on the smooth water than on the buildings and bridges. "I know there must be a lot of guys hanging around you," he said. "You're so pretty and smart." He was holding the steering wheel hard with both hands, staring straight ahead. "I think we should break if off now. I mean we'll still be friends. We'll always be friends, but no more pretending you're my girlfriend, like that." He sounded desperate. "I'll always love you, but I can't . . ." He sounded near tears.

I put my hand on his arm. "I'll always love you, too. And you don't have to."

He turned toward me then. The city lights were reflected in his glasses. "You know?"

I hadn't known, but neither was I surprised to learn he was gay. There had been no groping, no awkward attempts at intimacy, no quick kisses, nothing that I had learned to expect from boys. "I guess I must have known," I said.

He told me he had fallen in love with a camp counselor when he was thirteen, he had dreamed about him, how it had frightened and confused him. He never had told anyone, he said, especially the counselor. He was afraid to tell his father, who, he said, would kick him out. He made me promise to tell him if I became attracted to someone, if I wanted to go out with someone. "You know," he said almost helplessly. I promised to tell him.

That night he said I would always be his best friend. He had no more secrets.

After Amy left for UCLA early in September, the house was different. I heard the house noises that I hadn't heard in years. I left the television on when no one was watching it, or I played CDs until I was ready to go to sleep, and sometimes even left them on all night.

I wrote a story for Mrs. Corman's class that September. It was about a girl who lived in a village somewhere else. On a hill overlooking the village was a temple built by ancestors dead so long that no one knew who they had been or what the temple was for. It was a lovely airy building with soaring arches, all made of marble delicately wrought. The marble caught the sunlight at all hours of the day and turned from fiery red at dawn to deep gold, then to pale rose at sunset. By night starlight flickered on the smooth marble. The temple was taboo. It was said that some who dared to enter returned mad; a few never returned at all. Life was tranquil in the village; food was plentiful, and the villagers were contented, except for one girl, who tended sheep on the hill. She yearned to see inside the temple, just to see what it held. She wondered how a marble temple could drive anyone mad, or how anyone could get lost inside it and never come out again. It was not that big a temple, she thought. She was certain she could step inside, look around, then step out again. It became an obsession; she dreamed about it at night and thought about it by day, until finally she stepped inside. Instantly she was entranced. The walls were covered with beautiful script carved into the marble, flowing in line after line. The girl could not read; only a few elders in the village could read the holy texts, but she recognized that the flowing lines were words and more words, and that they were nothing like the words in the scrolls of the elders. She found herself sitting in the center of the temple, gazing at the strange letters and words, when suddenly a picture came into her head, then another. She saw things she had never seen before, places she never had heard of, animals without names, oddly dressed people. . . . She gazed at every line of flowing script on one wall, then another, and more and more pictures came into her head. As if from a great distance, she heard voices calling her name; they were so far away, she could ignore them. Finally, after she had studied all the words on all four walls, she stood up. Before her there appeared a tall lady who was gowned in shimmering silver; her hair, even her eyes were silver. She held out her hand. Although no word was spoken, the girl understood that she could go with the silver lady or she could go back to the village. When she didn't move, the lady said softly, "Only you can decide."

I ended the story there. The kids in the writing class wanted to know what she did, and if she went with the lady, where they went, and who the lady was. I didn't even try to answer the questions; I didn't know the answers. Mrs. Corman told me I should submit the story to a magazine that had a contest every fall for student writers. I mumbled that if I ever finished it, maybe then I would. She shook her head.

Kevin and Amy came home for the Christmas holiday, and Radix flew back to Philadelphia.

The day after Christmas, Mrs. Corman called and asked if she could come visit. Kevin teased me: I must be cutting up pretty bad if my teacher had to come out to the house to talk about it. But Mrs. Corman had startling news. She had known I would never submit my story to the contest, and she had done it for me. I had won third place and they would publish the three winning stories in the April issue. She had a check for one hundred dollars for me, my prize.

Later, Kevin went out and bought a bottle of champagne and we celebrated. Brian tasted his and said, "Yuck!" I didn't like it either, but I drank mine; after all, it was in my honor. We all laughed a lot that night.

But something was going on between Amy and Kevin. Several times over the holidays when I entered a room where they were talking in low, intense voices, they became silent and looked uncomfortable. One of the times, Amy asked if it wasn't too lonesome in the big house for just Brian and me. I lied and said no, that we liked it.

Kevin left two days after Christmas; he had to get back, he said. The program he was writing now, with three others, was at a crucial stage. Amy stayed a week longer.

The day before she left, she asked, "Has Brian outgrown it? He seems all right."

For a moment, I felt an intense hatred for her. He always seemed all right, with one exception. "Nothing's changed," I said.

The next day I drove her to Portland and she caught a plane back to California.

Radix hadn't hung around the way I thought he would when Amy was home, and I decided to give it up. It had become clear that they never would get together, and I found, to my surprise, that I was relieved. Amy was too single-minded for him. She would never go to a concert with him; she would be too busy. And she would be too busy playing with crabs to listen to him talk about his trips. They never would talk about Shakespeare or Jung, about Kierkegaard or Camus, or any of the things Radix and I talked about.

In January Brian told him about the contest. Radix was as excited as we all had been. "Another celebration is in order," he said. "How about dinner? Someplace really fancy." We agreed on a day and time, and he asked if he could read the story.

"In the magazine," I said, embarrassed at the thought of his reading it while I was in the same county.

"Liz," he said then, "let's sit down. We have to talk." We sat in the living room. "You have to go to a good school," he said. "At Yale, one of my instructors talked about studying under Nabokov, how important it was, how special. He'll never forget it. Think what it would be like for you to study with a writer like that."

I stole a glance at Brian. "You could do it,

Liz," he said. "I could stay here with Mrs. Inglewood."

"You could both go," Radix said impatiently. "You could live in an apartment together."

I shook my head and looked at the floor. "Maybe later," I said. "Right now I don't even know what I want to do, what I want to study. Just leave me alone."

Radix stood up swiftly. "Sure," he said. "I'll leave you alone. Be seeing you."

After he left, Brian said, "You should go, Liz. Honest, I wouldn't mind. And Mrs. Inglewood said she could spend the night if we really wanted her to. I think she'd like to live here with us, with me."

"Will you go with me?"

He shook his head. "I can't."

"You can take off to the coast. You can go down to Ashland. Why can't you go somewhere else?" Angry with him, tired of his nonsense, just tired, I heard my voice go harsh and mean.

"You know," he said quietly. "She knows I won't be gone long, and I don't go very far away."

"For God's sake, give it up!" I yelled at him. "It isn't cute or funny! Grow up!"

He walked out of the room.

Radix took us to dinner at the elegant Benson Hotel, and no one mentioned school. We talked about music, about books we had all read, about another coast trip one day, about civilized, grown-up things. When we left the restaurant, I asked him if we could go see his apartment, surprising him very much.

"Why?"

"I'm curious." I had imagined his apartment filled with beautiful art, statues and paintings, all originals. I wanted to see them. I wanted him to tell us where he got everything, tell us about Paris, Florence, London. . . .

He was looking at me with a puzzled expression. I shrugged. "If it's a bother, never mind," I said.

"No bother. Why not?" We got into his car and he drove us to a town house in Lake Oswego. In daylight there would be a nice view of the lake, he said, opening his door.

I was disappointed. The apartment was nearly barren. There was only enough furniture to make it livable, a leather-covered sofa, two easy chairs, reading lamps, a desk with a lot of papers on it. The walls were entirely bare. Bookcases held only books, except for one spot that held the piece of petrified wood he had found at the coast. No Persian rugs, only the nondescript carpet furnished by management. He was watching me.

"What did you expect?"

"I don't know," I said.

"You expected to see art, didn't you?"

I nodded, feeling guilty, like a discovered intruder, a voyeur caught at a peephole.

" 'When I became a man,' " he said softly, " 'I put away childish things.' Ready to leave? Or do you want to see the rest of it? It's more of the same."

Brian was gazing at me in bewilderment, then at Radix with the same expression.

"Let's leave," I said. Looking at Radix at that moment, I knew what it was he wanted to be when he grew up.

That night I thought about his apartment, how awful it must be to live there if his head was filled with beautiful art, how total his denial was, how he insisted that we, his pseudowards, follow our inclinations, wherever they took us. How he must have regretted ever telling me anything real about himself. That explained his staying away so much, I thought; it had nothing to do with Amy's being there or not; it had everything to do with my prying, my brutal opening of wounds that he must have thought were healed. I couldn't even tell him I was sorry; that would simply twist the knife another time.

17

I came to realize how naive we all had been to think that if we stayed in one place and attended school for a few years with the same kids, then we no longer would be out of step.

It was not only that I had deep secrets that could never be revealed, it was a general out-of-stepness. I went to two rock concerts and got a splitting headache each time and gave that up. I could not watch a movie in which characters died. I could not stand violence in movies or on television, except in grade-B horror movies, where nothing was real. When I saw how talkative, babbling, some kids got when they drank anything with alcohol, or smoked pot, I knew I didn't dare trust myself not to do the same. During our junior and senior years, when the other girls began to talk disparagingly of their parents, especially their mothers, or to talk openly about sex, their sexual adventures, I was silent. Everyone assumed that Boyd and I were a thing, doing it all the time, and I let them think that by denying nothing, admitting nothing.

I never dyed my hair a strange color, or wore out-of-the-ordinary clothes or jewelry. I did nothing to call attention to myself. I wanted to be invisible.

With Boyd I talked about music, my stories, his future, our fears about the coming years; it was good talk, but it got nowhere near my secret self, which was sealed off for all time.

Radix had taken Brian and me to Ashland to see Shakespeare, thus opening another door for me. Seeing the plays performed, hearing the magical language gave me the gift of Shakespeare, whereas high school had threatened to destroy him. Although we talked and argued about the plays, about books, about philosophy and Jung and Freud, about historical saints and devils, Radix knew there was something else, something I wouldn't or couldn't reveal. I could tell by the expression that crossed his face now and again, by the way he sometimes started to question me and quickly backed off, by the way he sometimes suddenly had to leave, had to go to work, had to go anywhere else. When he wasn't bossing me around, he was close to being my best friend.

In April of my senior year, the magazine with my story arrived. Mrs. Corman was jubilant; the other kids were all excited and praised me and the story lavishly. I was disappointed.

It wasn't the perfect story I had seen in my head; it had mistakes, wrong words, awkward phrases. . . . I was embarrassed by it, and I felt the editor must have been angry that it had placed third in the contest and he had to print it. I wanted to apologize to him. I wanted to cry.

The day after I received the magazine, when I got home, Mrs. Inglewood and Brian were talking in the kitchen. She hugged me.

"I'm so excited," she said. "You're a writer, a published writer. The story is wonderful. I love it!"

She released me and I glared at Brian. He shrugged and grinned. "I showed her," he admitted. "I knew you wouldn't."

Then Radix came in through the back door. He almost always came in that way, just as if he were family or something. He was carrying a copy of the magazine, smiling broadly.

"Liz, it's terrific! Congratulations!"

"Where did you get that?"

"I subscribed as soon as Brian told me you won. I thought I'd better, or I might never get to see your work in print."

"They're all geniuses," Mrs. Inglewood said. "Computer genius, scientist, writer, musician. All geniuses! I'm so proud of you all."

"And so am I," Radix said. "So am I."

"Well, I'm off," Mrs. Inglewood said as she pulled on her heavy man's jacket. "You've made my day, Liz. Made my day." She paused at the door. "There's plenty cooked if you want to stay and eat," she said to Radix.

After she left, Brian, without asking, got another plate and silverware out and put them on the table. "She said it would be another half hour for it to get done," he said. "I've got homework. Math. Yuck." He went to the dining room/study.

"What is it?" Radix asked then. "I thought I'd find you jumping up and down, excited. What's wrong?"

"I don't know," I said. "It's not how I thought it would be, I guess. I thought I had a better story than that." I picked up my jacket, which I had tossed over a chair back, and started to leave. He caught my arm and turned me to face him.

"Liz, it's a very fine story. Beautifully written. You should have won first place for it. When I think how a few careless words must have lodged in your brain, must have gathered image and mood and style, it makes me feel inadequate. I didn't see that story in my words, but you did."

I stared at him, aghast, as for the first time I realized where the story had come from, his description of the Alhambra. Not only was it full of mistakes, it wasn't even my idea. His grip on my arm tightened.

"You didn't know," he said in a low voice. "Oh God, Liz, I'm sorry. I thought you knew. You took something so mundane that you could have found it in a travel book, and you worked magic on it, made it yours, made it beautiful, made it meaningful for everyone."

I shook my head violently and tried to pull away. "I don't even know what it means," I said furiously. "It doesn't mean anything! I don't want it to be for everyone. It was for me. Mrs. Corman cheated and submitted it; I didn't."

He caught my shoulder and kept his grip on my arm, forcing me to face him. "No," he said. "Not just for you. Not this time. Keep your music, keep your secrets, keep yourself buried, but your stories are not just for you. You need to talk, and if you can't talk to me, or to anyone else, you'll talk to the world because you have to."

We were so close, we might have been dancing, intimately close, too close. Suddenly I felt his hand on my shoulder, his hand hard on my arm, and I felt a rush of fear. Abruptly he let me go and turned away.

"I'll leave now," he said. "Tell Brian another time." He crossed the kitchen and walked out the back door without looking at me again.

I ran upstairs, shaken in a way I couldn't comprehend. Afraid of Radix? Not bloody likely, I told myself, but I could still feel the pressure of his hand on my arm, his hand on my shoulder. Then I was angry with him again, the way I always was when he tried to tell me what to do. Besides, I told myself, it hadn't been his words about the Alhambra, it had been the pictures that formed in my mind as he talked about it. I couldn't even remember the words, only the pictures.

The next time he came around, I tried to be distant and cool, but he had a new computer game with him, and he, Brian, and I played Myst for a couple of hours. We were back on our usual footing, avoiding the subjects that were likely to send him away, or send me off to my room.

Boyd and I graduated; he took me to his prom, and later the same night to mine. In a few weeks he would be going down to his grandparents' place in Monterey, and from there on to San Francisco to get settled in before the fall term started. I was gloomy and he was apprehensive. The day he came to say good-bye, I cried.

Amy and Kevin came home, she to stay for a month, he only a week or so. They were both restless and discontented. Amy planned to move in with Jeff Hazleton, she said; he was a graduate student in marine biology. She missed him, and the only reason she had come home at all was that he was off visiting his parents in Wyoming; they spent hours on the phone every day. I told her she had to pay the phone bill and she smiled. She was prettier than ever, with a new softness in her expression, a dreaminess that reminded me of Mother when she and Dad danced.

But the uneasy feeling I had had over the Christmas holiday was back; they were conspiring about something, Amy and Kevin. And it was apparent that they did not intend to include me. I watched them carefully for a clue. Now that I was eighteen, I didn't feel threatened, but it made me nervous to come across Amy and Kevin in a low-voiced conversation that changed instantly at my appearance.

Then one evening Radix came over. We went out to the patio, all of us in shorts, three of us barefoot. Radix had on sandals. Brian was at the swimming pool with friends. It was sultry weather, airless; for more than a week, the temperature had climbed into the high nineties, up to a hundred on three days. Thunderstorms were a possibility, according to the weather reports, but they had been possible for days and had yet to materialize. My back was clammy against the plastic chair.

Kevin was telling Radix about the program he and three others had written. It was ready for beta testing, he said.

"So, it's set, ready to go, but how we'll release it is the problem. We could go share ware and collect nickels and dimes for the next five years or more; meanwhile one of the big companies would grab it, add a few whistles and bells, then release it with a lot of hoopla. Or we could put together a presentation and sell it outright to one of the big companies. No problem. It'll sell. But they'd own it. They'd want to hire us, more than likely. Or," he said slowly, "we could form our own corporation and release the program and be in business. And we'd get real rich, real fast."

Radix was watching him closely, his face expressionless, and Amy was gazing off into the woods. I felt certain she had heard all this before, but it was the first time I had.

"If we can raise from one hundred fifty thousand to two hundred, we could get matching money. That would be enough," Kevin said. "We'd need a lawyer to draw up papers and stuff," he said with a grin. "Your part."

Still Radix didn't move or comment. As far as I was concerned, Kevin might as well have been talking about a flight to the moon — unless his buddies were very rich.

"We would either hire you as our attorney or, after you see what we have, include you in the corporation if you want in. If you could put up some of the money."

"How will you raise your share?" Radix asked quietly.

Kevin leaned forward. "Mother's been gone for four years. No one believes she'll come back. If we could sell the house, I'd have my share. It's appraised at one hundred sixty thousand for taxes. We'd get more than that."

"You can't sell it," Radix said.

"I heard that there are ways," Kevin said. "A contract sale or something, contingent on finalizing the deal at a future date when the title is clear. There must be a way. And if it's really impossible, I could have you draw up a contract and let me borrow against my share when it does get sold." He glanced at me. "Liz needs to go to a good school, and she can't go off and leave Brian here with a paid housekeeper. And in a couple of years Brian should go to a good music conservatory. But they can't with this white elephant on our hands." His voice was getting husky. "You could arrange it, Bill. You know you could."

Radix stood up and walked to the edge of the patio to stand with his back to us. If I had been nailed to my chair, I couldn't have been more immobilized. Kevin knew we couldn't sell the house, not now, not ever; this was a crazy pipe dream. We all watched Radix. Out beyond him, some pale flowers glowed in the shadows of the fir trees that had eclipsed the sun and made pockets of darkness in Mother's garden.

"I'll have to discuss it with Martens," Radix said finally, turning toward us once again. "He makes the important decisions. You want to show me your program so I'll have an idea what I'm talking about?"

Kevin leapt up. "Yeah," he said, barely suppressing his excitement. "The computer here is pretty obsolete, but you'll get an idea."

Radix didn't move yet. "I'll have to tell Martens this is unanimous, that it's what you all want. Can I tell him that?" He looked straight at me. I didn't move.

"It will be after we talk it over," Kevin said. "Come on, let me show you."

Radix was still in the dining room with Kevin when Brian came home and went to the refrigerator. He looked at Amy and me uneasily as he made a sandwich, but he didn't ask any questions. Amy went upstairs, and I went to the family room to turn on the television. In a minute, Brian came in with his sandwich and a glass of milk. We could hear Radix and Kevin when they came out of the dining room. I strained to hear the words. Radix was saying, "Don't get your hopes up too high. It's a real long shot. I'll do a little research before I approach the lion in his den, then get back to you in a couple of days. I might have some more questions."

I heard the front door close, then Kevin yelling, "Amy! Come on down!"

He bounced into the kitchen just as Brian and I entered. Brian went to the refrigerator and brought out the milk. "What's happening?" he asked. He refilled his glass and put the jug back.

"Come over here and sit down," Kevin said. "We have to talk."

We crossed the kitchen to the table, but no one sat down. Amy came in and stood near Kevin.

"Listen, Brian," Kevin said, "it's time to think about tomorrow and the day after, and the years after. We have to sell the house. Bill is going to arrange —"

"No!" Brian yelled. "You can't do that!"

"We have to," Kevin said calmly.

"You can't," I said. "You know. We talked about it. We can't sell."

"You guys will all go to the coast for a few days," Kevin said. "I'll take care of things here."

"What do you mean?" I whispered.

"What do you think? Look, our mother's been dead for nearly seven years. I'll exhume her remains and we'll have a real funeral, maybe a burial at sea."

The glass slipped from Brian's hand and milk splashed out all over the floor. I had been watching Kevin; he was tense and determined-looking. I turned toward Brian. All the color had left his face. A shudder passed through him, then another. He had grown taller that year, and his arms and legs appeared abnormally long and thin. They were covered with goose bumps.

"No," he said hoarsely. "You can't do that."

"I can and I will," Kevin said. "We have to get out of this. Amy and I will never live in this house again. We've got our lives, and they're not here. As soon as Liz is out of school, she'll be gone. Then what? We have to do this."

Brian shook his head. He looked ghastly, he was so pale; his eyes were too wide, staring fixedly. Sweat broke out on his face and he kept shivering. "I'll tell," he whispered.

"You'll tell what? There won't be anything for anyone to find. They'll just think you're a nutcase. Get with it, Brian. We have to do this!"

"I'll tell. I saw you. Out my window. I saw you. She was in the tree and you yelled at her and pulled the ladder away. I saw you!" He started to sway.

Suddenly Kevin lunged at him, yelling, "You little shit! You're lying! It's a lie!" He knocked Brian over and was starting to beat him with his fists, yelling, "Liar! You fucking little liar!"

Amy and I grabbed his arms, screaming, and pulled him away. He rolled over and lay still for a second, then got to his feet, dripping milk, with milk running down his legs. I was kneeling at Brian's side.

"You've hurt him! You killed him!" I screamed.

"God, I hope so!" Kevin ran from the room,

and Amy pushed me away from Brian and knelt by him.

"He's in shock. We should get him to bed and cover him up. He fainted, I think. He's coming around."

Brian stirred and moaned, then he tried to sit up. Amy helped him. He got to his hands and knees and threw up, and nearly fell again. Amy and I caught him and half-carried, half-dragged him up to his room, where he collapsed onto his bed and, to all appearances, fell asleep. He didn't stir when I washed his face and hands. He was breathing easily, sleeping, his color more normal now, but he felt so cool, I put a light blanket over him. I went downstairs, where Amy was cleaning up the kitchen floor with paper towels. She was white, shriveled-looking.

Silently I got out the mop and pail, filled the pail with water, and added floor cleaner and bleach. The smell was awful in the kitchen. We worked in silence. Before we were through, Kevin came into the room carrying a suitcase; he was as pale as Amy. He looked like a stranger.

"Take me to town," he snapped at Amy. "I'll drive, you bring the car back."

Wordlessly, she went to the sink and washed her hands. Kevin started to walk out, and I cried, "Wait! He was hysterical. He didn't mean it! You shouldn't have sprung it on him like that."

"He meant it," Kevin said brusquely. "He's crazy. He belongs in an institution. The little shithead can stay here and rot!" He stamped out and Amy ran up the stairs for her purse. A few seconds later she was down again, and out the door. I listened to the sound of tires squealing on the drive.

18

I finished in the kitchen, then checked on Brian, who was sleeping and still felt cool. Back downstairs I went out to the patio and walked to the end of it, where the garage started. The garage was six feet from the house, with a roof over the passageway between the two buildings. At the corner of the house, the roofed patio was about eight feet wide, with another six or eight feet uncovered. I stood at the garage side and looked at it, remembering that day when Amy and I had come home late. It had been raining hard, I remembered, seeing the rain in my mind; we had been shaking water off our umbrellas in the passageway. Turning the corner onto the patio, I had seen the ladder on the concrete floor. House lights on, getting dark already. Kevin in the kitchen doorway, ashen-faced. I had dropped my umbrella on his boots near the door. I closed my eyes and saw the ladder again, all of it on the concrete.

I walked to the side of the patio, where the ladder had been, and looked up at Brian's window. One on this wall, the southern side, the other two out of sight, on the western side. Then I looked at the apple tree, large and overgrown, branches sagging with too much fruit that had not been thinned out, shading the entire patio from the lowering sun every day, the trunk ten feet from the concrete. And at the right, slightly behind the tree, the boulders where she had fallen.

We had bought the ladder when we moved in here. We'd need it, Dad had said, to keep the gutters clean of fir needles. It was an extension ladder, six feet, extending to ten. And it had been on the patio, extended all the way, the entire length of it on the patio. I could visualize it clearly, how it had been, where the rain had been falling on it, where it had been under the cover. I sat down in one of the web chairs.

I heard movement in the woods, the deer, or raccoons, or rabbits, possums. . . . It was growing cooler, the way it always did at night; soon it would be too cool to be out here in shorts.

Later, I heard the car return, heard the garage door close, then Amy's steps in the passageway. When she came around the corner, her shoulders were drooping, her steps slow, as if she moved with great effort. She jumped when I said her name.

"Sorry," I said. I had pulled my chair out of the light from the house; she pulled another one into the shadows and sat down. "Where did he go?"

"A motel. He said he'll fly out tomorrow if he can get a seat. He'll call Bill and tell him to forget it." Her voice was low, dull, and spiritless.

"Did he say anything else?"

"He said you probably believed the little shithead." There was a minute of silence; I could hear the high-pitched squeaks of bats. "Do you believe him?" Amy asked then in an even lower voice.

"No! He was hysterical. Kevin shouldn't have hit him with that out of the blue the way he did."

"You can't very well sneak up on the idea of selling the house," she said.

Not that, I thought. Selling the house would have been bad enough, but Kevin wanted to dig up Mother's body, take her away. I remembered the goose bumps on Brian's arms and legs, the sweat on his waxen face, the tremors that had shaken his entire body.

"What are we going to do?" I asked after a moment.

"God, I don't know." She put her hands on the sides of her head, as if trying to keep a headache from breaking out. I couldn't see her expression, just the gleam of her hair, the light blur of her skin. "Jesus, Liz, he could blow it at any time. He must be really insane. You know that, don't you?"

I nodded. I moistened my lips; my mouth had gone very dry, and now I was feeling the chill of the night. "That day, when we came home together . . . You know. Did you see the ladder?"

"What ladder?" Then, without pause, she said, "I'm not going to hang around. If he really believes what he said . . . I don't think I can be with him now, not right now. I keep thinking, What if Jeff finds out? What would he say? What would his folks say? I wonder if I should just go

184

ahead and tell him, clear the air, but I'm afraid to."

"If he really loves you —" I started.

She said impatiently, "You don't understand. He has a reputation to protect, and I do, too. This would be such a shadow, crazy little brother, what we did, how we lied. . . ." She jumped up, still pressing her hands to her temples. "Aspirin, lots of aspirin. I'll try to get a flight for tomorrow, go down and putter in the apartment alone, try to think." She went to the door and hesitated. "Are you all right alone with him? Does he do anything else?"

"We're okay," I said. She continued to stand at the door for another few seconds, then went inside. Hunky-dory, I thought. We're just hunky-dory.

I could have pressed her about the ladder, but I knew it would be useless. She seldom saw anything that wasn't of direct personal interest to her. But did I believe what Brian had said, or Kevin's denial? I looked up again at Brian's window, palely illuminated from the hall light upstairs. I didn't know what I believed.

Amy was already in the kitchen when I went down the next morning. She had deep shadows under her eyes, as I did. She examined my face and shook her head. "Bad night," she said.

"Yeah."

"Liz, I've been thinking about all this. You could go with me, you know. We can make arrangements here for Brian, but you don't have to stay."

I shrugged and went for coffee. I poured half a cup, added cream to fill it, and a lot of sugar.

"He doesn't need any of us," Amy said insistently. "He has everything he wants right here in the house. Let him have it. Come with me."

"Maybe later," I said, too tired to talk about it, too tired to argue about anything. I started across the kitchen to sit at the table.

We stopped talking when Brian appeared at the kitchen door. He seemed listless and as tired as I felt, and I had a flash of anger at that, because every time I had looked in on him during the night, he had been sound asleep.

"What happened last night?" he asked. "Did I pass out or something? Who put me to bed?"

I stared at him. "Don't you remember? You must be kidding!"

He shook his head. "All I know is that I had a sandwich and woke up in bed. I must have a bug or something."

Amy made a low noise, jumped up, and ran out. Brian watched her with a puzzled expression, then walked past me toward the refrigerator.

"Brian, don't you remember what happened? What you said?"

He peered at me. "Are you sick, too? You don't look so good."

"Answer me!"

He frowned in bewilderment; then he looked frightened, reverting in an instant to the little brother who always turned to me first. "What happened? What did I do? I don't remember anything."

"You threw up and passed out," I said wearily. He really didn't know; he never could lie to me, and he wasn't lying then.

Radix dropped in that evening. He came to the patio, where I was sitting with an unopened book; Brian was watering Mother's garden. I had made dinner and had not yet cleaned up the kitchen. During the summer that year, Mrs. Inglewood was coming only once a week; I missed her. As soon as school started again, she would resume her regular schedule; meanwhile Brian and I were doing the cooking and washing dishes, and I had no interest in either.

"Kevin called me," Radix said, heading for a second chair.

I put my finger to my lips and motioned toward the door. "He left some beer. You want one?"

"Sure." He followed me into the house. "You guys have a fight?"

"You might say that." I got a beer from the refrigerator and handed it to him. "We didn't mention Kevin's plan to Brian. No point in upsetting him," I muttered.

"Does that mean you're the holdout?" He moved past me and rummaged in a drawer for the bottle opener, then got a glass from the cabinet. "Kevin was pretty uptight."

I began to pick up plates and silverware from

the table. He watched me.

"Just the two of you? Is Amy out?"

"She's gone back to California."

"Ah. Big fight."

I began to scrape the plates, then rinsed them and shoved some of them into the dishwasher, which was already full. "Tell me something," I said, not looking at him. "Would it have worked? Kevin's idea?"

"I didn't have time to do any real research yet," he said. "I doubt it."

"Pie in the sky," I muttered. There was no room in the dishwasher for the glasses and cups on the counter. We had loaded it after dinner the previous day, but no one had thought to turn it on.

"Liz," he said, "leave that stuff and come talk to me." He pulled a chair out at the table and sat down.

After a moment, I joined him and sat on the opposite side of the table, where I could keep an eye on the patio. It was hot in the house, but I didn't want to talk outside, where Brian might overhear us.

"Whatever happened here won't make much difference right now to Kevin," Radix said. "I'm almost certain Martens wouldn't have gone along with either of his plans. So, if Kevin thinks you got in his way, he's wrong. I'll tell him so. Meanwhile, he has a very fine program. I think it'll sell. And I intend to put him in touch with a couple of people I know who like to back youth

188

and talent. One or both of them might be persuaded to put up venture capital. I'll do what I can, which won't be much more than giving him and his program a high recommendation."

"But no money?"

He laughed. "I don't have any money to put up," he said. "I think I told you guys years ago that my old man's pretty rich. He is. I have my salary. Period."

He poured beer into his glass and kept his gaze on it. "Nearly five years ago we had something of a blowup. He wanted me to go into his firm, just as he'd planned from day one, and I wanted to be on my own for a few years. He agreed finally that it was a pretty good plan, let me get a taste of working for someone like Martens, feel the pinch of not quite enough cash, and I'd be more than ready to take my throne. He thought five years would be long enough. Then I'd be mature, ready." He lifted the glass in a mocking salute. "To the wisdom of old men."

"When will the five years be up?"

"Ah, my practical Liz, always cutting to the point. January. But January comes a little early this year. I've been getting calls from my mother urging me to come home. My father's health is failing, she tells me. He's eighty-something."

His words were spoken lightly, but his face was troubled.

"When will you go?"

"Friday."

"If he . . . if . . . ."

189

"Say it, Liz. If he dies. And of course he will. We all die. When he dies, his money will go to a foundation he set up the week after our . . . discussion. There's a very generous provision for my mother, of course, and she'll need it all. She has expensive habits. After working for his firm for a few years, I'll come into some money, then in a few more years, more of it, and so on. And my salary will be very handsome with the firm, of course. He has been thoughtful and thorough. He wants William Radix the Third to take the helm."

I stared at him. How could he be so calm? So accepting? "It isn't fair," I said. "The dead shouldn't control the living. They should let go."

He nodded and stood up. "So they should. I'm sorry Amy and Kevin aren't here. I wanted to take the whole crew out to dinner tomorrow or Thursday. I'll settle for you and Brian. Are you free?"

We went to dinner and I alternated between misery and numbness. I had nothing to say; Radix and Brian talked. Radix had told Kimmelman to get a Cremona violin for Brian, he was ready for a very fine instrument. And, of course, the lessons would continue. For a going-away present, he had bought us season tickets to the symphony orchestra. He would stay in touch, and he might be back in a few weeks, but that was not certain, since he didn't know yet what the situation was back in Philadelphia with his father. His mother thought there had been a series of small strokes — TIAs, he called them.

Then we were back at the house and he was saying good-bye. He hugged Brian but didn't touch me. "I'm going to miss you," he said.

"I'll miss you, Radix."

He smiled at the name.

When he was gone, I thought, Everything ends. Everything changes.

19

That August I stopped my lessons with Mr. Kimmelman. I waited until the other students had left and talked to him in the studio, surrounded by empty chairs, music stands in disarray, and dust motes lazily dancing in shafts of sunlight.

"Are you sure, Liz?" he asked gently. "Is it what you want? I know your terror of public performance, but, my dear Liz, if you would agree to a little counseling, that would be controlled. I've seen it many times."

"I'm sure," I said. "I know I'm a good musician. I enjoy playing. Being good isn't being good enough."

"It isn't your heart's desire," he said simply. "I hope your music continues to give you pleasure."

I started to walk toward the door, then turned again and went to him, this little gnomelike man with a shiny pink head, and kissed his cheek. "Thank you," I said, and walked away from music.

When I started college, I resolved to do better than I had done in high school, but my resolution was as weightless as fluff, drifting away even as I voiced my resolve. I was bored and resentful. I didn't know what I was there for, where I was heading, what I would gain from stupid classes and stupid, meaningless work without end. Both

Amy and Kevin had gone with plans and carried them out efficiently. I had no plans beyond just getting through each day.

One night, while I was at the computer writing a dumb paper about democracy in ancient Greece, I was half-listening to Brian practicing, first Mendelssohn, then Schubert, then something new and unfamiliar. I went to the bottom of the stairs to listen. He stopped abruptly and after a brief pause started the new piece over, with a slight variation. The piece started off restrained, almost melancholy, reminding me of the *Siegfried Idyll*; a transition to gypsy music was unexpected and it worked, some of the same phrases were there, but wilder and almost exuberant, with a little bit of what Mr. Kimmelman called show-off music, like "The Flight of the Bumble Bee." Then it was as tender as a lullaby, a variation of the opening.

I realized with a feeling of awe that he had composed it. He had written it and I was his first audience. I started up the stairs just as he started down.

"It's wonderful," I said, meeting him halfway. "It's beautiful. Have you told anyone? Have you told Kimmelman? When did you compose it?"

He was smiling. Not the big little-boy grin he usually had, but a shy smile. His bright blue eyes were sparkling, his cheeks redder than I had seen them in months.

"After school, before you got home," he said, again with a new shyness. "I wanted to surprise

193

you. No one else has heard it yet. The first day of school, they were talking about the battle of something or other, and suddenly I began to hear it. I couldn't wait to get home and start."

I grabbed him and hugged him hard. "Kimmelman will pop!" I cried. "I want to be there when you play it for him. Promise!"

"Sure. Promise. There's a little rough spot I'm working on, but I think I know how to fix it." He grinned his old childish grin then. "Kimmelman will find a lot of things to fix, but that's all right."

"He won't! If he starts, I'll stuff a sock down his throat! What will you call it?"

"In the Garden."

I came down with a thud. Of course, he had composed it for Mother.

"Liz," he said softly. "It's all right. Honest it is. It's just that . . . I need her, Liz. It doesn't hurt anyone."

"Why do you need her?" I demanded, hearing the harshness in my voice.

"You know. I told you. She keeps the others away. She promised she would always keep them away from me. It doesn't hurt anyone."

I jerked around to go back downstairs, unwilling to discuss his obsession, and he said, "You hear them, Liz. I know you do. Sometimes I do, too. But I used to see them all around until she made them leave me alone. They're here, but she makes them leave us alone."

Facing him again, I said furiously, "When we

194

moved here, you heard the house noises and got afraid. Dad told you all about the noises houses make. That's all you heard then and it's all you hear now."

He shook his head and went back up; I returned to the dining room and my homework. In a little while I heard his music again and I closed the door.

But I could no longer concentrate. Was his obsession the result of witnessing his brother killing his mother? Was he keeping her alive because he had not been able to do anything that day? Or, I thought bitterly, was he simply crazy? Or was I? Because — But my mind closed as if someone had hit an off button. I was terrified of what was happening to my mind, something that left little gaps of nonawareness, and the knowledge that I had been thinking of something, then nothing. Absolutely nothing.

I was in the studio the day he played his composition for Kimmelman, who was ecstatic and didn't criticize a phrase. I was there when Brian played it for his fall recital and received a standing ovation. I applauded wildly, the first to start, the last to stop. I hardly heard any of the others after that; I was so proud of my little brother. Brian never had shown any of the fear that paralyzed me before an audience; that night, he looked especially mature and handsome in his strange phase between being a boy and a man. I realized that he, like Amy and Kevin, knew where he was going, knew what he wanted. I felt very alone, sitting among strangers.

Brian had sent a program to Radix, with his name and his music circled in red. Radix called and said if it was possible, he would be there, but he didn't come. Instead, we got a terse little note with his congratulations, and an apology. He wrote that his father was very ill and he would not be able to get away. He hoped we were well. I wondered if his father was ill because Radix had told him he didn't want to be a lawyer. Or if, because his father was ill, he hadn't felt he could tell him that. "William Radix the Third," I muttered, and threw the letter away.

That fall, for the first time in years, I began having nightmares again; once or even twice a week, I was jolted from sleep with a racing heart, in a clammy sweat, and with no memory of a dream.

On a cold gray day in November, as I was heading toward my obligatory composition class, Dave Gwyer caught up to me in the hall. "You interested in that stuff?"

"Are you kidding?"

"Let's blow," he said.

He was a couple of years older than I was, and this was the only class we had together, but I had seen him eyeing me several times. That day I didn't hesitate a second, and we left together.

It started like that, with no forethought, no

plan, and no hesitation. I lost my virginity. After Dave there was Warren, then Izzy, then Michael. . . . I could measure the weeks of the month by the guys who drifted in and out of my life. Neither Amy nor Kevin came home for Christmas that year. I drifted in a semidaze through the winter, on into spring.

The crocuses had come and gone, the jonquils and daffodils were in bloom. I was in danger of flunking out of school, and couldn't have cared less. Brian and I hardly talked any longer, but I could feel his eyes searching, searching, and there was something hurting in his gaze. I didn't care about that, either. One day Mrs. Inglewood put her arms around me and held me against her; I resisted for a moment, and she stroked my back and murmured, "My poor Liz. Poor baby." Without warning, I cried like a baby against her warm plaid shirt.

Then one night I was at a party with a lot of loud music, quite a lot of dope floating around, beer, and hard liquor. Tip Lundgren and I were dancing, or at least we were plastered together, swaying to the music. His hand was under my T-shirt, moving up and down my spine, my ribs, my breast. "Let's take off," he whispered. I nodded. We walked out; at his car I started to open the back door, and he grabbed my wrist and opened the front. I didn't care — here, somewhere else, it didn't matter.

I didn't pay any attention to where he was driving until he got near South Hills. His hand was under my skirt, inside my panties. I usually wore skirts then; it made things easier.

"Where are we going?"

"Your place," he said. "Not in the car. In a bed. Your bed."

I pulled his hand away, rearranged my skirt. "I know a place. Just keep going through the village."

"In a bed. I want you naked in bed."

"No."

He kept driving, through the village, onto our blacktop road, into the driveway. As soon as he stopped, I yanked my door open and ran to the porch; he caught me before I could get my key in the lock. "You'll like it in bed. I promise you, you'll love it in bed."

"You can't come in. Let me go."

He shook my arm, hurting me. "I'm coming in. Little brother's asleep. In bed." He made a grab at the key, and I twisted away.

"Let me go! I said you can't come in! Get out of here! Leave me alone!"

He was going to kiss me, force the key out of my hand, force me inside. . . . Furiously, I cried, "If you don't leave, I'll call the police and say you raped me. You'll have to fight me and I'll have marks to show them. Do you hear what I'm saying! Get out of here."

He pulled back, then he slapped me and called me filthy names. He turned and dashed back to his car and took off, gunning the motor, squealing his tires. Shaking hard, I leaned against the house for minutes, until I could open the door and stagger inside. I wasn't hurt; the slap had stung and I might have a bruise, but I was shaking as if he had tried to kill me.

I didn't make a conscious decision any more than I had in the beginning. Something had happened, then it stopped happening.

20

During spring break the next week I went to the coast. I didn't invite Brian, and he didn't suggest going with me. He knew something had happened, but he asked no questions. He helped me inspect the tires and take out the backseat in the van so I could spread my sleeping bag there. No last-minute reservations were possible at campsites or in motels during spring break, but that didn't matter; I knew dozens of places where I could park and sleep.

"I'll be home by Wednesday night probably," I told Brian when my gear was all stowed away.

"Take as long as you need," he said. He looked very much like our father at that moment, his expression grave, his eyes knowing, no details, of course, but he knew something.

I arrived at the coast before noon on Monday and parked at a day-use area and started to walk. It was misty and cold, with a sharp wind blowing. Later, I drove again, and the next time I stopped, it was near Amy's cove. The whole stretch of beach was exposed; it was low tide. I hadn't consulted a tide table and as I went down the cliff I had no idea when the water would come rushing in again. Halfway down, the wind stopped buffeting me. A few other people were fooling around at the tide pools; they didn't stay long. There were many people at the coast, as I had known there would be, young, loud, playful; I ignored them all. I sat in the same place where Radix and I had sat that day.

It seemed a long time ago, yet not time as measured by the dance of stars and planets, or the sifting of sand through a pinhole, or the movement on a dial, but measured in a deeper way. Time as measured by the birth of cells, their division, death, dissolution. Or even deeper, at the level where atoms collide, are created or destroyed, and everything is indeterminate, and time itself is uncertain. I felt as if I had nothing to do any longer with the girl who had sat here with Radix; I had her memories, but I was no longer she. She was dead, and this new person, this new I, was altogether different in ways I could not comprehend.

I closed my eyes and remembered getting lost in a castle, and then finding the magic of the Alhambra. The pictures were still in my head — the magnificence of *David*, the compelling power of van Gogh, the cool perfection of Gainsborough — the pictures were there, but the mystery and enchantment were gone. Now I felt only sadness. And I felt fear, afraid of what was happening to me, to my brain, afraid of the nightmares that continued, afraid of the memory gaps. Afraid I had whatever Brian had, that I was going insane.

I opened my eyes when spray hit my face. Papa Bear was taking his dive; the tide was rushing in. How easy it would be to stay here, I thought then, to cry, "I do! I do!" To adorn myself with the billowing bridal veils and dance in the froth of the sea. When another, bigger spray of water hit me, I stood up and started back, the foamy water lapping over my boots.

I was only halfway up the cliff when the beach was completely underwater again. The surf was crashing into the cliff, sending spray high into the air, even as high as I was, drenching me. It was icy.

I changed my clothes in a rest room, then wandered the beaches until I knew it was going to be dark before I found a place to sleep. I headed for a logging road that wound up into the Coast Range and ate dinner in a turnoff with towering trees pressing in so densely and understory growth so thick, it was like being in a sheltering black cave.

All day Tuesday I wandered, climbed hills, followed trails to waterfalls, climbed the coast cliffs down to the water, back up. I realized I was retracing the steps we had taken with Radix when we showed him the coast that we all loved so much. Unbidden, my feet were taking me to all the same places. That was where we had our kite war. Over there he found petrified wood in the stream. Here we made a fire on the beach. I even drove into Newport and had coffee in the same restaurant we had eaten in, watching the harbor seals at play.

Tuesday night I returned to the turnoff and heated canned stew on the camp stove, then sat in the front seat of the van with coffee. It started to rain, not serious rain, but a pattering of drops that was soothing. And I said to myself, "You love him."

Pictures crowded one another in my head: the day he had appeared so incongruously in his shorts and grinned when I asked if he was billing us for the visit. His triumphant laugh when he beat me at chess, the rueful laugh when I won. His serious expression when he said he wished I could trust him. How the fire had played over his face when he talked about ghosts and God at our campfire. His anger when I said I wouldn't go away to school. I hadn't known that I had been storing every image so carefully, so completely, yet there they were.

I remembered my fear the night he had held my arm and my shoulder, his intensity when he said I would write my stories because I had to talk, that I would talk to the world.

Had he touched me again after that? Not really. He had hugged and kissed everyone else, but not me. He must have thought I was really afraid of him.

I remembered my relief when I realized he and Amy would never get together. I felt heat on my face when I recalled his amusement at my efforts to push him and Amy together. "Liz the match-maker," I said under my breath. "Not."

It was all right to be in love with him, I decided that night: He was unattainable; he would never know. I crawled to the rear of the van and sat cross-legged on my sleeping bag for a long time, listening to the soft rain.

Some girls fell in love with rock stars, or movie stars, with sports stars. I had fallen in love with the Radix I had known, not who he was now, turning into a Suit, on his way to becoming a Gray Man, but the Radix who had given me music and Shakespeare and a castle and the Alhambra. That Radix.

Then I thought, If it was all right, the same as when girls fell for rock stars, why did it hurt so much?

When I finally got inside the sleeping bag, as I drifted toward sleep, I thought that I had come to the coast because I had been lost, and now I wasn't. I didn't try to make sense out of it, but I was comforted by the thought. Then I promised myself that I would pull my grades up, not flunk out, as inevitable as that had seemed to be. It would be grueling. I had a lot of catching up to do, papers to write, chapters to read, whole books to read, a test or two to make up, plus the continuing day-by-day stuff. But I would do it. It wasn't that I cared particularly; it would just be too embarrassing not to make passing grades.

When I got home on Wednesday, Brian came out to help unload the van. He took a close look at me, then said with a grin, "Hi." He knew I had been gone and that now I was back.

By the time school was out for the year, I was exhausted, but I had passed all my courses. Not merit-scholarship grades, but good enough. I had talked to Boyd several times; he wouldn't be home that summer, he said. His folks were going to Monterey, and he'd visit with them there. He was in love, he said softly on the phone; the guy's name was Gary. They were living together. Radix called a few times, but I didn't talk to him; I told Brian to say I was out. Radix told Brian his father was paralyzed from a stroke. I supposed Radix was fully entrenched in the law firm by then, carrying on his father's mission.

The first week of summer vacation, I did little but sleep. Then I cleaned my closet of all the things I no longer could or would wear and boxed them up for Goodwill. I had no dates, and there were no girls in town that I wanted to hang out with; our paths had diverged during the year. One night, when I played my violin for the first time in months, I was dismayed by my ineptitude, by how much I had lost. I began practicing again. I should get a job, I told myself often, but I made no effort to do so, and rationalized by telling myself that the part-time and temporary jobs were already taken by the time I got out of school.

Brian stayed busy most of the time; he practiced for hours, and he was composing a new sonata that, even unfinished, was hauntingly beautiful; he went to Mrs. Inglewood's place to ride and groom the horses; he rode his bike to the swimming pool most days, and, of course, he tended the garden. His days and nights were full, but by the first week of July, I had a serious case of cabin fever.

"Remember how we used to talk about going to Yellowstone Park?" I said to Brian at dinner one night. "Let's do it."

He shook his head and mumbled something unintelligible about Kevin.

"He isn't coming back," I said. "He'll probably never come back. And maybe Amy never will, either. We can go anywhere we want."

"You go," he said. "You know, you went over to the coast. You can take off and stay as long as you want to." He carried his plate to the sink and rinsed it, put it in the dishwasher, came back to get other things.

He had grown and was now several inches taller than I was, but he was still only fourteen. I knew I couldn't go away and leave him alone more than a day or two. It would be years before I could really leave him alone, especially in the summer, when Mrs. Inglewood was there only once a week, but I had to go somewhere. I didn't even care where, just away. Everyone else had gone: Radix had turned into a regular full-time Suit; Boyd had a lover in San Francisco; Amy was going to spend the summer with Jeff in Hawaii on a marine project; I didn't even know where Kevin was. With Radix's help, and I didn't know what else, his group had raised the money they needed, and they were now in business, getting ready to launch their second program. Everyone had something.

"Brian, we both need a change," I said, pleading with him.

He didn't respond; he picked up the butter and salt and pepper and took them across the kitchen.

"This has to stop!" I yelled, slamming the tabletop with the flat of my hand. "It's gone on too long! It has to stop! Brian, our mother is dead. She's been dead for eight years. She's gone! You have to give it up, admit she's gone and that she won't come back."

Silently, he put the butter in the refrigerator.

"If she knew what this was doing to you, it would break her heart. She wouldn't want this. She wanted us to have a real life, a good life; that's all she ever wanted — for her family to be happy and have a good life."

His oblique look and his silence infuriated me further. I screamed at him, "Give her up, Brian! You don't need her anymore. You were a little kid when she died; maybe you needed her then, but you don't now. Give it up!"

He walked past me to the stairs in the back hall. I knew he would go to his room and play the violin for her, that he would stand at the window and play and watch her dance, and he would smile. I jerked away from the table and ran out to the patio, out to Mother's garden. With deep pockets of shadows, stripes of sunlight, flowers blooming, it was very beautiful.

I felt breathless, as if I had been running hard for a long time. I whispered, "You have to leave him alone. Go away and leave him alone. It isn't fair. Go away!" I heard my voice rising and couldn't control it. "You're killing all of us. Is this how you wanted it? Kevin's gone. Amy's gone. You're killing us! Mother! Go away and leave him alone! You're killing him, Mother!"

I was shouting, gasping for air. "You wanted us to be a family. You always said we were a family, together. But we're not a family anymore. We're nothing. We're dying! You're killing us!"

Suddenly Brian flung himself at me and wrestled me to the ground, not hitting, not fighting, just trying to get his hands over my mouth, to make me stop.

"Mother, if you love him, tell him he doesn't need you! Tell him good-bye," I cried, warding off Brian's hands. My words were broken, incoherent. "Tell him good-bye! Let him go!" Brian was on top of me; his hand covered my mouth. I pulled it away. "Mother! Look at us! Is this what you wanted? Tell him good-bye! Let him go!" He got both hands on my mouth and I couldn't move them. Suddenly he went rigid and then fell down on me like a dead man. His head hit my forehead and the earth beneath me seemed to tilt and there was no light.

The moment passed; I could focus my eyes again, but I could hardly breathe beneath his weight. I was terrified when he didn't move, and more terrified when I realized he had passed out the way he had done before.

I struggled to move him so I could get up; then

I ran to the house for a washcloth and a glass of water. He had come out of it before, I kept telling myself. He would wake up and I'd get him to bed, and he would be all right, just like before. He didn't move when I washed his face. I lifted his head and tried to give him a sip of water; it rolled down his chin. I kept saying things like *"Please wake up. I'm sorry. I won't do that again. Please!"*

I started to drag him to the house, but I couldn't. There were rocks that would dig into his back, hurt him; he was too heavy, too awkward. I remembered what Amy had said — that this was shock, to cover him up — and I ran to get a blanket. He was breathing, just sleeping, I told myself, but he wouldn't wake up and he felt cold; even with the blanket on him, he felt cold. His skin was like ivory, cold, dead ivory. At last, in desperation, I went in and called 911.

21

They said he was resting comfortably. They said his vital signs were all normal. They said they probably would keep him a day or two for observation. They said they would start some tests in the morning, a CAT scan, an EKG. Their words were like raindrops falling on the ocean, leaving no trace afterward.

"Is he awake?"

"No. We need to ask you a few questions about what happened to him. Do you want coffee, a Coke or something?"

I shook my head.

"Okay. What exactly happened?"

I had to swallow before I could speak. "We were in the garden walking, and he fell and knocked me down. He wouldn't wake up. I couldn't wake him up."

"Take it easy, Ms. McNair. Try to relax."

I saw him then, a middle-aged doctor with sparse gray hair, tired eyes. We were in a little cubby off the emergency room. I didn't know where they had taken Brian. "I'm okay," I said.

"Good. Did he fall forward or backward, crumple straight down? How did he fall?"

"I don't know. My back was turned."

"Did he become violent, hit you?"

"No!" I cried. I touched the spreading bruise on my forehead; I felt bruised all over, but that one showed. "I hit the ground, a rock or a stick or something. He never was violent."

He didn't believe me, but he let it go and asked other questions. How had Brian been that afternoon, that evening? Had this ever happened before? I said no. What had he eaten? Had Brian been stressed by anything? On and on. Then he said, "You might as well go home. He'll sleep through the night. And tomorrow, we'll run some tests." Then, very kindly, he asked, "Do you want something to help you sleep tonight?"

"Can't I stay with him, sit by him? When he wakes up, he'll be afraid in a strange place. He won't know how he got here."

He shook his head. "He's in a ward with two other people. I'm afraid that wouldn't be a good idea. We'll take good care of him, Ms. McNair. Go get some rest."

I couldn't leave the hospital, despite his assurances that they would call me if there was a change, that I could call as often as I wanted to check on Brian's condition. He gave me Brian's room number, the name of a nurse I could call. He left me finally, and I sat in the waiting room, waiting, waiting.

People came and went. A woman sat next to me and started to talk; after a time she moved away again and talked to someone else. I got cold and hugged my arms to myself. I had on shorts and a T-shirt, sandals; I couldn't get warm. I walked on the first floor, trying to get warm, went outside, back in, and finally up the stairs to the

211

fourth floor and to the nurses' station. A nurse was behind the desk; another one was carrying a tray of medications down a darkened hallway. It was very quiet.

"What are you doing here?" the nurse at the desk asked, glancing at me. "You're not allowed up here this late."

"Is Brian awake yet? Is he all right?"

She frowned.

"Brian McNair. He just came in this evening. My brother."

She smiled. "Sleeping like a baby. Go on home and get some sleep. He'll be okay."

"Can I see him, just for a minute?"

She stood up and came around the desk, reached for my arm, no doubt intending to herd me to the elevator and see that I started down, but when she touched me, she said, "For heaven's sake. You're freezing." She looked me up and down. "You brought him in alone?"

I nodded.

"Okay," she said after a moment. "Come with me." She led me to a tiny room overcrowded with several chairs and a padded bench. "Ain't the Ritz," she said, "but you can rest in here. I'll get you a blanket."

I could only nod numbly. I never learned her name, and I never saw her again.

I wrapped myself in the blanket she brought back, then stretched out on the bench, and I dozed finally. A different nurse woke me up and pointed down the corridor toward a lounge. I washed my face and hands, looked at the bruise on my forehead, which was already turning purple and yellow. Then I was sent to another room, where someone gave me coffee, and I waited again.

No one would answer any questions; when I asked, the nurses said I had to wait for the doctor. I was left in a small room like the one in which I had passed the night, a conference room.

At nine the doctor came in, and with him was Mr. Martens. I felt stupid and uncomprehending until I remembered I had given his name as Brian's guardian.

"My dear," Mr. Martens said. "What a terrible thing. Terrible. I called your sister and brother; they'll both be here later today." He looked grayer than ever.

"How is Brian?" I whispered, terrified.

"He's sleeping," the doctor said. Dr. Pierce was his name, a neurologist.

I stood up. "I want to see him. I have to see him."

Dr. Pierce shook his head. "Have patience, Ms. McNair. Brian woke up very early this morning, and he was violent. Hallucinatory. He is under sedation now. We have run some tests and the results will be coming in as the day goes by. Preliminary reports indicate no lesion, no tumor, nothing of that sort. But we have to wait for the final results."

He stood up. "I'm afraid that's all I can tell you at this time. We will keep him in seclusion today, and by tomorrow we may have something concrete to report." He reached out and clasped both my hands. "I'm sorry. They tell me you slept here last night. Go on home now and get some real rest. No one can see him for at least twenty-four hours, and you can do nothing here. You may need your own strength in the days ahead."

I had gone to the hospital in the ambulance with Brian; Mr. Martens took me home in his Lexus. Neither of us talked on the way. Mrs. Inglewood met us at the door; Martens had called her, to my surprise.

"My poor baby," she said, and held out her arms; she held me while I shook and told her the same story I had told the doctors. "That poor little feller. My heart just breaks for that poor little feller. And you, poor child, you're exhausted. Go take a nice long bath and try to relax."

Kevin came home that afternoon, and we both assured Mrs. Inglewood that we were all right, that she could go on home. She said she would be back the next day, and every day for a while, as long as we needed her, just to see to things. As soon as she was gone, I told Kevin what had happened. For a time he sat motionlessly, then he took my hand.

"You had to do it, Liz. He had to give up that fantasy. You know it as well as I do."

I pulled my hand away. "They think we were fighting, that he hit me, I hit him. He has a bruise on his forehead." I touched my bruise. "We weren't fighting. We weren't! He would never try to hurt me!"

Kevin regarded me with a sober expression; he touched my cheek. "Not knowingly. Of course, he wouldn't hurt you if he was in control."

I fled to my room.

Later that night Kevin went to the airport to pick up Amy. As soon as the car left the driveway, I heard footsteps, rustlings, slight wheezing noises like muffled whispers.

"You goddamn things!" I screamed. "You goddamn fuckers, get out of here! I'm not some scared little kid you can drive batty! Get out of here!"

For a moment, the house was absolutely silent; then it started again, exactly as before. Enraged, I turned on the kitchen radio, put a CD on in the living room, turned on the television. I rinsed dishes and put them in the dishwasher, then started a pot of coffee. A noise sounded like a man's booted footsteps on the bare floor of the attic, Kevin's room. I got out cups.

The power of suggestion, I thought grimly. Folie à deux. Mother had been stronger than Brian's fears; she had vanquished them, and I could, too. I was as strong as she had been. I was! The noises became old-house noises again.

On the drive home, Kevin must have told Amy what had happened. As soon as they entered the house, she ran to me and put her

215

arms around me hard.

"It isn't your fault, Liz. You know it isn't. He's been on the edge for so many years, it was bound to happen sooner or later." She drew back and examined my face. "Kevin said Brian hit you."

"Oh Jesus!" I cried, wrenching away from her. "Kevin's full of it! He didn't hit me. His head hit me when he passed out."

Wordlessly, Kevin took her suitcase upstairs. She followed him up to change her clothes. Afterward, we sat at the kitchen table, exactly the way we had done so many times, the committee of three, plotting.

Kevin was relieved that this had happened, I realized. He even said it: "They must know by now that it's a mental problem, not just a head injury. No matter what Brian says, no one's going to believe him. Not if he's unstable."

Amy swirled coffee in her cup, keeping her gaze on it. "The real question is, How much are we going to tell them? Did you tell them about last summer?" she asked me.

"No."

"Did you tell them what happened between you and Brian out there?"

"No!"

"They'll want to know what set him off," Amy said, not looking at me. "We have to think of something that might have triggered all this, something that could have been the precipitating event."

"How about if we start telling the truth?" I muttered.

"Right," Kevin said meanly. "Listen, we're home free now. It won't matter what he says, no one's going to come poking around. Not now. I don't give a shit if we sell the place or not anymore. So let him talk. If they need something to account for this spell, just say you were talking about clearing out of here! Weren't you?" When I didn't respond, he said angrily, "Then just don't say anything! Just keep your mouth shut! I think you can do that after all these years!" He was flushed, veins pulsing in his temples.

Watching him, I said, "The day Mother died, who put the ladder on the patio?" I heard Amy gasp, but I ignored it, kept my gaze on Kevin.

For a second he looked too stunned to understand the question; the color drained from his face and he jerked upright, knocking his chair over. "You believe him!" he whispered hoarsely.

"It was all the way on the patio when we got home," I said, jumping up. "How did it get there?"

He looked about wildly, as if searching for something to grab, to throw, to break; his hands were twitching.

"Kevin, listen," I said. "If you didn't put it there, who did? Think! There was only one other person here!"

He sat down again as if his legs had given away. "What are you getting at? You mean Brian?" he said hoarsely. "Brian moved the ladder?"

I nodded numbly. I had said it finally. Admitted to myself what I had known to be true, what I had denied, put out of mind, buried, refused to look at. The off button in my brain had finally disconnected. I watched my hands shake on the tabletop and couldn't make them be quiet. Amy put her hands over mine.

"Tell us what you've been thinking," she said in a low voice.

"Kevin said Brian was cool that day when he checked. Cool or cold? And he didn't wake up all evening. We were making noise, but he didn't wake up. Like last summer, like yesterday, cold and sleeping. And he wouldn't wake up."

Amy refilled my cup, put it in my hands. The heat felt good.

"He could have seen her climbing up the ladder from his room," I said, "and decided to help or something. You know he would have done that. He might have wanted to move the ladder to a different spot, help her pick apples. But when he moved it, she must have fallen. Maybe he panicked and dragged the ladder to the patio and ran to hide in his bed and passed out. And he didn't wake up for so many hours."

"He was cold," Kevin said. "I shook his arm a little, but he was sleeping and cold. I put another cover on him."

"He doesn't know," Amy whispered. "Last summer, he must have almost remembered, but he couldn't let himself. So he said it was Kevin."

I knew she was working through it the same

way I had done. "That's why . . . That's why . . ." I started, but I couldn't finish.

"That's why," Amy said. "My God, he was a baby, only six!"

"He had to keep her alive, deny what happened," I said in despair. "And I sent her away."

I knew what denial, forgetting could do; I had gone crazy myself that year. Kevin got up to pace restlessly, and Amy was looking into the distance, no doubt seeing connections she had not noticed before.

The question tormenting me, and I suspected Amy and Kevin as well, was: How much would Brian remember this time when he came out of it? Even more frightening was: What would it do to him if he did remember?

Finally Kevin came back to the table and sat down heavily. I realized only then how tired he was; working so hard for so long had drained him. "What now?" he asked helplessly, looking first at Amy, then at me, as if he no longer had the will to scheme and plot.

"We can't do anything until Brian comes out of it," Amy said. "Even if he tells the truth now, no one's going to believe him. There's just too much circumstantial evidence that Mother abandoned us of her own free will."

"Unless we all corroborate what he says," I said in a low voice. "Maybe he needs the truth to come out before he can get well."

They both looked at me, Kevin's gaze dull and hopeless, Amy's distant, as if she were seeing through me to something else. It was uncanny, unnerving how much she looked like Mother. Was she seeing the wreckage of her career as a marine biologist? Her fiancé, Jeff? Maybe even her little brother, who probably had accidentally killed his mother and might now be completely insane?

Amy pulled her gaze back to focus on my face. Gently, she said, "You're closer to him than anyone. What will the truth do to him? Can he live with it?"

Almost desperately, Kevin said, "Liz, are you sure about the ladder? That it was on the patio? You didn't move it there? Maybe you or Amy moved it and forgot."

I shook my head. Amy stood up. "Liz, you're so beat. You couldn't have slept last night in the hospital. Let's leave it for now. We all have to think."

But I didn't sleep that night, either. I thought incongruously that I would paint my room again, and the living room, maybe Brian's room, if he wanted me to. I thought of Amy scuba diving, looking for sea urchins, sea slugs — we used to call them "sea turds" to make her angry. Slug-ologist. I thought of Kevin working for years on his computer program, starting his own company, fame and wealth almost within his grasp. And Amy getting engaged, planning to marry in a year or two. I got up and stood at my window and thought about Brian.

When the house got too noisy, I told *them* to get the fuck out, and the noises became boards creaking, a stair step adjusting.

We weren't allowed to see Brian the following day. Dr. Lomans was in charge now; he said vaguely that they were making adjustments in Brian's medications. None of the tests so far had revealed a physical problem.

The next day, accompanied by Martens, we had a conference with yet a new doctor, this time a psychiatrist, Dr. Sheryl Redmond. She was in her fifties, with dark reddish hair streaked with pure white. Her body was heavy and thick, her arms and legs were thin. I hated her from the start.

"This is a most unfortunate occurrence," she said. "I'm very sorry. We believe your brother is suffering from acute adolescent paranoid schizophrenia. It's treatable, but it will take time. He has not talked to anyone yet, and it would be most helpful if I can get some family history from all of you. Is that agreeable?"

"Why can't we see him?" I cried.

She looked at me calmly. "You're Elizabeth, I believe? You brought him to the hospital?"

"Why can't we see him?" I demanded.

"It would do him no good and might do you harm," she said quietly. "We have been forced to put him in restraints while we try to find the medications that will allow him to relax. You see, Elizabeth, as soon as his medication begins to wear off, he becomes hallucinatory and violent.

He sees figures and hears voices that are threatening him and he tries to fight them off. After we have stabilized his condition, of course, you may visit." Then, without changing her inflection, she asked, "Did he hit you?"

"No!" I cried. "How many times do I have to say it! He never hit anyone in his life!"

Still calm, she turned to Kevin and started to ask questions about Brian's childhood, his parents. When she asked if Brian had ever done anything like this before, if he had passed out, had a seizure, gone into an abnormal sleep, I tensed and held my breath.

"I can't decide," I had told Amy and Kevin. "I can't." The choice was to sacrifice both of them and their brilliant futures they had worked so hard for, on the faint possibility that it might help Brian. I was more afraid of what the truth would do to Brian than afraid of what our lies would do.

When Kevin said no in a low voice, I let out my breath. The decision was made. I looked up again to see Dr. Redmond gazing at me.

I didn't say another word during that meeting. I listened to the questions and answers numbly, heard them discuss necessary arrangements; Brian had to be moved from the general hospital to a specialized institution, a private hospital, where he would receive the necessary attention. Dr. Redmond said it would not be for long; cases like this usually responded in a few weeks, several months at the most, and, of course, most patients had to be kept on medication and be seen as outpatients after they were released, often for short periods, but sometimes, she warned, for the rest of their lives. In Brian's case it was too early to tell.

She had a lot of catchphrases — *hormonal imbalance, vitamin deficiency, electrolyte imbalance.* . . . And they had very good medications now that had not been available in even the very recent past. She was optimistic. She would let us know when we could visit.

Kevin had to leave after a few more days, without being allowed to see Brian. He was reluctant, but Amy and I urged him to go, since there was nothing he could do. He promised to fly back instantly if there was any change. Amy said she would stay with me the rest of the summer; I was grateful.

We were permitted to visit Brian the following week, ten days after I had taken him to the general hospital, one week after he was moved to Woodhaven. It was a pretty place, high on the flank of Mount Hood, with a magnificent view of the Columbia River. The building was stone; there was a high security fence, and a gate with a guard. Prison, I thought, when I first entered the grounds. A few people in street clothes were out walking around; others in wheelchairs were being pushed by people who must have been visitors.

"Your first visit will be in a private room," Dr.

Redmond had told us. "Your brother will be observed to determine how he accepts visitors. He's quite stable now. Just act natural."

They had told me to bring some of Brian's clothes, personal things he might want; I had packed a suitcase for him. A male nurse took it from me, then led us down a corridor. We passed a room with two televisions turned up too loud, and half a dozen people in chairs; no one was watching the television.

The nurse opened a door and motioned us in, and I saw Brian in a chair by a window. He didn't turn to look at us, even after I called his name. I hurried over to him, then came to a halt. His eyes were vacant, lifeless, with no luster, like dull slate; his gaze was toward the wall; he was pale, and a nerve was jumping in his cheek. His hair was combed wrong. He was dressed in faded blue hospital pajamas and an open lightweight robe. One slipper was on and one was off, on the floor.

"Hi, Brian," I said, and touched his hand. Finally he looked at me; it seemed to take a great effort. "How are they treating you?" I asked.

"Hello, Liz," he said, slurring the words.

He was a zombie, living, breathing, but a zombie.

22

We went to Woodhaven every day for a week, then I told Amy she might as well go on back to Hawaii, back to Jeff. We talked about it forlornly, hopelessly; staying here was doing no one any good, and doing her harm. Brian didn't seem to notice if she was there visiting; he didn't seem to notice if I was there most of the time. He would say hello in that thick, strangled-sounding voice and then become silent and remain silent, staring off into space or, more often, at the floor. On Wednesday of the following week, I took Amy to the airport. She wanted me to promise that I would return to school, that I would get my own life moving again, that I would stop blaming myself. . . . Promises you can't keep, you shouldn't make, I thought, but I didn't say that; Dad's words seemed to come from a place and time so distant they might have been in the air when pharaohs walked the earth.

I began to know other patients at Woodhaven — Mr. Lampkins, who had Alzheimer's; Gloria Beson, who smeared strawberries on her face and tried to put them in her ears; Mrs. Grayling, who recited psalms and sang church songs without end. . . . I got to know Andy, the friendly male nurse. "Talk to him," Andy told me early on. "Tell him about the past, when things were good for him; remind him. He can hear you. Read to him, or tell him stories. Touch him, hold his hand. Take him for walks. He needs the exercise."

So I read to him, and talked to him about the good times, and every day I took him out for a walk. At first, he acted as if his hands and feet were too heavy to move; walking seemed to tire him rapidly, almost as soon as we started. I urged him on, just to the bench, over to the fence, where we could see the barges on the river, to the oak tree. . . . Without protest, he did whatever I told him, like a robot.

"Why is he so tired?" I asked Andy one day when I arrived. Brian was sitting in the common room, where two televisions played all the time. His head was lowered and his hands were dangling. I had handed over my purse and a grocery bag to Andy.

"It's the medications," Andy said. He was a big gaunt-looking man with powerful shoulders and arms, in his forties. Every day he looked through the packages I brought, looked into my purse, as if I might be trying to smuggle in contraband. He handed my things back to me. "The more you can get him walking, the less sleeping pills he'll need; that'll help."

I got to know every tree, every bench on the grounds. There were places where the broad blue Columbia River was visible and we could watch the tugs and barges; every afternoon between three-thirty and four a freight train rumbled on the tracks close to the river; the engineer always sounded the whistle, as if in a friendly greeting to the folks up at Woodhaven. Many of the patients stopped whatever they were doing and watched the train pass out of sight, heading eastward, heading away.

Now and then other patients joined us at a picnic table when I read to Brian; he never seemed to notice them, and I continued to read. They ate the cookies and cakes Mrs. Inglewood sent, and the candy or fruit I bought. Sometimes one or two of them tagged along when Brian and I walked, but not far. We covered the grounds, followed the high fence to the rear of the stone building to a fenced-in delivery yard where trucks could pull in. At the rear, the high security fence stopped at lava stacks that rose fifteen feet or more, straight up, a reminder that we were on the flank of Mount Hood, a dormant volcano poorly concealed under a carpet of towering fir trees. No fence was needed there. It was like a black wall. The grounds were immaculately maintained, with stretches of lawn, mammoth, mature trees shading benches, occasional picnic tables. No shrubs, no flowers, nowhere to hide. Walkways were hard-packed shredded bark, but the patients wandered on the lawn as often as they walked the paths.

One day Mr. Kimmelman arrived while I was reading to Brian. He sat silently, listening for a few minutes, then spoke to Brian in a low voice. Brian was gazing off into space. When Mr. Kimmelman got up to leave, his cheeks glistened with tears.

Brian had been there a month, when one day the receptionist told me he was not allowed visitors that day. I felt terror rising in my chest. "What happened?"

"Sorry, you'd better talk to Dr. Redmond," she said.

"Hi, Liz," Andy called, coming toward me. "I tried to phone you, but I guess you'd already left."

"What happened?"

"Nothing to be alarmed about. He just had a little bit of a bad spell. Be right as rain in a day or two."

He took my arm and started to propel me toward the entrance. I pulled free. Now and then a patient had disappeared for a day or two, only to reappear more wan and listless than before. Patients had told me things; other visitors had told me things. A bad spell usually meant an outbreak of violence, a relapse, a convulsion, a bad reaction to a medication. . . .

"I want to see Dr. Redmond," I said.

He nodded at the receptionist. "See if she's free," he said.

I had to wait over an hour before I was taken to her office. She was behind a desk that was barren and shiny, more like a prop than a piece of useful furniture.

"What happened to Brian?" I demanded at the door.

She motioned me toward a chair with a green leather seat and wooden back. I ignored it.

"Nothing of consequence," she said calmly. "He has been very resistant all along. We tried a new medication and he reacted badly. It will take the medication a day or two to clear his system, and we're monitoring him closely, of course. There is no emergency, believe me. He will be fine."

"He isn't fine," I cried. "He's worse than ever! What all are you doing to him? What kind of drugs are you giving him? What do you mean by 'resistant'?"

She sighed and her expression became strained. "You must leave the care of your brother to the professionals who have experience in this field. Surely you understand that. If I told you the names of the medications, what would you know? Believe me, we have his best interests in mind, and we know what we're doing. Until he is able to face the truth about his mother, he will not be well. And perhaps he won't be afterward. There's never a guarantee, but it's his only hope to recover."

"What do you mean?" I asked, my voice hoarse suddenly.

"Surely you know he believes she is waiting for him at home, and that he is besieged by evil spirits of some sort that he thinks only she can control. This is a fantasy on which he has constructed his belief system. Until he admits that she abandoned him, that she is truly gone, and that he is not to blame, he will continue to be ill. Even if we control his hallucinations with medications, he will continue to be ill until he relinquishes his fantasy."

"He told you all that?"

"Elizabeth, we have drugs that allow patients to talk about their fantasies." She sounded impatient now, and she glanced at her watch. "We are doing what we know is best for him. Believe me."

"I want to take him home," I said.

"Of course that cannot be allowed," she said, and rose from her chair.

"He isn't a criminal, he hasn't been committed here! You can't hold him! I want to take him home!"

"That decision rests with his legal guardian. It is not yours to make," Dr. Redmond said coolly. "I have reported our diagnosis and prognosis to Mr. Martens. Brian is inclined to violence, even if you continue to deny it, and that violence could be turned inward upon himself, as well as outward, toward others, as he has demonstrated more than once. I'm afraid I have to end this interview now, as I have other engagements."

I went straight in to see Martens and got nowhere. First I pleaded with him to let me take Brian home, then I yelled at him. He believed Brian was violent and suicidal and had to be in an institution. He said he would like to talk to Kevin and Amy in another week or so, possibly other arrangements would be necessary. He was thinking about a state hospital, I realized; he was concerned about our dwindling funds. I had no idea how much Woodhaven was costing, but it was probably very expensive, too expensive to continue indefinitely, and with that thought, I knew he didn't believe Brian would get well. Dr. Redmond must have told him that. My hatred for her burned like acid behind my eyes, in my throat, in my stomach.

Every afternoon Mrs. Inglewood came to the house. "You've got enough on your mind," she said the first afternoon I arrived home and found her making dinner. "If you'll just leave me out a little grocery money, we'll be fine. Mr. Martens doesn't have to know a thing about it."

Every day she stayed to have dinner with me, then cleaned up the kitchen and left. She would have spent the nights, but I told her no, that she had to be home to take care of her horses. She agreed. "Can't ride Betsy anymore," she said regretfully. "She's getting too old and stiff, but she likes her rubdowns and sugar cubes. That horse knows no limit when it comes to sweets." Then she would say, "There's a little bag of cookies for Brian. Tell him I'm praying for him."

When she was gone, the house felt empty, echoing. I heard *them* sometimes, and cursed and yelled at *them* until I heard house noises again. I knew it was my imagination, and told myself I was venting my frustration, my fear and loneliness, my guilt.

I was not allowed to see Brian for three days.

I kept thinking of what Dr. Redmond had said: He believed his mother was home waiting for him. Did that mean he had forgotten what happened in the garden? Had he forgotten that I exorcized Mother's ghost? And I thought, His demons have followed him to Woodhaven; I freed them when I banished her.

I went back to Woodhaven on Friday. Brian was duller than ever and very pale. "Well, it's out in the sun for you, kiddo," I said cheerfully, and watched Andy relax a little at the open doorway. I took Brian's hand and led him outdoors; his hand was cold and flaccid in mine. It was quite hot in the sun, but fresh and breezy in the shade.

We sat under a tree where the tugs were visible, and I looked at the grounds, at the fence, at the patients, all the while chatting to Brian. I understood the high security fence now; patients like Mr. Lampkins could be as lucid as anyone one minute and quite mad the next. Sometimes he would go from person to person, asking if his wife had come for him yet. She was coming, he would say, any minute now, and she would take him home again. He might wander away, I understood, fall off a cliff, or get lost in the woods. . . . So they needed the fence. And the guard who looked over my car each time — probably they needed him, too. No unauthorized persons were allowed, no reporters, or photographers, no vengeful victim of someone inside. So I understood the need for security. The question in my mind was how good was it, because I had to get Brian out of there, and soon, before they transferred him to a state hospital, where escape might be impossible.

The parking area adjoined the truck-delivery yard, fenced off from the rest of the grounds, off-limits to the patients. A door from the parking area led directly to the reception room. We couldn't get out that way. I watched everyone, and talked to Brian about the garden.

"It has so many weeds," I said. "And I don't know what's what out there. You remember? I pulled up a nicotiana once and you were furious with me. I'll bring a flower next time and you tell me if it's a weed."

He might have heard, might not have. I couldn't tell.

"Come on, let's walk. You have to get more exercise, get your strength back so you can come home." I walked him around the hospital building and studied the volcanic stacks. Straight up. The volcano had erupted here. This whole area had been molten lava; then time, rain, weathering had stripped away the surrounding softer rocks, leaving the stacks. Straight up fifteen feet. I craned to see what was on top, but I couldn't tell from the base.

There were many windows on the back of the building, all draped or covered by venetian blinds. The crazies could walk back there, but they couldn't look in. Neither could anyone see out.

"Remember how we used to climb the cliffs at the coast?" I said, starting back to the front of the grounds. It was three-thirty, nearly time for the freight train. We were near a bench when I heard the whistle.

"Sit down and rest here, Brian," I said. Obediently, he sat down, and we watched the freight train come into sight. "I'm leaving now," I told him. "See you tomorrow. I'll play the violin tomorrow."

He kept his gaze on the train rumbling slowly far below. I left him on the bench and walked back to the building. In the reception room I told Andy that he had been too tired to come back right now. We both stepped outside and looked at him at the far end of the grounds, his shoulders rounded, his hands loose, gazing straight ahead. "I have to go," I said. "Will he be all right?" Here and there others had stopped to watch the train heading east, heading away.

"Sure," Andy said. "Wish he'd do a little more walking, to tell the truth. I'll make sure he comes in when visiting hour's over."

I detoured into Portland on the way home and went to a bookstore to buy a topo map of the area along the Columbia. Dad always had used topographical maps when we went camping; he would know where every water spigot was, every cabin, every chasm.

I had to get tires for the van, I thought, driving again. Maybe it needed a tune-up. I decided to have that done, too. No flat tires, no stalling out.

The van was over ten years old, and although we had not put many miles on it, neither had we done much maintenance.

I didn't know exactly what I intended to do yet, but I knew I needed the map, and the van. In my head was a picture of Brian going up the volcanic stacks. The rest would come to me.

23

I made an appointment to have the van serviced and then went to the hospital, this time with my violin, and an old cap for Brian. It was very hot and sunny again; he would burn, he was so pale.

When I played at one of the picnic tables, several patients walked over to listen; Mr. Lampkins sat down at the table with an intent expression. I faltered when I realized I had an audience, but then I saw that Brian was looking at me, not just staring into the distance but looking at me, and I played.

After I finished, I took the violin case to the receptionist and retrieved a flower wrapped in damp paper towel inside a plastic bag. "This is what I was asking about, Brian," I said, back at the table, where he had not moved. "Weed or flower?"

It was a white nicotiana, one of the flowers that glowed in the garden and perfumed the air every evening.

Staring, he reached for it, then dropped it on the table. I picked it up again.

"Ni . . . nico . . ." he said hesitantly, the fragment so thick, it was hard to recognize the vowels.

"Is it nicotiana?" I asked then. He nodded slowly. "Well, thank goodness I left it alone. Here, it's for you." I put it into his hand, and this time his fingers closed over it.

When we took our walk, I thought he returned the pressure of my hand, but it could have been my wish-fulfilling imagination. That day I again left him at the farthest bench, watching the freight train. With the baseball cap on, he was just another slumping, formless figure, except for the flower clutched in his hand.

But he had looked at me, and he had recognized the flower.

The morning after the van was serviced, I left the house very early and headed for U.S. 26, then the turnoff to the Government Camp Road, up the mountain for twelve miles toward Timberline Lodge, and another turn onto a forest service road. It would be winding and hilly, I knew, but it should be in relatively good shape — this was too close to civilization to let the forests on Mount Hood burn. They would keep the road passable. It was adequate, a dirt and rock road with hairpin curves, dips, steep climbs, sometimes skirting an abyss too close not to worry. It wasn't much worse than the winding road up to Woodhaven from the interstate. I made a note of both mileage and the time it had taken me to reach this place where the woods thinned at the edge of the lava, and the growth was mostly vine maple and huckleberries and ferns all dusty from the hot, dry summer. I stopped and got out. There were no tall trees between me and forever, just the understory growth struggling in the thin lava-rock soil. A hundred feet from the road was the edge of the volcanic stacks, rimrock, and down below was Woodhaven.

The ground was flat enough and firm enough that I had no hesitation about backing and turning to head out again. You could pull off, park, and be safe, I thought, satisfied.

The picture of Brian coming up the stacks was now accompanied by one of him climbing into the van and hiding there.

I varied my routine on my next visit. Before, I had walked Brian to a distant table to read to him, or to play. Now I chose the table closest to the building and played the violin there. Other patients and a few visitors gathered for the impromptu concert, and when I finished, they milled about while I took the violin case to the reception desk, to keep it safe until I was ready to leave. Then I walked with Brian on the path closest to the building, to the far end, and around the corner. A few patients stayed with us for part of the way, but they dropped off before we reached the end of the building. We walked along the side of the building on a path, then around it, and to the lava wall. I walked him along the fence, back toward the front of the grounds, and we sat on the farthest bench, where we could see the train when it appeared. I thought the entire distance from the reception room, around the building, along the fence, and back was a little under a mile; it took us nearly an hour. No one paid any attention to us.

Andy was on duty most afternoons, along with a male orderly and a female nurse, all keeping an eye on the patients and visitors. They paid more attention to the patients who didn't have visitors than to the ones walking with companions or being pushed in wheelchairs.

My routine became to leave Brian at the distant bench, collect my violin, and walk out through the exit from the reception room to the parking lot.

I planned the entire scenario, filling in details, going back and forth over it all, planning what music I would play, how long, what I would say, what I would wear, just as if I was writing a story, and when I had it all in my head, I called Kevin.

I left a message on his machine; when he called back, he couldn't mask his anxiety. "Has something else happened? Is he worse?"

"He's the same," I said. "Kevin, he still believes Mother is here, waiting for him."

He groaned. "Martens called me a day or two ago. He wants a conference. The first day we can all three get together is a week from Friday. I'll come up Thursday next week. Amy will come, too. Do you know what he wants?"

"He won't tell me anything. Kevin, they're really hurting Brian in that place. He should be home, not there."

He was silent for a long pause, then he said

gently, "Liz, you have to face it, admit it. He's insane. He's suicidal. Who knows what might set him off again, or what he might do? He could hurt you, even kill you. Or kill himself."

My hand on the phone was hurting; I loosened my grasp slightly. "Okay. I'll see you next week."

He was talking when I hung up. I should have known, I told myself. Almost absently I yelled at *them* to get out, and the house became very quiet. Not Kevin, and not Amy. Neither of them really knew Brian the way I did. Probably they both believed Brian had attacked me, as Martens believed, and Dr. Redmond.

It was nine o'clock, Tuesday. A week from Friday Martens would tell my sister and my brother that Brian was hopeless, that he had to be put in a state institution, maybe for the rest of his life. He had not invited me to the conference. He must want it settled before September, before another monthly payment to Woodhaven would have to be made.

Nine o'clock, midnight in Philadelphia. I didn't care. I looked up the number in our phone book and called Radix.

I told his machine: "Radix, it's Liz. I need you. I'll sit by the telephone until you call back."

He could be in bed with some whore, I thought; he could be in his own bed, sound asleep, or keeping vigil by his father, or out of town, out of the country even. I made a pot of coffee and sat at the table waiting for it. He called five minutes later.

"Liz, are you all right? What's wrong?" He sounded out of breath, or as if he was trying to breathe and couldn't.

"I'm okay. It's Brian. They put him in a mental hospital and they're killing him with drugs. He needs help. I need help. We need you."

"Jesus Christ! A mental hospital? What happened? Never mind. I'll fly out there tomorrow. Sit tight."

"I'll be at the hospital until about five."

"I'll rent a car and drive out to the house. Tomorrow, the first flight I can get on. Are you all right, really?"

"I think so. Yes, I am. But please come as fast as you can."

The rental car was parked in front of the house when I got home the next day. Radix and Mrs. Inglewood were waiting for me in the kitchen; he was standing by the table when I entered the back door. He didn't move.

"Hello, Liz. Mrs. Inglewood filled me in. Why didn't you call me?" His gaze was intent, searching.

"Now, don't go fussing at the poor child," Mrs. Inglewood said, then turned to me. "I made up Kevin's bed for Bill, and supper's in the oven. Rosemary chicken, potatoes. You two will have a lot to talk about and I won't stay and be in your way. Bill, don't fuss at her. She's had enough to put up with. And see that she eats something."

He nodded, but he kept looking at me as if searching for something. Mrs. Inglewood patted my arm, then said, "I made some of those muffins Brian likes so much, you know, with the apples? I don't think they're feeding that child enough. Skin and bones. It breaks my heart to see him."

When she left, Radix said, "I bought some wine. Let's have some, and you tell me what's going on."

I sat down at the table and he uncorked a bottle of chardonnay and poured for us both, then sat down opposite me. "Did she tell you anything?" I asked then.

"What little she knows. I doubt she knows much. You tell me."

Then, sipping the wine when I remembered it, I told him what we had done, from the day we moved in.

He looked stunned, then incredulous, and once he left the table to stand at the door and gaze out at the garden, where the nicotiana was blooming, the only flowers out there that bloomed so late in the summer. Pale, ghostly flower heads with long, fragrant, tubular blossoms. Brian had been quietly triumphant; even the deer knew enough not to mess with tobacco.

"You were just children! You buried her out there? In the garden?"

"Yes. It wasn't a garden yet. Brian made the garden."

Radix refilled the glasses, sat down again, and

I told him the rest of it.

"You have to eat," he said when I finished. "I guess dinner's pretty cold by now. I'll turn on the oven again. Just sit still, it shouldn't take long."

At the stove, he asked, "Why didn't you call me sooner?"

I ducked my head, only then remembering his father, who might be dying, or might have already died. "You had your own problems," I mumbled. "Is your father . . . How is he?"

"He's dying," he said. "There's nothing I can do for him. Nothing anyone can do for him. Why did you call me now?"

I didn't look at him. "I have to get Brian out of there. They'll kill him. One of the visitors told me that if someone can't give up his hallucinations, they resort to shock treatments. They'll fry his brain. But first they'll keep trying to brainwash him to admit something he knows is a lie. He knows Mother didn't abandon him, us. He can't admit it. And they think he won't be cured until he does. They'll have to kill him to save him." I took a deep breath, and went on in a lower voice. "I could tell the truth. They wouldn't believe it at first, but if they investigated, they'd know. Aside from what it would do to Amy and Kevin, I'm terrified of what it would do to Brian. From the day we moved here, he heard things; he said there were noises of people walking, talking. We all tried to talk him out of it, Dad, Mother, all of us, but he heard them."

I closed my eyes, remembering the evening we buried our mother. How soft the ground had become under the composting grass, how warm the ground still was. In a whisper, I told Radix about the burial. "Mist and fog were gathering in the trees, rising from the warm ground, meeting, making wraithlike shapes. Before that evening Brian had heard noises and voices and that evening we freed demons from the earth. The rising fog, the fog drifting down from the woods met and formed shapes, and that was when he started to scream. He was terrified of the wraiths we had released. He lived in terror of them until Mother came back and promised to keep them at bay, to protect him. Mother protected him from devils. He believes that! He knows it's true! The devils followed him to Woodhaven, and she's here, where she can't protect him any longer. He has to come home! It was an accidental death. It was! But even if he is forced to admit any part in it, the devils are still waiting for him."

Radix came back to the table and put his hand on my shoulder. "Take it easy, Liz. Try to relax a little." I had gone stiff at his touch; he pulled his hand away and picked up his wine. "We'll figure out something. Where do Amy and Kevin stand?"

"They're scared," I said. "They think he really is crazy, that maybe he'll flip out again unpredictably, that maybe he'll start telling the truth and maybe someone will believe him. Or that he's homicidal, or suicidal. I don't know what they think!"

I looked at him then. He was grimmer than I'd ever seen him, with deep lines on his forehead, his mouth tight; he looked hard. "You know him better than either of them," I said. Pleading with him? I was afraid of him suddenly, afraid he would side with authority, with the experts, afraid he would dismiss me as guilt-stricken, misguided, overly protective, wrong. "You know him, Radix," I said again.

He rubbed his hand over his face and didn't respond.

"I think we should go ahead and eat, it's warm enough," he said after a moment. I started to speak, and he shook his head. "I need a little time to think," he said gently. "No more for right now."

He ate and I picked at the food. Unaccustomed to wine, I felt lethargic and light-headed, and impossibly tired. I kept thinking that if I could put my head down on the table for just a minute, then I would doze a little, not long, and wake up all the way again.

"I meant to put on more coffee," I said. Or had I done that a long time ago? I remembered vaguely that I had made coffee and filled the thermos carafe and had not touched it again. But was that today or yesterday? I yawned.

Radix smiled. "What you should do is haul yourself up the stairs and drop into bed. I'll be up for a while. If you hear me moving around, pay no attention."

I protested halfheartedly, then I went to bed. That night when I heard footsteps, heard doors open and close, heard the stairs creak and groan, I shifted my position and went back to sleep, content.

When I went down the next morning, it was nine o'clock. Radix was on the phone. He waved to me and pointed to the carafe, listening to someone else. "Right," he said then. "About an hour." He hung up.

"Sorry to be so late," I mumbled. "The wine did me in."

"You cut yourself a very long rope weeks ago, but it wasn't long enough," he said, "and you were perilously close to the end. Better after a real sleep?"

"Much better," I admitted. I poured coffee and sat down with it. "What are you up to?" He was wearing a suit and tie, his lawyer uniform.

"Martens," he said, pointing to the phone. "I have an appointment to see him around ten. I told him I'm here on personal business, staying in a motel. I checked in with you and learned about Brian, and I'm deeply shocked and disturbed, and feel a resurgence of my responsibility to the family. Okay. He buys that. It's better than saying I was summoned; that might put me in an adversarial role, and he would instinctively close like a clam. I'll check into a motel, just to

246

give him a phone number and address." I must have signaled dismay; his voice became gentle when he said, "I'll check in, but I'll stay here, if you don't mind. Okay. Next I'll suggest he sign over guardianship to you, with me as adviser."

"He won't," I said. "He doesn't trust me."

"I'll try that first," he said. "I'll ask to see the medical records, the medications, diagnosis, prognosis, whatever he has, and I'll make copies. I haven't thought of a reason to give for wanting the stuff yet. And he might not have it."

"You're a lawyer, you'll make up something," I said when he paused.

He laughed. "I've missed you, Liz. Okay, I'll think of something. If he doesn't have the material, I'll get him to authorize the release of it all from the hospital. One way or another, I'll get it. Even if we have to use the old one of getting a second opinion before anything else is done." He nodded, then said, "And I'll go to the hospital this afternoon to see Brian for myself."

"Not with me," I said quickly. "They shouldn't associate you with me."

"What a reputation you must have gotten," he murmured. "But you're right. Alone. What's your usual routine?"

I told him. He glanced at his watch and stood up. "One more thing. Would you mind showing me where the ladder was, and where your mother fell?"

We went to the patio. The apple tree was over forty feet tall, its branches drooping with too much fruit. I pointed to the ground, where the large boulders were half-exposed. "That's where Kevin found her," I said. "She must have climbed up there." The lowest branch was eight feet high; the tree was dense now, but in the fall there had been no leaves, only the fruit out of reach of the deer.

He nodded. "And the ladder?"

I showed him where it had been lying diagonally across the patio floor.

Again he nodded. "And you don't think Kevin could have done it?"

"No. It was raining by the time he got home; he left his boots out here and went upstairs to put on dry shoes. She . . . she was soaked all the way through, but she wouldn't have been in the tree in the rain."

He looked at the tree, at the boulders, and then he looked up at Brian's window.

"His room," I said in a low voice.

He glanced at his watch again. "Okay. I've got to beat it. Go on in and have yourself some breakfast. I'll see you this evening, and if plan A isn't working, we'll invent plan B."

I went to the patio door and paused. "It won't work. Martens won't give me custody. And I already have plan B. That's why I called you."

"Want to give me a hint?"

"Sure. I intend to sneak Brian out of there, and you will help me."

"You're out of your mind!"

248

"That's not a smart thing to say right now in this house."

"What you're talking about is a criminal offense. It's called kidnapping."

"I call it saving a life. See you at dinner, Radix." I went inside, and after a minute, I heard his car tires spinning in the driveway. Even his car sounded angry.

24

That day I found several long-sleeved white shirts in Dad's bureau and washed them, and when I went to the hospital, I took one with me. I left it and the box of muffins at the reception desk when I went out with Brian to play the violin in the shade, but before we started our walk, I retrieved the shirt and slipped it on him. "I'm afraid he'll burn, the sun's so hot. But he needs to walk," I had told Andy when he looked over the shirt. I left the box of muffins on the picnic table, and various patients helped themselves, as I had known they would. We walked, and I told Brian a story.

He can hear, I kept telling myself, and he understands, he just can't respond. But he knows what I'm saying.

"Once upon a time," I said, "there was a prince who was given a birth gift of a magic lute. He could play it so beautifully that the wind stopped blowing when he played; the birds stopped flying; roosters stopped crowing; dogs stopped barking; silkworms stopped spinning; anyone who heard his music was entranced. This made an evil magician so jealous and angry that he commanded an eagle to carry away the prince to a castle high on a mountain. And when the boy was inside, the magician cast a spell so that he could not find his way out again. He was lost in the castle.

"He wandered the hallways and vast rooms, and every time he thought he saw a door, it turned out to be no more than a shadow on the wall. He became weak and despairing."

I kept telling myself that he was listening. My words were registering in his mind, pictures were forming. I told myself that he would remember. He would.

"His sister, who was grief-stricken," I said, "begged the wind to help find her brother, and the wind roamed the world until it found the castle and entered through a high window, far beyond the reach of the boy. It told the girl, 'You must weave a silk ladder as strong as steel and as light as a feather, and I will carry you to the high window. There you must let down the ladder and he must climb up before the clock in the tower strikes twelve, or you will both fall to your death, because at twelve, the eagle will come to pluck you and your ladder off the castle wall.' "

I stretched out the story to last until we reached the bench where he could rest and watch the train. "So, back at home again, he played his magic lute and his mother danced for joy in the garden."

I left him sitting there, his shoulders slumped, the cap low on his forehead, his hands swallowed by the long sleeves of Dad's shirt, which glowed white in the shade of a towering pine tree.

Radix drove into the hospital grounds as I drove out.

Mrs. Inglewood left us alone again, the dinner in the oven, and Radix mixed himself a drink; he had brought bourbon this time. I had wine. We sat at the kitchen table, the way we always did, and he told me about his day.

"Martens," he said, "is an ethical man, a moral man who will do the right thing, no matter how much it hurts."

"I knew he wouldn't go along," I muttered. "I shouldn't have exploded at him like I did."

"Not just that, although it's a factor," he said. "But everyone is convinced that you and Brian had a real fight, a rolling-on-the-ground-punching fight. You were filthy, front and back, according to the hospital report, and you had a bruise on your face and another on your arm, and Brian's forehead had a lump. That's why they thought at first that it was a concussion." He drank more bourbon, then moved his glass back. "Anyway, they think you lied to protect him, and in their eyes, you became an obstructionist from then on. But Martens wouldn't turn the guardianship over to Kevin or Amy at this point, either. He thinks it would be a cruel and impossible burden for any of you guys to have to make the tough decisions now."

Martens had given him all the medical records; he even agreed that a second opinion would not be unreasonable. Radix had taken them to a doctor he had become friends with in Lake Oswego. "Antipsychotics, tranquilizers, sleeping medications, hypnotics. I claimed to be looking into a possible malpractice suit, and he said there wasn't a chance to win, if the diagnosis was right. I'll come back to this. Anyway, then I went to see Brian." He looked very troubled and drew his glass back and drained it. I had become used to Brian, had forgotten what a shock his condition had been the first time I saw him. "They play chimes when it's time for the patients to go back inside," he said in a low voice. "It was like watching a bad movie about zombies, watching them shamble and shuffle back to the hospital. Some of them had to be collected and practically dragged in, but most of them just began to move, like automatons. Like Pavlov's dog."

I nodded. That's how it was with Brian. He simply got up and started his slow, dragging walk when he heard the chimes.

"I had an appointment with Redmond after that," Radix continued. "She explained the medications a little. The reduced dosages indicate when they tried to find the minimum amount of any given substance that would keep him free of hallucinations. And they keep trying different drugs, different combinations, trying to find something that works. The doses he's getting are very high, she admitted, but with a reduction, he starts hearing voices and seeing things, and he fights hard to keep them away from him. She thinks now that he isn't going to recover without shock treatment. The success rate using it is not particularly good, but his chances without it are worse." He looked at me steadily then as he said, "The doses he's on now can't be tolerated for long. Side effects will start taking a terrible toll on his body. And some of them will be permanent. That's what my doctor friend was concerned about."

"I told you," I whispered. "They'll kill him."

"Don't you see the problem?" Radix asked in a tired voice. "If they take him off the drugs, they'll have to put him in a padded room, probably in restraints, and whatever demons he has will be in there with him. That's the alternative. Or try shock treatments. It's a last resort, Redmond said, and they wouldn't do it for another month at least, but after that . . . She doesn't see much choice after another month or so."

Before I could say anything, he went on. "I talked to my doctor friend about this in very general terms, no particulars, no names. It's his opinion that if Brian needs the doses he's getting at this time to control his hallucinations, no reasoning will get through to him. Even if you decided to tell them exactly what happened out here, nothing would really change. He comes down from the dope and turns violently hallucinatory. Martens isn't prepared to do anything except follow Redmond's advice, and he isn't prepared to maintain Brian in a private hospital when he believes his case is hopeless. He doesn't see any alternative to the state hospital and whatever treatment they recommend."

"There's another alternative," I said. "I want

to bring him home, detox him."

"You don't know what will happen when the medications wear off."

"Did she tell you what he said when they used the hypnotics and made him talk? Did she tell you that?"

"He thinks his mother is here waiting for him, that she will protect him." He reached across the table and took my hand. His hand was colder than mine. "And that's insanity, Liz. You know it is."

I leaned forward. "He lived with Mother's ghost for nearly eight years. You knew him for nearly five of those years. Was he crazy when you first met him, when you came over here and played games with us, when you heard his music? Tell me, Radix, was he crazy those years?"

His hand tightened on mine, then he let go and stood up, walked to the door to gaze out. "I don't know. God, I don't know. Tell me your plan B so I can tell you why it won't work," he said bitterly.

"When belief systems defy reality, and definitions no longer define, then chaos sets in," I said softly. "You know he was not insane during those years, yet he must have been. Cognitive dissonance, I think they call it." I drew in a deep breath. "On Saturday you will take the van to a point overlooking the hospital. I'll follow my usual routine. While Brian and I take our walk, you will lower a ladder, and when we get to the back wall, Brian, with your help from above, and mine from below, will climb up and hide in the van. You will come down the ladder, put on the white shirt and cap, and I'll walk you to the usual bench and leave you there. I'll go back to the reception room, out through the door to the parking lot, and out of the grounds, alone. In exactly ten minutes, you'll wander back to the wall and climb up it yourself and pull the ladder up after you, and you will bring my brother home."

He had swung around to stare at me as I spoke; his face registered disbelief, dismay, incredulity, anger, all chasing one another in a furious mix of expressions that changed and changed and changed. "You're mad!" he said.

"I'm not!"

"You'll kill him."

"They'll kill him in that hospital or in a state hospital. The devils we set loose will kill him. The only thing that might save him is his own belief that Mother will protect him. I took her away, now I'll give her back to him."

"It won't work, and he'll die here," Radix said harshly. "You'll be guilty of voluntary manslaughter, at the very least. Kidnapping and manslaughter."

"As soon as you deliver him here, you can get in your car and take off, go back east, go anywhere. No one will ever suspect your part in it. If they come, if anything goes wrong, I promise never to say how I did it, or who helped, anything. I promise."

His expression was murderous, his hands clenched hard as he glared at me. "Forget it. There won't be anything to tell. I won't help you, and you won't do it. Period."

I stood up. "Radix," I said reasonably, "I know he has to face the facts, just not now, and not when he's pumped full of dope. In his own time, his own way, he'll face the past and accept it. I intend to keep him alive long enough for that time to come along. And right now, I intend to heat the lasagna."

"Damn you, Liz McNair. Goddamn you!" He yanked the door open and stalked out.

I tossed the prepared salad greens with the prepared dressing, warmed the lasagna, opened a bottle of pinot noir, got out bread and butter, started a pot of coffee, and when it was all ready, I went to the door and called Radix to dinner.

He washed his hands in the kitchen, and we sat down to eat in complete silence. He was grim-faced.

We didn't speak as we cleared the table together and he got out the coffee mugs and I brought the carafe. Only after he had sipped coffee did he break the silence.

"I'll ask questions and poke holes in your little scheme and then we'll think of something real we can do," he said brusquely. "Why Saturday? Aren't there more people, more visitors?"

"A few more. Sunday's the big visiting day. And the staff is reduced on Saturday. It's Andy's day off. He's the nurse who takes care of Brian

most of the time. None of the others know Brian
as well as he does. He might suspect an impostor,
but the others will see a slumping figure in a
white shirt and cap."

"Someone might see you out back and blow
the whistle."

"No one follows us all the way. It's too hot
and sunny; the patients hang out in the shade
most of the time, and the visitors always do. The
rooms in the rear are offices and treatment
rooms, conference rooms, things of that sort, all
with drapes or blinds drawn, and not used on
the weekends."

"Brian's in no shape to climb a ladder. He'd
never make it."

"You'll buy a harness, the kind mountain
climbers use, and make sure he doesn't fall backward. He can't weigh more than a hundred
twenty by now, he's lost so much weight. And I
planted the idea in his head that he has to climb
out to save himself. He'll make it."

"Someone will notice if the impostor walks
toward the back instead of the front of the building."

"You won't wait for the chimes. Ten minutes,
remember? That's twenty minutes before visiting
hour's over. No one will try to collect him until
the chimes sound. You'll be long gone before
that. And there will be a diversion or two. By
the time they get things sorted out, I'll be gone,
you'll be driving the van down the mountain,
and Brian will be safe."

I had no doubt he would do it. In my head the story had finished itself, complete with mini-movies, and he was the third character.

He argued a long time, and tried to find weak spots, but by midnight he knew he would do it as well as I did. "One stipulation, Liz," he said tiredly. "I'll talk to my doctor friend and ask about those medications. It could be too dangerous to stop them all cold turkey. If that's the case, everything goes on hold. Agree?"

I got out the reports he had received from Martens, and we interpreted the marks, the dosages, the times as best we could. Then I said, "It looks like they gave him more tranquilizers when they reduced the other junk. We could do that."

"I'll talk to the doctor," he said. "We're out of our depth here and you know it."

I knew it, but he overlooked the fact that I had not agreed to any postponement. In even a week the weather might change or they might try a different drug and keep Brian in isolation, or he might become too weak to climb the ladder. And after a week he might be transferred to the state hospital, where I suspected they had real security. We had to get him out this week, Saturday.

We studied the map together and agreed to drive the route first thing in the morning in order to allow Radix to familiarize himself with landmarks and to examine the problem of the lava stacks.

At one we stopped talking and I headed for

the stairs and bed. He said he would go up in a minute or two. I paused at the door to look back at him; he was going over the doctor's reports again. "For a Suit and a pseudoguardian, you're okay, Radix."

He grinned fleetingly. "For a snot-nosed pseudoward, you're not all bad, either. But, my God, have you ever become bossy."

We followed the route I had driven before, U.S. 26, up Government Camp Road through the forests, onto the forest service road. He drove, and I suspected he was paying as much attention to landmarks, distances, and time as I had done. At the lava-flow rimrock, we kept behind the scrub vine maples almost to the edge, where we both dropped low to the ground and crept forward. There was the hospital, a delivery truck at the rear fence, a landscape-maintenance crew doing some work out near the front fence.

Radix eased himself closer to the edge, to where he could look over and down. "A rope ladder would be easier to manage," he said.

"Easier for us, harder for Brian. An orchard ladder, an extension ladder will work. They telescope down to a few feet, aluminum, not too heavy."

"We'll have to spray-paint it black," he murmured, still studying the grounds below. "What if he doesn't cooperate?" he asked then, backing away from the edge. "He'll stand out like a beacon up here."

260

"Keep him low. He'll do whatever you tell him to," I said bitterly. "When you lower the ladder, toss down a dark shirt. I'll keep the white shirt down there and put the dark one on him. And you wear dark clothes. Who's going to look up here?"

Back at the van, I put my hand on his arm before he got behind the wheel. "Radix, you'll be watching. If anyone sees him climbing up, if anyone comes yelling, take off. Don't hang out and wait. They'll know there's an accomplice up here, and they'll send someone up the ladder, no doubt. Don't let them find you."

"I won't," he said grimly. "You'll need a good lawyer on the outside if that happens. I'll cut you a great deal."

I became aware of my hand on his arm, and hastily pulled it away, then hurried around the van to the passenger side.

On the way home we stopped at a farm-supply store and bought the ladder and spray paint. At the house he helped get the ladder to the patio and open it all the way. It was sixteen feet long, six feet longer than our old ladder, and much heavier than I had thought it would be, but he said it was okay, that he could manage it alone. Then, carrying his briefcase with the medical records, he took off in his rental car.

I changed clothes, put on old jeans and a long-sleeved sweatshirt and gloves — no paint on my hands, I remembered; I brought some logs to the patio to prop the ladder against for it to dry, spread a lot of newspapers, then I spray-painted the ladder black. I would have to think of something to tell Mrs. Inglewood, if she asked, but I had no idea of what that something would be. How could anyone explain a sixteen-foot-long black ladder?

Then it was time to change my clothes again and start the hour drive to the hospital, where Brian would be sitting in the common room with his head bowed, his expression vacant. I couldn't even say waiting for me. I didn't know if he anticipated my visits or not.

As I drove, my mind was whirling with things I still had to do: pick blackberries as soon as Mrs. Inglewood left, bake muffins, prepare the back of the van for Brian, remember to take an extra shirt tomorrow. More often than not the things I took to Brian vanished without a trace. I kept an extra cap in the car. His room was ready, nothing to do there. I had to remember to tell Mrs. Inglewood not to come tomorrow, Saturday, because, I would say, Radix would take me out to dinner. Sunday was okay; she didn't work on the Sabbath. By Monday either it would be almost over or it wouldn't matter what she did, because there wouldn't be a job for her at the house anyway. Thoughts of Radix kept crowding in. What was he learning? He could still back out. What if his father died and he had to leave suddenly? And I thought of my hand on his arm, his hand on mine on the table, his hand on my shoulder. All in all, it was a miserable drive.

That night Radix said we would have to give Brian tranquilizers and painkillers when the drugs started to wear off. The only hopeful information his doctor friend had given him was that the patient hadn't been on any one drug long enough to have become dependent on it. Even so, there would be physical effects, and they could become serious. Round-the-clock care for three, maybe four days. What we proposed to do was the equivalent of detoxifying a drug addict; he could become violent, nauseated, throw up. He would need adult diapers. We had to give him liquids, nourishment. The doctor said intravenously, but, Radix said, we weren't prepared to attempt that. He stopped, regarding me with an unreadable expression. "He could die, Liz."

"He won't. Not here. In there he'll die."

He nodded. "That's what my doctor friend said. Okay. It's on. Why are you baking muffins? I don't think he'll be eating anything like that for quite a while."

I glanced at him, then quickly turned away and said, "I told you there would be some diversions while you're heading back toward the ladder. The muffins will provide one of them. There's a poor woman in there who isn't allowed any red foods at all, or berries, red or not. She smears them on her face, tries to stuff them in her ears. The muffins are filled with blackberries. Someone will have to collect her and clean her up. It's cruel, I know, but I'll do it. I'll see that she has several blackberry muffins just before I leave, a minute or two before you start moving."

He shook his head. "The other diversions? You said more than one."

I studied my fingernails, ashamed and unhappy. "One more. It's cruel, too. Mr. Lampkins has Alzheimer's. He keeps thinking his wife will come to take him home, but she won't. He asks everyone if she's there yet, and I heard that when she used to come, he would scream and cry, begging her to forgive him, to take him home. He would forget the whole thing every time, but she couldn't. She had to stop visiting or she might have ended up in there with him. I'll tell him I saw her in the parking lot. He'll go to the fence and —" I looked up then and said, "He'll forget almost instantly. He doesn't remember anything more than a minute or two, not in his lucid periods, or the others. But they'll have to tend to him, calm him down, take him inside."

When he didn't speak, I said angrily, "It won't do any real damage to either of them. They'll just have to wash Gloria's face and hands, and clean out her ears. No one ever told me not to give her blackberry muffins. And Mr. Lampkins won't remember after a minute or two. He does worse things than yell for his wife."

Radix nodded. "Right. Actually, I'm relieved. I was afraid you might set off a bomb in the parking lot, or start a fire in the common room. You know, something ordinary in the way of a diversion." Then, surprising me very much, he added, "You'd make a hell of a terrorist. If you

264

ever decide on crime as a life career, the rest of us will be in deep trouble."

We went over the whole plan several times. Radix had bought Gatorade, juice, and broth. He had codeine and tranquilizers, and I didn't ask what lie he had told to get them. He had bought a plastic sheet and diapers. I had put a foam pad and lightweight cover in the van. He had gray sweatpants like the ones Brian wore every day, and running shoes that from any distance would look okay. He had picked up two navy blue shirts, one for Brian, one for him, and the harness. In the morning we would put the ladder in the van. Ready,

25

The next day Radix left the house half an hour earlier than I did. He wanted plenty of time to wrestle with the ladder and get everything ready. At the van, he said, "Whatever happens now, Liz, you're not alone. Okay?" His eyes were so dark, they looked black, without a hint of blue.

"Thanks, Radix," I said. "You're really a great guy."

"Well, it took you long enough to come to realize that," he said, and got in the van. "See you back at the house, five, five-thirty."

I stood there until he was out of the driveway, out of sight. It hadn't taken all that long, I thought. I went back into the house and gathered my own things, my stage props.

At the hospital I played for fifteen minutes, with the usual audience of three or four patients, a visitor or two. When I stopped, I said, "Too hot. Wait here, Brian. I'll be right back." I took the violin to the receptionist, who put it under the counter, then I returned to the table, where Brian, in the white shirt and cap, was waiting. I held his hand and we started in our usual tortuously slow manner. Although it was ninety-five degrees at least, I felt cold as we walked.

"Remember the story I told you? About the prince who was lost in the castle? That's you,

Brian. You're the prince with the magic lute, except you have a magic violin. And you'll have to climb a ladder to save yourself. But you can do that. You know you can do that." He might have heard, might not have. I couldn't tell.

At the corner of the building, I saw a hunched figure on top the lava-stack wall; he vanished, and the ladder eased down the wall. If I hadn't been watching for it, if it hadn't been moving, it would have been nearly invisible, black on black.

I walked a little faster, and Brian did, too. I had let him set the pace before, but he kept up now. "You're the prince, and you have to climb the ladder, and then you'll be out of the castle and home again. You'll play your magic violin and Mother will dance in her garden."

The harness and shirt were being lowered to the ground on a length on nylon rope. Brian's steps were slowing, but we had nearly reached the wall by then. As soon as we got to it, I pulled the white shirt off him and put the dark blue one on, then buttoned it enough to keep it from tangling, from flapping. "Remember, you have to climb before the clock strikes. You have to climb up the ladder. Radix is up there. He'll help you." I had the harness on him in a flash. It was like dressing a doll.

"Here, Brian, take hold of the ladder." I put his hand on the ladder. "Both hands." He moved his other hand to it. "Hold on. Lift your foot, higher. Good boy. Now the other one."

He couldn't do it, I thought in despair when

he seemed uncomprehending, or unable to move, but then he lifted his foot to the next rung. He lifted his first foot and shifted one hand, and he was climbing. I held him from below until he was out of reach; he faltered and stopped moving and I saw the nylon rope tighten, become taut, and I knew Radix was supporting him with the harness. Brian lifted a foot again, resumed climbing.

It was taking too long, much too long. Someone would surely come around the corner. The eagle would pluck him off the wall; we would both perish. Suddenly the nylon rope slackened and for a moment I thought he was falling, but I saw Radix's hands on Brian's wrists, then Radix pulled him up over the edge.

I let out my breath and waited another eternity for Radix to get Brian to the van, to get back to the ladder, come down it. I wanted to climb up to make sure everything was all right, that Brian hadn't passed out, or that someone had not come along to see what was happening. It was taking too long. Too long. Then Radix started down the ladder, moving very swiftly. He let go and dropped down lightly the last few feet. I handed the white shirt to him; he pulled it on and slapped the cap on his head, and we were ready to walk.

"You set the pace," he whispered when I took his hand. His hand tightened almost painfully on mine. "He's okay, in the van, under the cover."

He was on my left, the way Brian always walked, next to the fence, with my body between him and anyone who might glance our way. He slouched and shuffled, and I looked over the grounds in a swift search. Had anyone noticed the long delay? Was anyone paying any attention to us? It was so hot and sunny, hardly anyone else was walking around; they were staying in the patches of shade cast by the big trees scattered on the lawn.

"You're shaking," Radix said in a low voice. "Stop it."

"Still telling me what to do," I muttered, but I stopped shaking. "Did you lock the van?"

"Yes. Does it always take this long?"

"This is normal," I said. We were keeping our voices whisper-low, but he shouldn't be talking at all, and someone might notice. "You should shut up," I said.

I thought he chuckled.

Neither of us spoke again until we got to the bench and he sat down. He was sweating heavily, and no wonder — he was wearing two shirts. "Exactly ten minutes," I said, tugging to free my hand from his grasp. He held on another moment, then let go, but he kept his head lowered, and his shoulders drooped exactly right. "See you back at the house," I whispered, and left him.

It took me a minute to get back to the reception desk, another minute or two to wait for the woman on duty to hand over the violin and discover the box of muffins. "You leave these here?" she asked, setting the box on the counter.

"Oh, darn. I forgot them. Muffins. I'll take

them out and be right back." She shrugged. She knew they were muffins, she had checked them herself. I took them to the nearest picnic table and opened the box. Two or three patients drifted over; Gloria Beson was with them. She always came for the goodies, never for the music. I put a muffin in each of her hands and left the box for the others to help themselves. I saw Mr. Lampkins approaching. He always came for the music and never for the goodies. He probably had already forgotten that I had played earlier. I greeted him, then said in a low voice, "I believe your wife is looking for you in the parking lot." He looked puzzled for a moment, then an intent expression came to his face, the same expression that he had when I played, as if he was trying to remember something.

"My wife is looking for me," he said. "She's coming to take me home."

I went back to the entrance to the reception room and stood for just a moment, gazing at the figure at the far end of the grounds, slumped, head lowered, one hand dangling. I heard the train whistle in the distance, and a Saturday orderly said, "He'll be all right. They like to watch the train."

"I know." I went inside and collected my violin and then walked out the exit to the parking lot. At my car door I heard Mr. Lampkins calling Louisa in a high-pitched, frantic voice.

The guard at the gate glanced at the backseat of my car, said it was another hot one, wasn't it, and waved me on. Driving the winding road to the highway, I thought, Seven minutes: Soon Radix would leave the bench, start toward the back wall and the ladder. I was out of it, but he was still at risk.

Then, through the trees, on a curve lower down the mountain, I saw a truck. The road wound close to the side of the mountain, then back among the trees, back to skirt the outside curve. The truck was coming up.

"No!" I cried. "No!"

It would be waved through by the guard and go straight back to the utility yard, where someone might come out, where the driver and one of the hospital employees might stand and chat a few minutes, have a cigarette, where Radix would appear on the other side of the fence, a conspicuous figure in the white shirt and cap.

Panicked, I swerved to the center of the narrow road and turned off the key, then pressed my forehead down against the steering wheel, trying to think. Radix needed time to walk around the building. Three minutes? Five? He couldn't rush that part and draw attention. Then he would move fast, but he needed time to take off the white shirt, climb up the ladder, pull it up out of sight. Three or four more minutes? The truck couldn't get around my car on the road. But how long could I stall here?

A flat tire, I thought in desperation, and I opened the glove compartment and pulled out the pressure gauge we kept there. I jumped out of the car, ran to the rear-right tire, and started letting out the air. I pressed my head hard against the car. The air hissed, but then I heard the truck. *Faster!* I thought at the escaping air. *Faster!* The truck noise was getting louder as it came slowly up the curvy road. I felt laughter rising in my throat, hysteria, at the thought of deliberately flattening a tire, after all the times we had worried . . . I bit my cheek hard enough to draw blood. The truck sound changed at the last curve and then it was idling. I didn't raise my head until I heard a horn, a light tap only, like a gentle nudge.

Just a little more, I thought, but I didn't dare crouch there any longer. I stood up, thrusting the pressure gauge into my pocket. Very slowly I walked around the car.

A florist's delivery truck had come to a stop fifteen feet away. The driver was leaning forward, his chin resting on his arms, which were crossed on the steering wheel. He was young, a teenager, Hispanic, and he was grinning at me. He raised both hands, palms up, as if to say, It's your move.

"I'm sorry," I said, walking toward him. My voice was too high-pitched, quivering.

"Hey, it's okay," he said. "Car trouble?"

"I shouldn't have stopped there. I just . . . I don't know. I just couldn't seem to control it, and I stopped. I was trying to get the hubcap off."

"Don't sweat it," he said, getting out of the truck. "You're really bummed out. Take it easy, right? It's no big deal."

"I'm really sorry. I kept thinking I could get to a gas station. I was afraid to keep going."

He started to walk toward the Toyota. "Hey, it's okay. Don't get in a panic. A flat tire's no big deal." He looked at me, then asked, "You got someone up there?"

"My little brother. He's only fourteen." I turned away.

"That's really rough. I've got a little brother, too, and a little sister. That's really rough. But they'll fix him up. You'll see."

We stopped to gaze at the tire, noticeably flat by then, flatter than I had thought it could get in such a short time.

"What were you using on the wheel cover? I'll change it for you."

I shook my head and held up both hands.

For a moment he stared, then he grinned again. "Okay, get the keys and let's have a look in the trunk. You got a spare?"

I felt panic start. Was there a spare? What if it was flat? What if I was delayed here for hours?

Gently he said, "Maybe you left the key in the ignition? I'll have a look. Why don't you go sit on a rock in the shade, close your eyes, and take some good deep breaths. I'll have this fixed in a jiffy."

I stumbled away, to the edge of the road, and sat on a rock, exactly as he had suggested, and I closed my eyes, trying to think. I had to stall him until ten minutes before four, ten more minutes. I prayed it would take him that long to

273

change the tire, but it didn't. He was at my side again in seven minutes.

"All set," he said. "You feeling better now?"

I got to my feet. "A lot better. I don't know why it hit me so hard. Just all at once, everything seemed to come at me."

"Yeah, that happens."

"You've been awfully kind, and your hands are filthy now. I've got some paper towels in the car. And I'd like to take down your name and your company. You know, write a letter to your boss saying how much you helped me. Sometimes it's good to have a letter like that." I babbled on, walking slowly back to the car, then taking my time rummaging in the back for the roll of paper towels, finding a notebook and my pen. He protested; his hands were okay, he said; I didn't need to write a letter. I insisted. He was clearly becoming annoyed, just wanted to get on with his business. He must have thought I was the one who belonged in Woodhaven by the time I got back inside my car and he returned to his truck.

I eased over to the side of the road; he eased his truck around me and we both waved. I had delayed him for ten minutes. Had it been long enough?

At the highway, I had to wipe my hands on tissues. We should have arranged some way for me to know if Radix got up the ladder safely, if he got everything up and out of sight before anyone missed Brian, if he and Brian were on the way home. I thought of the white shirt. What if he forgot to take it off again before he started up? How would he carry it and climb the ladder? Had someone spotted him on the ladder? On the top?

By the time I reached the house, I was so nervous, I could hardly get the key into the lock. I paced until I heard the van coming up the driveway, then I ran out as Radix pulled into the garage. Before I had the garage door closed, Radix was opening the back of the van; together we supported Brian as he climbed out.

He was so tired and unsteady that we half-carried him into the house. I doubted that he knew where he was; his face was vacant, his eyes dull, and his head kept lolling and dipping down.

As fast as I could move, I scrambled eggs. He had to eat something now; he might not be able to for a long time. He managed a few bites, a few sips of milk, but he was exhausted, without any appetite, and we had to let it go at that little bit. Radix helped me put him to bed, where he seemed to fall asleep as soon as he was prone. We knew that wouldn't last, and were grateful for any rest he could get before his nightmare started. I sat with him while Radix went down to clean out the van and carry the ladder over to the brambles to hide it there out of sight. When he was done, he ate before he came up to relieve me. Brian was still sleeping. Now and then he twitched in a whole body spasm, but he didn't wake up.

"Go eat something. Soak in the tub for a while, try to relax," Radix said. "I'll call you if anything changes. If you can rest, that would be good. It might be a long night."

Back downstairs I put on a CD, Mozart's Violin Sonata No. 75, one of Brian's favorites. I would play music constantly, and he would hear it. It would help him, I told myself. It had to help him.

At seven-thirty the long night really started. Brian began to moan and his twitches became spasms that were harder and lasted longer. He cried out and woke up, struggling with the sheet, flailing out with both hands, crying inarticulately. I hurried downstairs for the tranquilizer. He wouldn't be able to swallow a pill, Radix had said, and I had honey ready, already warmed slightly in a pan of warm water. I mashed up a tranquilizer in a spoon with the back of another spoon and put it in a custard cup, then added a little honey and mixed it. In his room again, with Radix holding him, I got the mixture into his mouth, on his tongue, hardly more than a drop at a time, until he had all of it. He kept twisting his head away, tried to bat the spoon away, but he swallowed it all. Within a few minutes he began to relax again and sank into a stupor that was not really sleep, but he was quieter.

It got worse as the night dragged on. Ten-thirty, one, three. He was in a cold sweat at three, shaking all over, spasming hard. We washed him with warm water, changed his bedding, force-fed him another tranquilizer. We would give him one every four hours, as the doctor had recommended, or as often as every two hours if he seemed desperately in need. That was the fifth one that night. "Toxic waste," Radix murmured, carrying out the sweat-soaked bedding and towels. At five in the morning we did it again.

At nine the telephone rang. "Go on and hear who it is," Radix said. Brian was curled into a fetal position, his eyes open and staring. I ran downstairs as a message was being left on the machine.

"— haven calling. I'm afraid that Brian had a bad night and won't be able to receive visitors today. Thank you." It was the voice of the weekend receptionist. I stared at the phone in wonder, then slowly went up the stairs again. They seemed to have become steeper and longer.

When I told Radix the message, he nodded. "They don't want to admit they've lost him. They're probably out scouring the woods right now. I tossed the shirt by the fence to the utility yard, and his cap halfway across the delivery parking lot. Maybe they think he got out over there."

Throughout the morning Brian spasmed and sweated hard, or lay curled in a fetal position. In the afternoon he had a convulsion, then cramps that made him scream in pain. We massaged his legs and back and made him swallow another tranquilizer, this time with codeine mixed with

277

it. I was afraid each time that the next time it would be impossible to open his mouth, force the honey mixture into it. I wasn't sure they were helping, but it was all we had to give him. We tried to give him water, Gatorade, broth, and he might have swallowed a drop or two, but mostly it ran down his cheek.

Late in the afternoon, I was massaging Brian's legs when I heard, "Just as I suspected."

Mrs. Inglewood was standing in the doorway. I stared up at her, and Brian screamed. "Let me do that," Mrs. Inglewood said. "You go get me some olive oil." Gently, she pulled me up from my kneeling position at the side of the bed, and she took my place and began to knead Brian's leg muscle. "I came to help," she said. I hurried to get the olive oil. I could hear her voice in a low rumble: "Oh, you don't know what a real cramp is until you've worked one out of a horse's leg. I've worked with Betsy more times than I want to remember. How that poor old mare used to cramp up. . . ."

Radix came down the stairs on my heels. He had been in the bathroom when Mrs. Inglewood showed up. "How did she get here?"

"She has a key," I said, then realized he meant how had she known. I got the olive oil from the cabinet and ran to take it to her. "I don't know how she knew. She said she came to help."

She poured a little oil on her hands and rubbed them together, then resumed massaging Brian's legs, talking in a low voice all the while. "Almond

278

oil's good, too, but I know there isn't any in this house. This will do." She glanced at Radix, then at me. "Take a little break," she said. "I'll manage for a time."

Brian got worse as the day passed. His cramps increased until his entire body was cramping, and he was dehydrating, his eyes sinking into his head; he was getting weaker minute by minute. Mrs. Inglewood told Radix to fill the bathtub with warm water, and together we got Brian into it. Radix held him in the water, held his head above the water, and Mrs. Inglewood fed him juice, half a spoon at a time. He relaxed a little then.

"We'll do that again in a couple of hours," Mrs. Inglewood said when we had Brian back in his bed. "And you two have to rest. Liz, go to bed. Just two hours. Then Bill will rest for two hours. Or you'll both fall down, and I can't manage him alone."

She was so matter-of-fact, and so right. Every time Brian quieted even a little, I felt myself slip into a semiconscious state that was not restful but seemed compelling. I stumbled to my room, left my door open and stretched out on my bed, and fell asleep. Radix woke me up two hours later.

We bathed Brian again before Radix went up to rest. The hours crept by. I put on CDs whenever I noticed the music had stopped. I watched my dying brother. After this ended, I thought during that long second night, I would go to the coast and visit all the places I loved so much, and then I would walk off a cliff and find peace in the ocean. Not here, not in this house. No more ghosts in this house. At the coast. I had done this to Brian, started him on a death spiral, and the nightmare would end after I was gone, not until then.

Toward dawn Mrs. Inglewood came up to relieve me. She had been resting on the living room couch. "Go get yourself some coffee," she said. "Try to eat a little something."

Radix was in the kitchen, his forehead pressed against the glass door to the patio. He pulled himself away and faced me. "Another day," he said.

"You never know what someone else means by bad, do you? When someone says it's going to be bad, you don't know what that means, not really."

He came across the kitchen and held me. "You never do," he said, his breath warm on my cheek. Then he kept his arm around me and guided me to a chair. "I'll bring you some coffee. Can you eat some toast?"

I shook my head.

He brought coffee but didn't sit down. It was his turn to stay with Mrs. Inglewood and Brian. He started to walk toward the hall, then asked, "If you had known, would you still have done it?"

In my mind a picture formed of Brian restrained in a wheelchair, his liver destroyed, his

280

heart permanently damaged, his brain burned out by shock treatments, his body shaken again and again by uncontrollable spastic movements. And always the devils waiting to pounce on him, because no matter what they did, the demons would be there, waiting.

"Yes," I said. I wanted to say that here he screamed not because there were demons but because he was in pain from toxins, from withdrawal, from God alone knew what. But not demons, not ghosts. They were being held at bay by Mother. I was too tired to explain, and Radix went upstairs. Brian was screaming.

At nine that morning the hospital called to say that Brian would not be allowed visitors again today. I stood by the phone and listened to the message. Then Radix called the motel he had not slept in once to inquire about messages for him.

"One," he said. "From Martens."

I turned off the CD player and looked in on Brian, who was curled in the fetal position. Mrs. Inglewood put her finger to her lips. Brian was sleeping. We all thought he drifted into sleep now and then, but it was hard to tell for certain. For now, at least, the house was quiet. Radix called Martens.

I could tell little from his end of the conversation. When he hung up, he said, "The hospital got in touch with him to report that Brian's missing. He wants me to come as soon as I can to the office. I don't think he knows what to do next." He rubbed his eyes.

"You have to go," I said. "We have to know what they're doing, what they're planning. What if they call Amy or Kevin and they turn up?" Radix looked terrible, with deep dark shadows under his eyes, a two-day beard black on his cheeks; he was haggard and drawn and at least as tired as I was. But he had to go.

He nodded. "Shower, shave first. And more coffee. I won't stay a minute longer than I have to."

"I know."

Brian lapsed into the deep comalike sleep and we couldn't rouse him for liquids. Then he spasmed, or cramped and cried out, and slept again. The hours crept by. Mrs. Inglewood dozed in a chair near Brian's bed and came wide-awake instantly when he moved or made a sound. I had been sitting on the floor, holding Brian's hand, talking to him in a low voice; unresponsive, he slept. Finally I got up and walked out, down the stairs, and then to the garden, where I sat on the bench. The garden was dry and unkempt, un-tended, unloved now. Weeds were rampant, and dead flowers clung to stalks.

"Mother," I whispered, "please help him. I was wrong. I'm sorry. Please, don't let him die. Help him, please."

The air was hot and still and very quiet. I remembered how, when he was smaller, he used to kneel in a chair and look out the back window and watch her dance. How he smiled then. I looked up at his windows, two at the back of the house, and I thought, But he can't see her from his bed.

I went back inside, upstairs, to stand in his doorway; he hadn't moved and Mrs. Inglewood was still dozing. There were three windows, one overlooking the patio, two facing the garden. A bookcase was under the double windows, and a chair. By day it was a bright corner for reading. The foot of his bed came almost to the bookcase, but it was too low; even if it was moved to the windows, he couldn't see out. We would prop it up. Or add another mattress. That would make it just right.

Radix didn't return until almost two; he came upstairs while Mrs. Inglewood and I were working cramps out of Brian's legs. Brian was crying.

"Just in time," I said. "Fill the tub, will you? Maybe we can get him in it before he goes back to sleep."

He hurried out to fill the tub. I let him and Mrs. Inglewood bathe Brian, who had already started to go limp before they lowered him into the water. I yanked the covers from his bed and started to tug it the few feet to the windows. It was heavy, hard to move, but I got it there against the bookcase, and then I ran to my room to pull my mattress to the door. I had it off the bed, stripped, ready to move already. I pushed and shoved and lifted it into place on top of Brian's bed, and then I put on fresh sheets and put his pillow under the windows. It was exactly high enough now for him to see out.

After a startled look, neither Radix nor Mrs. Inglewood asked what I was trying to do when they carried Brian back. She was breathing hard. "Go get some rest," I said to her. "He'll be quiet for a bit now. And you," I said to Radix, "should get on some dry clothes." He had taken off his suit jacket, but his pants and shirt were drenched. I was breathing hard myself, and I needed to sit down a few minutes before he told me any more bad news.

When he came back, dressed in jeans, a T-shirt, and sandals, he pulled a chair close to mine and said in a low voice, "You won, Liz. Martens signed over the guardianship to me, the trusts, Brian, all of it. It's official and legal. You don't have to be afraid any longer. You won."

I looked at Brian, drawn up in his fetal position, and shook my head. Not yet, I thought. I hadn't won anything yet.

That evening, when the shadows striped the garden and the fragrance of nicotiana was strong, I set up the music stand in the doorway of Brian's room and put his music on it, the music he had written for Mother, then, sitting in the hall outside his door, where the music would drift through the house and not be too loud in his room, I played. I didn't know this music; I had to watch the notes; I couldn't tell if Brian was hearing it. When I finished and looked up, Radix was watching Brian fixedly. He motioned to me, then mouthed, "Again." I played it again.

I wanted to look, to see what was happening, but I would miss a note, flub it, so I read the music and played, only distantly aware of movement across the room. The next time I looked, Mrs. Inglewood had her arm around Brian's shoulders, supporting him. His face was turned toward the window and he made a low, inarticulate noise, not a cry of pain or anguish, just a soft noise. Radix handed a glass of water to Mrs. Inglewood, and she said, "There, there. Your mouth's too dry to try to talk. Take a sip of water, child."

He took a sip, another, then she lowered him to the bed once more, and he lay there facing the window.

26

It wasn't over, but the worst had passed; we all sensed that. His body was still reacting violently to withdrawal, but now, in between spasms and cramps, when he opened his eyes, it was with awareness and recognition. He knew where he was, who was with him. Now, when he slept, still curled in the fetal position, he could be roused enough to take a drink, and we began to give him juice, Gatorade, clear broth. With Radix and Mrs. Inglewood supporting him, he tottered to the bathroom. It exhausted him, but he walked there and then walked back.

I had lost all track of time; when it was twilight, whether the dusk of dawn or evening, I could no longer tell, I played the violin and ended with his music. She would not come to recorded music, I understood.

I had played, then when I stood up, I nearly fell down again, and Radix caught my arm. "To bed with you. Come on." I didn't protest, just let him lead me to bed, let him pull off my sandals, and I fell asleep.

Sunlight was brilliant when I woke up and found myself in Amy's room, in her bed. Then I remembered that I didn't have a mattress any longer, and with that thought, I bolted up. How long had I slept?

As it turned out, I had slept for only a few

hours; it was midmorning, Wednesday. I ran across the hall to Brian's room and found him propped up with extra pillows, gazing out the windows. I sat down on the side of his bed.

"How are you?"

"Pretty tired," he said weakly. "Sore."

I hugged him, and he tried to hug back. Now all he needed was coddling, I thought, and rest, and lots and lots of food. It was over.

That afternoon Mrs. Inglewood made dinner again, then she said she would go on home and see to her horses.

"Oh God," I cried, "I'm sorry. Who's taking care of them?" I had forgotten all about her two old horses. Her babies.

"A neighbor. He's good about their food and water, but he's no hand at rubdowns, and they'll be missing me. There's soup in a bowl in the fridge. And a pork roast in the oven, be done about six or six-thirty. Don't rush it, it won't overcook. And I'll be back around noon tomorrow. Might get myself to bed real early tonight, real early."

I put my arms around her and we held each other. "Thank you. Thank you. We couldn't have managed without you. How did you know to come?"

"Oh, you would have managed," she said. "I have no doubt about that. When they said I couldn't see Brian on Sunday, I thought that was a bit peculiar. They don't start anything new on weekends, not that I know of anyway. And you'd been there Saturday, and he must have been same as usual then. And I remembered that ladder on the patio, the one you painted, and I knew. But I knew all along you weren't about to leave the poor little feller out there and let them kill him. I just didn't know when or how you'd get him home."

She went up to tell Brian good-bye, and then she drove off in her old rusty truck. I still didn't know if it had a gun rack. Brian came down for dinner that night. He came down the wide front stairs, where Radix could stay by his side, just in case he needed a hand, but he walked down without help. It was obvious that he was sore — every muscle must have been inflamed from all the cramping — but he walked to the kitchen and sank into a chair with a satisfied grunt. He said he guessed he wouldn't sit up and play cards with us just yet.

Sometime during the day Radix had gone out and bought a bottle of wine. We drank it that night, talking at the kitchen table.

"I probably won't see you alone again," he said. "Amy and Kevin will arrive tomorrow and be around for a few days, and I have to get back to Philadelphia."

I nodded. He had to, we both understood that. Tomorrow Amy and Kevin would come, expecting grim news from Martens, but instead, they would find that the world had shifted while their backs were turned. "How much should we tell

Amy and Kevin?" I asked.

"As little as possible. I don't think they'd approve of your methods. They're both pretty straight."

I laughed, and he did, too. "Okay," I said, "just that Martens made the deal with you and we brought Brian home and dried him out. Right?"

"That sounds about right." He became serious again. "You understand that Brian might still have some pretty bad times ahead? We don't know how much he'll remember when all the fuzz clears. If there's a problem, will you call me right away?"

I nodded.

"Promise?"

"I promise," I said. Then I asked, "How did you talk Martens into the deal?"

"I didn't. He brought it up. He didn't know how to tell Amy and Kevin that Brian had gotten loose, and they expected to find his body in a ravine. He dreaded having to tell any of you, but he would have faced them. He was terrified of facing you with the news. You scare the bejesus out of that man."

I ducked my head and mumbled, "It wasn't that bad."

"He thinks it was. Anyway, he brought it up and practically pleaded with me to take this whole crew off his hands. I let him talk me into it."

"Do we have to pay you?"

He laughed a long time. "Oh God, Liz. You know the first time I remember seeing you? It was when you were going up the stairs, and you asked if my visit was billable. You, a scrawny, bony, snot-nosed kid. Straight to the point even then. And the answer is no. I'll consider this outfit my pro bono work, a rung in my ladder to heaven, Good Samaritan and all that."

"What are you going to do now, Radix?" I asked, ignoring his levity. "Have you moved into the big corner office?"

He sobered instantly. "No. I told my father I don't intend to. The provisions of his will haven't changed, and I don't know what I'm going to do. Satisfied?"

"Of course not. Why don't you paint, or sculpt, or do whatever it is you really want to do?"

He regarded me for a long time without speaking. Then he said, "I'm not good enough. The desire without the talent is a cruel gift."

"How do you know how good you are? And what if you don't show the world your art? Who's it for, the world or for you? Be a Sunday painter, just like I'm a Sunday musician. So I'm not good enough for a symphony orchestra. So what?"

He drank his wine and set the glass down carefully. "I think we should go to bed, we're both pretty wiped out. If Brian wakes up and needs anything, we'll hear him; he doesn't need watching overnight. Tomorrow we'll shift mattresses back to where they belong and get things ready for Amy and Kevin. I'll talk to them about

the new situation, and on Friday, I'll take off."
He stood up.

"Okay." I stood up, too, across the table from him. "I owe you a lot, Radix. No way can I ever repay you. I know that."

He waved his hand in a dismissing gesture, then started to move, to walk away.

"Wait, I'm not through. Something else. I love you, and I've loved you for a long time. You should know."

He looked stunned, or, as Mother would have said, he looked poleaxed. Then his face became expressionless. He shook his head. "You're very tired, and you're grateful, even if your gratitude is undeserved. You did it, not I. But now you're mistaking gratitude for an altogether different emotion, the way a child does. Go on to bed, Liz. It's late."

"I tell you something profound and meaningful, and you give me drivel. What a dope you are. Lolita is dead and gone, and so is Humbert Humbert. Think in different categories. Good night, Radix. See you in the morning." His face turned scarlet, and I left him standing like a stick by the table.

He was right, though: We were not alone together again. Brian was with us early, then Mrs. Inglewood. Radix called the hospital and told Dr. Redmond that Brian was in good hands and was no longer her patient. We got the beds back together and made up; Mrs. Inglewood started dinner for the whole bunch of us, and Radix went to pick up Amy and Kevin at the airport. He talked to them before they got to the house, so they were prepared and not as shocked by Brian's twitchiness and emaciation as they might have been.

That night, after Brian went up to bed, we sat in the living room, the committee of three, plus Radix. Kevin said, rather stoutly for him, that he absolutely would not permit me to stay here with Brian.

I made a rude snorting sound, and Radix looked amused for a moment. He sobered quickly. "I think we should clear the air so we can talk freely. Liz told me what happened to your mother, what you did, and how it affected Brian. That needs to be out in the open."

Amy and Kevin were shocked into stillness, and I was probably as surprised as they were by his words.

"So, I know where you've been and what you've done. No more secrets among us. Okay?" He didn't wait for a response. "Now, in my opinion, Brian has always been a perfectly normal kid ninety-nine percent of the time, until he was threatened. Obviously he needs a home, and this is a fine one. In a few years he'll be legally of age to make any decisions by himself, and until then, I'll be his guardian. And as his guardian, I decide what I think is best for him. He stays put here, with no threats of any sort. As for Liz, I seriously doubt that she will let you tell her what she can or can't do. If she remains here or goes somewhere else is her decision, and hers alone. If she wants to leave, we'll make arrangements for a live-in housekeeper until Brian's older."

Kevin looked ready to argue, but Amy put her hand on his arm and shook her head. "What are you going to do about . . . You know, about us?"

"This situation is unique in my experience," Radix said thoughtfully. "I need to do a lot of research, find precedents if they exist. It will be a time-consuming job, and quite frankly, my schedule won't give me enough slack to get to it right away."

I stopped another rude noise before it could escape my lips. He knew, and again I caught a hint of amusement in his glance. "You could take years on such a project," I said with as much innocence as I could get into my voice.

He shrugged, and on the couch Amy seemed to relax; she was regarding him with a new expression, one I'd never seen her turn on him. Tough, I thought at her. Too late.

After a moment she nodded. She patted Kevin's arm and said, "Leave it alone."

Radix got up to go soon after that. He had told Brian good-bye earlier and now he hugged Amy and kissed her forehead, then bear-hugged Kevin. He looked at me, and for a moment I thought he would hold out his hand for a good hearty handshake, but he didn't. Neither did he touch me, and something in my expression seemed to make him angry. Or possibly bewildered, or, I thought, perhaps he was angry because he was bewildered. "I'll be in touch often," he said stiffly. "And feel free to call me day or night if you need anything."

"I'll remember that," I said.

"I'll pay a visit in the fall. No later than Christmas. Maybe for Christmas."

"We'll hang an extra stocking."

His expression was murderous, and he stalked out.

Amy and Kevin stayed only a few days; they left satisfied that everything was back to normal, at least as normal as we ever had been.

Now we're alone again, Brian and I. Tonight he played his violin. He had picked it up several times, but he had a tremor in both hands, and he merely held it. I stood in his doorway and listened to him play, the way he used to come to listen to me. Although he didn't play Mother's music yet, when he finished, he was peaceful.

"I've had a dream a few times," he said, sitting back in his chair, holding his fine Cremona violin. "I was in a dungeon. Like a well, a mile deep. It was black and gray all around, without any light, except straight up above me. I couldn't get out. I couldn't find the door. Then Dad was at the top, and Mother was in the bottom with me, and she began to float with me in her arms, and when we got high enough, Dad held me, and we all floated out."

He knew he had been very ill and that for a while he had been in the hospital. That's all I had told him, and he hadn't asked for more. He would, and I would say he had fallen and hit his head. I hadn't decided if I would suggest amnesia, which would be romantic and pleasing, or if I would say brain fever, the favorite affliction of so many people in nineteenth-century novels. Whatever I ended up telling him would not be the truth, not yet. I thought he would ask questions then, after he told me about his dream, but he didn't.

Now it's very late, and I have been pondering the problem again of what to tell Brian and when to tell him. He'll have to know what he went through and why. It would be cruel for him to become an old man and die without knowing why he was haunted. When the day comes, I'll tell him the truth, even though I have to admit that I don't know what the truth is, actually. Whose truth? His? Mine? Do we ever know for certain?

Radix calls every day, always with the pretense that he is inquiring about Brian. Tonight he called for the second time in one day, ten o'clock here, one back there in Philadelphia. At first I thought it was about his father, but he said nothing has changed.

"Brian said earlier that you both went up in the woods today and found a perfect tree for Christmas," he said. "Christmas seems a long way away."

"I know."

"If I get there in time, two, three days before Christmas, could you wait that long to cut the tree? I'd like to help."

I doubted that he had ever even held an ax, but I laughed and said, "Sure."

"Liz . . ."

"I'm here."

"Christmas seems a long way away." There was a pause; then he said, "Liz . . ." He cleared his throat. "I won't hold you to anything you said when you were so tired. I just wanted to tell you that."

"I didn't say anything I didn't mean."

The pause was longer this time. "Liz . . ." In a rush he said, "I never was anxious about Christmas before, never in my life. It seems a long time away."

"For me, too."

"Liz . . . Damn. It's late, I should get to bed. Are you all right? Sleeping enough? Resting enough? Do you need anything?"

"I'm fine. Are you?"

"No. It's cold and gray here." Suddenly he laughed, then he said, "You're not going to help a bit, are you?"

"It's your move."

"I . . . I miss you, Liz. I just wanted to hear your voice. Good night." He hung up.

Poor Radix, I think, still holding the phone; they probably don't leave him alone long enough for him to work through it all, to sort out his categories. I had three days alone on the coast;

he has to find a few minutes here, a few minutes there, but he's doing it. After his father dies, I decide, he will come back here and be a country lawyer, or a consultant, or a handyman, and study art with a teacher like Mr. Kimmelman. If he turns out to be a Sunday painter, that will be okay, too. He'll learn to live with it, and he'll enjoy doing it, not for the world, but for himself. His self will demand that he do good work, and he'll work hard to satisfy that interior critic.

Of course, we'll have to travel; he'll need to see more art, and I'll need whatever it is I need. We'll manage it somehow.

I can hear my own interior critic mocking me: Daydreaming again, Liz? And I can honestly say no. I'm writing the story of my life to come. Then it hits me, how to tell Brian.

I'll write it all for him, starting with the day the four of us kids waited for Mother and Dad to come tell us they bought the house. There will be things I'll have to back up and explain, since Brian was too young to know them, and of course all the times the committee of three excluded him when we plotted and schemed. . . . I'll change the names to protect the guilty, and one day when he's ready for it, I'll hand the manuscript to Brian to be read as our true story, or as a novel, a piece of fiction. When he's ready.

And I have a deadline: Christmas. It will be my present for Radix. There are things about me

297

that he should know before we get married. It's not for the world, I'll tell him. It's for you and someday for Brian, not for the world.

About the Author

Kate Wilhelm was born in Toledo, Ohio, and grew up in Kentucky. She published her first novel in 1963 and has gone on to publish more than three dozen novels and story collections. Her books include the classic science fiction novel *Where Late the Sweet Birds Sang*; the fascinating psychological portrait *Margaret and I*; the Charlie Meiklejohn and Constance Leidl mysteries; and the popular Barbara Holloway courtroom thrillers. Her works have been honored with three Nebula Awards, the Hugo Award, the Prix Apollo, the Jupiter Award, the Kurd Lasswitz Award, and many other distinctions. Her short fiction has been published in such magazines as *Redbook*, *Omni*, *Fantasy & Science Fiction*, and *Ellery Queen's Mystery Magazine*, and a number of her stories have been adapted or are in development for film and television, including "The Look Alike" and "Forever Yours, Anna." She and her husband, Damon Knight, helped found and run the influential Milford Writers' Workshop and the Clarion Writers' Workshop, which have shaped and launched the careers of many of today's leading writers. Kate Wilhelm lives with her family in Eugene, Oregon.